News from the Volcano

News from the Volcano

Stories by Gladys Swan

University of Missouri Press
Columbia and London

Copyright © 2000 by Gladys Swan
University of Missouri Press, Columbia, Missouri 65201
Printed and bound in the United States of America
5 4 3 2 1   04 03 02 01 00

Library of Congress Cataloging-in-Publication Data

Swan, Gladys, 1934–
    News from the volcano : stories / by Gladys Swan.
        p. cm.
    Contents: News from the volcano — Backtracking — Sloan's daughter
    — The chasm — Gate of ivory, gate of horn.
      ISBN 0-8262-1296-4 (alk. paper)
        I. Title.

    PS3569.W247 N49 2000
    813'.54—dc21   00-036409

♾™ This paper meets the requirements of the
American National Standard for Permanence of Paper
for Printed Library Materials, Z39.48, 1984.

Design and composition: Vickie Kersey DuBois
Printer and binder: Edwards Brothers, Inc.
Typefaces: Leawood, Lingprint

For Leonard Zellar

And in Memory of Robert G. Brooks and Ella Snodgrass

Contents

Acknowledgments

I would like to express my gratitude and appreciation to Beverly Jarrett, Jane Lago, and Clair Willcox of the University of Missouri Press for their support and encouragement over the past decade.

The stories included in this volume have been previously published as follows:

"News from the Volcano" in the *Green Mountains Review*, in *Walking the Twilight II: Women Writers of the Southwest* (Northland Publishers, 1996), and in *World Wide Writers* (England).

"Backtracking" in *Writers' Forum* and in *Where Past Meets Present: Modern Colorado Short Stories* (University Press of Colorado, 1993).

"Sloan's Daughter" in the *Southwest Review.*

"The Chasm" in *Studia Mystica.*

In a dark time the eye begins to see.
—Theodore Roethke

News from the Volcano

News from the Volcano

Rising up from land flat as sheet metal, the rock, sheer and huge, unprecedented, is a ship moving across the desert, its dark shape bearing straightaway, wherever it is headed, not to be put off course. Aeons ago it rose towering above the land, lava overflowing from the molten core. Now the core is all that remains, the rest worn away by all that time can do. Only the core—a relic of ancient catastrophes, before any were present to know what they might mean. Hardened now and silent.

But now and then the moon rises blue in the dust of ancient memory. A haze of particles hanging suspended in the air, as though from that time when the volcano erupted. Who knows how they've gathered or where they came from? They gather above the rock, above the desert, above the occasions of earth below, as though reminded by the original disturbances of the air. So I see it now, as the moon rises three-quarters full. And with a light that comes somehow from beyond it.

The moon sends its bluish haze over a huddle of adobe houses, from which the small lights float in the surrounding indigo, and the smells of chili and beans and fry meat mingle with the evening chill. The light touches on the headlights of the trucks parked alongside, as though they were closed lids, gives a sheen to their metal casings, and leaves the land beyond a dark sea. Prickly pear and yucca, ocotillo and scrub cedar raise dark silhouettes from darker pools. Along the road cars are moving, and among them is a stranger moving this way. He moves the way a shark moves toward a school of fish, a dark rush in the direction of the unwary.

Up the road a neon sign sets its glare against the landscape: a gas station–grocery–café, still open. Many times I have gone past, watched the customers enter and leave. Sometimes I've taken my loaf of bread and left change on the counter. Lupe I know from hearsay, for she does not speak much, at least to me. Perhaps she feels my gaze upon her and draws away, not

1

wanting anyone to know too much. But I cannot get enough of certain faces, wanting to know what has shaped them. I only know I must not look too long. There is something frightening in too close a scrutiny. I keep close to myself and see things as they come.

Tonight Lupe sits inside as she usually does, on a stool behind the counter, waiting for Lorenzo to return to help her close up. He'd left her alone all that afternoon, away on some errand. He may have driven all the way to Gallup—he does that sometimes. She had already cleaned the grill and wiped the counter, totaled up the day's receipts. Whatever came in now belonged to tomorrow—it is good to begin the day with something.

A truck pulled in, three boys in front, two more sprawled out in the bed. Lupe knew the truck—Manuel's. They were headed to the dance in Farmington. She could hear them outside. "No, man, you're drunk already." "Look with your eyes, man." "It's the Russians—they've set something off." "Why them?—maybe it's us." "You're crazy, man. We'd have heard it." "It's from outer space. A spaceship—a huge one." "Not that big—don't you know any science?" "I know the moon when I see it—only that's different." "I want another beer."

It was a game, of course. But there was a difference in the cast of things. They could tell as they stood in front of the truck, looking at the sky. They broke their pose just as Lupe reached them. "See, look how strange it is," they showed her. And she stood with them, her arms hugging her shoulders over her thin blouse. She'd never seen the moon like that. Just now a plume of cloud fanned its surface, trailing across like a scarf. Splotches of light and shadow lay over the dark vegetation.

A different moon. Where had it come from and what did it mark? Perhaps it was a sign if she only knew what it meant. That is always the way—it could be this or that. Her grandmother had been one to know. She could read the world like a map of secret journeys—there are some who can do that, who seem to be born knowing. She could enter certain moments like a doorway and see what pulsed beneath, even if she could not tell the exact·shape of what was coming. She could tell people where sickness came from, the violence in the flesh, and if an ill wind was blowing. It was something. Though perhaps not enough—perhaps it is never enough. One keeps looking for news; perhaps that's why I stare so at the things around me, waiting for them to speak.

Lupe's grandmother was dead now. Lupe had seen her lying at the threshold of her hut, left behind by the soldiers who carried off her chickens. They laughed as they caught the squawking birds. And the one who struck her down, who can tell? Or the others they left, scattered in the postures in which they had closed with death, set upon with the marks of whatever impulse or intention had overtaken them. Rumor caught these things and breathed them on the wind. But the soldiers had disappeared as they had come.

Lupe turned to go inside, and Manuel followed her in to pay for gas. It was his truck, he'd bought it used and took jobs hauling. He had a sister and a mother to support. Though he wanted to go off on his own, down to Albuquerque to look for work and perhaps for a certain freedom, he didn't stray, not even for better wages. Lupe liked him—he was older than his friends, held something in his face she could trust. "You going to the dance?" he asked her.

She gave a shrug. She didn't know, Lorenzo was so late in coming.

"We could wait," he said. "You could ride with us—in front."

She'd have liked to go with them. But she didn't like to leave when Lorenzo wasn't there. "I'd better stay," she said.

"I could come back," he said. He wanted her to go. "Unless," he said. "You have someone else."

"No, there's no one else."

Very likely it was Willie he meant. Willie was always asking her to go with him. He had a motorcycle and liked to roar down the highway with a girl at his back holding on with her arms around his waist. I've seen him many times, getting in his brags, you might say. There'd been a number of girls eager for the thrill, but Lupe was the one he wanted. It was easy to tell by the way he looked at her, as though he were trying to take her with his eyes. But she'd never sent a glance in his direction, was never lured by his roaring down the road.

Willie was trying to make a special link between them: they knew more than the others. They were above doing what the spoilers had done. He had found Indian somewhere in his blood, past the blue eyes and white skin that had corrupted the original purity, and he'd come West to find it. He brought his camera with him, and his power lay in that. He took pictures of road kill—that's what the hunter's skill had come to. Having left the buffalo to die by thousands, this was what civilization had brought—dead creatures in the road, and the effete beef steak. He took pictures of junked cars and litter and dumps and faces from which every dream had fled. Warnings and reminders.

There is always laughter in his eyes, when he turns his glance on Lupe, though when I've passed him I've caught something cold and sharp that goes right through and doesn't disappear. And he turns away as though he's already revealed too much. I too draw back. I have no wish to meddle. There is always something back of his expression when he's flirting with the girls, taking in their measure, taking the square root, storing things away for the next time—something quite beyond them that perhaps he doesn't see himself. But his attraction works like a scent drawing to him all that might speak to his contempt.

Perhaps Manuel was relieved to know he didn't have a rival, for Willie was always asking her to go. "Maybe you'll come later," he said, taking up his beer and the change. "Save a dance for me." And he gave her a smile that she held on to after he had gone.

The truck started up, moved out onto the highway, and was gone. It was quiet now but for the refrigerator making cold, and the buzzing of the fluorescent lights inside taking the beer cans into their glare. She doubted she would go to the dance: Lorenzo would be too tired.

Once or twice a month he took her: she knew it was for her sake. He'd come through the door around closing time and say, "Let's go have some fun," and they'd climb into his pickup and go to join the crowd. Lorenzo didn't dance himself, but stood on the edge among the spectators, drinking a beer and talking intently to whoever might be standing next to him, man or woman—he knew everybody. But he always kept an eye out for what was happening on the dance floor. If things started to get rowdy, Lupe had only to look for his nod, and they would leave. There were always those who hung around the edge, usually outside passing around a bottle, sometimes hooting and laughing, hoping for a fight. It was a question of whether they'd get bored and go off to further adventure or start something there. More than once the sirens came shrieking down the road, and someone got carted off to the hospital. Lorenzo kept a sharp eye in his head.

Lorenzo had had a wife once, but she'd run off to Denver with another man. Her lover had disappeared long since, and others had followed. But somehow she'd remained in Lorenzo's life, even though she never came back. If he went to see her, he never said. She called him at least once a month and told him her latest round of troubles and asked for his advice, and some-times money. For a time he'd given her both, but the money blew away like scraps the wind had brought and would, as far as she was concerned, bring again. Now he gave neither, but listened to her stories. From time to time, he was with a woman. Now he had no one, though there were women who'd have been glad to have him. He was a generous man, who liked people around him, but who kept back a certain melancholy he never imposed on anyone. People liked him.

A restless mood came over Lupe. The night was growing too long, and the lights were not strong enough to keep certain shapes from invading from the darkness outside, nor the cans of beer and the packages of snacks and loaves of bread solid enough to keep her solidly among them. She got these moods. And you could watch her struggle against them. I can remember when her look spoke only of this.

When they had first arrived, she and her mother, it felt strange to her to stop moving. She felt the moving still in her body, and a danger of falling over if she stopped. It was strange not to see one landscape shifting into another, whether they were on foot or in the waddling buses. She could not believe that if she closed her eyes the same objects would be standing in front of her when she opened them again or that she would wake in the same bed in the same room, the mountains beyond the window still solidly standing, and Lorenzo's place down the road.

She refused to go to school—they had to bring her home. She wouldn't be separated from her mother, though in many ways she was no longer a child. When the two of them came into the store, Lorenzo gave her sweets. When her mother sank into the drunken stupor that lay at the end of her pursuit of safety and could no longer take care of her, Lorenzo gave her credit. And when her mother went off with the man who took her by the hand and led her to his car, Lorenzo took her in and taught her to make change and add figures and how to brew the coffee and cook hamburgers. She had finished growing up there.

The other girls envied her. Like one chosen, she had been given a place where she could earn her own money and put it in the bank. She had a future. She could go where she pleased, though she seldom left her place behind the grill or the cash register. She could lead her own life and didn't need a man if she didn't want one. She sensed their eye on her, their gaze as sharp as desire. But what was there to envy? The dark rush of her dreams? Sometimes she dreamed of animals devouring one another that lived like a menace just under the surface. She'd crossed boundaries where she'd had no wish to go, and who would care to follow? For she'd had experience, and no one could wipe it away. And what was there to be done with it?

She heard a car door slam and hoped it wasn't Willie come to lean over the counter to try to lure her in his direction. She had no idea why he continued to pursue her. Lorenzo never spoke to him. She was always pressed back by the tightness of a face that seemed to close behind some secret scorn, while his eye let nothing escape his notice. Then, unexpectedly, his face would break into a grin and he would tell her a joke, a bit of gossip he'd been saving up: who Manuel was sleeping with and which of the boys liked Lupe. He had something to tease everyone with, those he wanted to get the better of. He tried to tease her about Manuel, but she never blinked an eye.

He never had enough to do, it seemed. He was always around. Sometimes he showed off the photographs he took of mountains and desert plants to sell to tourists. Compliments made him smirk. There were times she saw Willie every day. He'd come in and pull down a loaf of bread, a can of soup, a jar of peanut butter, as if eating were a matter of indifference to him, slap some bills down on the counter, and leave without a word, sometimes without his change. Or he might come in for beer and disappear for days on end. He'd be off in his room, chain-smoking, his music turned up loud so he wouldn't have to listen to the noise of cars. Sometimes he slept all day and went prowling out at night. Sometimes he stayed drunk until he felt like being sober.

But it wasn't Willie come to pass the time. It was a stranger. He stood with his back to her as he filled his gas tank, then replaced the hose and came inside: a tall man with a ponytail pulled back from a narrow, bearded, hawk-nosed face. He closed the door and surveyed his surroundings as though to take a reckoning. She caught the restless glitter of his eyes, a film of weariness over something leaden and driven.

He did not offer to pay but placed himself on a stool at the counter. The lights were off in the kitchen; it was too late for food, but Lupe did not tell him so.

"What do you have to eat?" he wanted to know.

"Omelette," she said, "or a sandwich. Ham or cheese."

He considered the choices as though they were the only things he'd ever be tempted to eat.

"Till tomorrow morning," she explained.

"I could be lying half starved on the slope of Pike's Peak by then."

She didn't deny it. One could be anywhere, without so much as a piece of bread. He wanted an omelette with ham and cheese and coffee—lots of coffee. She put on a pot on the Silex in front and went back into the kitchen to beat up the eggs, take out the cartons with the ham and cheese. She watched him while she worked. He drummed impatiently on the counter, glanced in her direction when any noise came from the kitchen. He took out a cigarette, lit it, took a long, deep drag, and let the smoke out slowly. He set it in the ashtray and left it. She saw him reach toward his belt, draw a hunting knife from its sheath, and lay it on the counter. She hadn't seen it under his jacket. It had what looked to be a bone handle with dark streaks, perhaps a design carved into it.

He gazed at it for a moment, then took it up, ran his thumb across the blade in a way that suggested that he wanted her to take notice. He glanced up in her direction, but she'd felt his attention coming and had ducked away in time. This was something she had no business with, she knew it under her skin, but it would be hard to keep away from it. He turned the knife over in his hand, familiarly, as though he'd gotten it as a bargain and he could take pride in whatever the knife might bring him. A certain energy pulsed out of his weariness as he turned the knife back and forth cutting the light into metallic slices.

She didn't want to look at it, the way it cut the light, the restlessness of it in his hand, as though straining in the direction of what it had been shaped to do. It knew killing. Lupe saw at once. The knife had killed someone. It had leapt into the place where killing was and caught the secret scent. Who knew how it had happened? But it was glutted now with what it knew, even if it had blundered into that space, been caught blindly or risen up and driven forward in a flash. The man was hectic with the consequences, but he could not get rid of the knife. It was joined to him now like his flesh.

He set the knife down, then pushed it to one side when she brought him his food. This gesture was for her benefit, she was no fool—to show her it was subject to him. She asked him if he wanted ketchup, then came with his coffee. She wondered why he hadn't threatened her before, hadn't robbed the store of what he wanted and gone on his way. There was food enough to cram into his maw. The threat itself was enough to get him whatever he wanted.

But maybe he wanted to be reminded of something, the smell of cooking in the air, the aroma of coffee. She filled his cup. His hand trembled as he took the mug, raised it to his lips. A bit spilled over the edge. It was the knife—it had him in its power and wouldn't leave him alone. The knife had no interest but itself.

Every now and then he paused, his fork poised as though he were listening, perhaps for something that pursued him or something that had momentarily stopped, as though a buzz had been set ringing in his ears that wouldn't shut off. Till he was weary of it, sick to death of it. She could see how he was trying to push it away, rid himself of it as he tried to eat, as he tried to chew his food back into savor and to warm himself with coffee. He craved the ordinary and was working to get food to his stomach before it gagged him and turned to sawdust.

She breathed sharply. The knife was greedy too, as it strained against its moorings. It would spare nothing. In the fullness of its impulse it was trying to get her to form the image of her death, make it coalesce before her eyes. It wanted her to reach toward a source of terror, where its power lay. If she tried to run away, it threatened to pursue her. Not because of anything she would do, but because she was there and had seen it. It wanted her powerlessness. If Lorenzo wandered in, heedlessly, it could rise up against him. He could walk right into it. She saw that and stepped into uncertainty.

She put herself back into what she knew, those nights when the countryside had turned into the shadows of fleeing forms. They were all joined together in the shadows, pursued and pursuer, having shed everything but the one impulse that bound them. It lay at the bottom of the world. Out of it she could imagine her death. The absence of herself standing there—that was her death. It formed a space of stillness. The part of herself she was most familiar with would die. And whatever it was that lay behind it— that would leave her too. But she let go of that. She would not give it to him. It did not belong to him. Though she was looking at him, she seemed not to see him at all.

When he'd stopped eating and made a swipe with his napkin across the last of his food, he stood up and took his knife. "I'm finished now," he announced. "You can open up that drawer and give me what's in it."

"I'll give you nothing," she said. "You'll have to pay."

He looked at her like a snake risen in his path.

She did not let go. Neither did she pretend to innocence. She had passed beyond that long ago. She looked directly into his eyes with the knowledge of what he had done. "You have to pay," she insisted. "You've eaten, you've filled your car with gas. Now you have to pay."

She had no pity and asked for none. The knife had no pity. It was looking to make an excuse of her weakness, to bury itself in that. But she had let go of her life—it did not matter.

"I have no money," he said, as though it were a joke. "When you have this, you don't need money."

She stood there like a wall: he could kill her if he wanted.

He didn't move. Perhaps he caught a sense of what she knew and how the space between them joined them now. She was no accomplice. Or perhaps it was her voice that struck him, twisted inside him. It had found him out, gone to the bone. That can happen—I have seen it. It made him want to let go of all he knew, as if there were a moment in which both of them might rise above their images to something else. Everything wavered in that effort, that possibility. Then in a sudden movement he flung down the knife, reeled as though it had taken all his effort, and threw himself out the door. He stumbled and nearly fell before he reached the car.

Lupe did not move. For a long moment she seemed to stand outside her body. The knife had put her there, and now it was lying on the floor. She would not look at it. Dizzily she sat down, trying to regain herself. She tried to call to mind whom she'd seen that day, who had come for gas, for food.

She did not notice when the door opened again. And when Willie came up behind her, he startled her.

"You falling asleep?" he said with a teasing laugh. "Who's the guy who left—friend of yours?"

"I never saw him before."

Nothing to make a difference. "I thought you'd be closed up now. Why hang around. Let's go to the dance."

"No," she said. "Not tonight." She wanted to pull the grin off his face like a mask.

"You always dance with me. Just to tease, I bet."

"I dance with everybody."

"You don't trust me."

She shrugged. "Lorenzo would take me, but he's not back. I won't go till he comes."

"He's not your father—he doesn't own you," he said meanly. "What's he saving you for—himself? The big man." His foot struck against the knife. He bent down for it.

"Don't pick it up," she warned him.

"Why not?" He stood up with it.

"It isn't yours," she said.

He turned it in his hand, watching her as he fingered the blade. "It's a good knife," he said. "You don't find one lying around like that every day. Finders, keepers."

"Fool," she said, turning away, as he toyed with it.

"I've always wanted a knife like this."

She tried to ignore him.

"Look. Go with me," he insisted.

And if she went with him . . .

"Or you'll be sorry." Willie turned away, as though the threat would hold force without him, and strode out the door.

Now he had the knife. He would go where it took him. She would be sorry, he'd promised her that, when he turned again in her direction. He was asking her again to reach into the fear that filled the space the knife was ready to make. To live in that darkness. If she looked into the space, would she see only the blank tearing of flesh, the deep wounding that asks for revenge, the endless chain? What was to be saved, and what would save her? She stood for a moment as though waiting for news, for something else beyond her to come to speech, if it were there to speak. That was the question, the one that takes us to the depths, nailed by the moment, as though to listen for our lives. She could hear, she could almost see a great struggle roaring in the dark on the verge of some upheaval. She expected it to appear in front of her, but when she ran outside, into a brisk wind that was raising up the dust, the road was empty. The moon was still rising.

Backtracking

Salida, Colorado. He stepped down from the Greyhound on stiff legs and looked around raw-eyed from a night of broken sleep. He was there. Home: on the concrete of its bus station, in the very exhaust fumes and restaurant smells and fluorescent glare of it. Welcome home, Jason. Bring out the brass band, folks—here I am. But first tell me where the rest room is . . .

He combed his hair in front of the mirror, picked up his satchel, gathered himself together, moving parts still intact, and outside the bus station took a scan of the street to get his bearings. Where to first? Not to the house. Save that for the last. What he wanted to do was look, wander around loose, get the feel of the place fresh coming back to it, before he got hooked into some new situation and the focus shifted and things darkened perhaps, threw up walls, turned strange. He started off along the main street with an open eye, tracing around cornices and taking in signs and studying the fronts of stores, not even trying to catch hold of anything, connect himself—if there was anything left to catch hold of. . . . Strangers, he thought, glancing into faces—like everywhere. Yet an impression gathered, despite storefronts having been remodeled, things coming in and going out—a hardware store where he remembered a grocery, the theater he used to go to on Saturday afternoons closed up, cage boarded: the scratch house, as the kids used to call it. The town had kept a certain flavor. Nor had everything been carried off in the flow of change. He found himself opposite his father's place—still a bar. Whose place now? he wondered. They'd kept the same name: The Spur. The spur you wore or the spur of the moment or the spur of the taste for drink? He decided to go in. The spur of curiosity—at least nothing so definite as desire nor so vague as impulse. He crossed the street.

Inside: a heavyset fellow tending bar. Widow's peak, tight face, narrow eyes, as though whatever they looked at, it was all the same to him—somebody Jason didn't recognize. He ordered a draft and looked around. They'd pulled out all the old wooden booths and put in tables with Formica tops and a jukebox and a TV. But they'd kept all the old woodwork around the bar, curlicues and all, and the chandeliers with the colored glass shades. The two sets of things drew sides and let you have it in the cross fire. He'd liked the old booths.

"Who runs this place now?" he asked the bartender.

"You're looking at him. Own it and run it."

"Used to be a guy named Avery."

"So they tell me."

"You don't happen to know what became of him?"

He looked at Jason as though he were trying to get a rundown on whoever the answer was going to, why he might be wanting it, and what he might be going to do with it—all in a glance.

"Drank himself to death."

"It figures. Broke the first rule—"

"You knew him?"

"A little."

"Got his liver finally. They said he used to chug down a quart a day."

Poor bastard. Ironic. He thought of how his father had lost the place to Avery in the poker game. It had been Avery's luck—and his fate. "How long's it been?"

The bartender seemed to loosen up a little, let through a sort of low-grade affability: "I've had the place seven, eight years now. Closed it up for a while after he went bankrupt. Had to get the lawyers to quit hassling over it. You always got to pry them loose of a thing. You live here?"

"Just visiting," he said, drained the glass, and left.

He had to cross the river to get over to Victor Street, where the house was. He paused on the bridge to contemplate the Arkansas. The old river. It had never been a big town, but it had the river. Cross plain and mountain in a wagon and there it is: precious water. You don't let go of it—you plant a town down on it every chance you get, even a little town. Every boy growing up will go fishing in it, as he had done, and, grown up and gone, carry the river along with him, running through memory, always there. The river was still there, always the same and always different. But looking at it, he felt somehow disembodied, the ghost of whoever he had been. Some few still had a memory of him—unfortunately. That thought alone had prevented him from coming back for his mother's funeral. He'd have had to stand there among them, their eyes on him.

Well, better get there and get it over with, he thought, leaving the river and turning down the street. Nearly fifteen years. God Almighty, where had the time gone? He'd walked down that street so often, he fell back into the old frame of mind, seemed to fall back into the time when it had all been familiar. But when he came to the old neighborhood, the mood collapsed. He scarcely recognized it. It had cut leading strings with the past and gone off on its own. Nearly all the other houses had been torn out. Gone without a trace, leaving not so much as a shell of the life that had gone on in them. Old Miss Pennuel, his fifth-grade teacher, who spent nearly all her life indoors pumping out hymns on her organ. Vern Grider, who'd put the cat up into the canary cage one morning for the sake of experiment. . . . A filling station took up part of the block, next to that a hamburger stand. Only the white frame house on the corner stood like a relic. The moment he saw it, something collared him: he'd done it, all right, and just let him walk in the door and the roof would land on his head.

He walked past the house and on to the end of the next block, crossed to the other side of the street, and came back. One of the pillars was gone, he noticed, and the porch, a clutter of tricycles and broken rockers and crates, had weakened to the point of collapse. The rest was all of a piece with the porch, the white paint a dirty dull, chipping, bare boards showing through. So that was what he owned half of . . .

Not that he gave a rat turd for it, he thought, crossing the street. Callie could have it and welcome to it. No doubt she'd earned it, nursing the old woman through her last bout of illness. God knows he'd done nothing for her, hadn't even come back to see her. So he couldn't figure out all the pestering, the letters that kept following him around for months, from his sister and from some lawyer named Jackson—Curtis Jackson, or Jackson Curtis, whatever the hell it was—the envelopes bearing a freight of postmarks and cancellations and addresses crossed out and smudges and creases from fingers clean and dirty. Every letter seemed to come to him with a weight of unknown humanity impressed upon it—a transaction with an anonymous fellowship—as he turned it over and tried to figure out how many hands it had passed through. He'd written letters back and signed papers—asserted and sworn and disclaimed—but the outcome of it was his being stuck with half a house that Callie and her kids were living in, and which, by all rights, ought to be hers. They were going to have to settle it one way or another, Callie wrote him: he owed her that much. Opening the last letter as he stood in the lobby of the flea-trap transient hotel in Albuquerque, he wondered at the faith or desperation that would make a woman suppose he'd come back there a second time. Inside he found a bus ticket home. So from a sense of some obscure obligation he'd come back—it was a matter of inheritance.

He rang the doorbell. A little girl of about six opened the door and stood there staring at him. Dinah, was it? He felt a sudden impulse to sweep her up and whirl her around, but thought better of it. It might scare her and, besides, Callie might not approve.

"Hello, honey, is your mother home?"

She left him standing in the doorway and disappeared. It was dark within, and on the blaring TV dark shapes jumped on the light patch of screen. As he adjusted his vision, a woman appeared in the darkened interior, tall, rather gaunt, and for a moment he saw his mother.

"Hello, Callie," he said, a tightness in his chest.

She looked at him, much as his mother would have done, sharply, as though nothing she saw made things any better or worse than she had expected. "Come in, Jason."

He went into the living room among the shapes of furniture. The child had returned, and now he saw another in front of the TV. "This Dinah?" he said, bending down on a knee so that he could look at her.

"Diane," she said, giggling. "My name's not Dinah—that's a funny name."

He was sure that went over big. He put his hand into his pocket and pulled out some chocolate.

"Don't spoil her with candy," Callie said. "I got enough to worry over without trips to the dentist."

"Just this once," the little girl pleaded. "Please."

"All right," Callie said, wearily, "but go play somewhere out of here and take Billy with you. Billy," she said, "you go on with Diane."

"I wanna watch."

"Look what I got, Billy. Come on, you can have a piece."

"Go on, get on out," Callie said. "She'll give you some. Give him half, you hear. And no fighting, or I'll paddle you both."

When the children were gone, Callie turned off the television and pulled open the shade.

The same wallpaper, Jason noticed, surprised to recognize it. It had been a silver-gray in an ivory background, but aged now to the color of yellowed parchment it trapped the light, made the room dim.

"Sit down," she said to Jason.

An uncomfortable silence followed after he had done so. He found himself staring at her and shifted his gaze to a spot on the wall. She was only three years older than he, but the years had not been kind—she looked forty. She'd been a pretty girl, he remembered, though in a rather severe way, and even now you could catch something of what had faded out, like the design of a piece of goods that had gone through the wash too often.

"Well, you're back," she said.

"Got your letter just the other day. How are you getting on?"

"Much as it's been a concern of yours all these years," she said, with half a smile. "Well, never mind that. I didn't send that letter or ask you back for old time's sake—it's a matter of business and a matter of money, and right now that's all I care about."

He didn't say anything.

"You know the will. Half the house is yours—"

"I thought we got all that straightened out," he said. "Take it, it's all yours. I don't want any of it."

"That'd make you feel good, wouldn't it? Big and easy brother. Well, don't think I wouldn't take it. If Mother had wanted me to have it, I'd have taken it all. God knows I earned it. What do you think it was like these last years with her on my hands? And the kids. And Sam running off. Why they haven't carted me off is the wonder of it."

"I'm sorry," he said.

"Yes, that's a good word. Covers a multitude of sins. You think it does any good?" she demanded. "You think it makes up for anything?"

She waited, apparently for him to think it over.

"Anyway," she continued, "she made me promise. 'It's his and he's got to have it'—she was that pigheaded about it. Or maybe senile. Or maybe, Gene being dead, she didn't want to write off the men in this family as a total loss." She gave him a straight look. "I wasn't to take it and you had to come back and settle it."

He shrugged. "I'm willing."

"All right. I'll give you five thousand dollars for your share of the property."

"Whatever you say."

"Yes, Jason the bighearted. It'll be a satisfaction to me to cheat you. They've offered me thirty thousand dollars for the land, to put in a supermarket. And I'm going to get the kids out of this hole and go to California and start over."

He said nothing.

"And you wouldn't stand up to me, would you? Not even insist on what's yours by rights—half after it's sold. No, you'll come home, your head all down in sorriness, wanting me to say, 'Welcome home.' But you won't stand up to me, will you?"

"Goddamn you, Callie," he said. "Don't push me too far. You got what you want. And you don't know what I want. Push me far enough and I'll change my mind."

She laughed. "So I got a rise out of you after all. I just wanted to see how long it would take you to get down off your high horse and start acting like people." She looked at him with contempt. "Oh, yes, I see I got to be nice to you, don't I? I was forgetting how you got to coax and wheedle a man, though maybe he'll run off anyway and leave you high and dry." She sat back, her face a blank.

"Good lord, Callie," he said, his anger gone. "Don't let it all get you whipped."

"I've suffered, Jason," she said, quietly. "All my life. You could get out—you got out and didn't look behind you. I been here all the time."

She held that against him—all his greener pastures. He went over and sat on the arm of her chair and took her hand. It was like ice. For a moment she let him hold it and smooth it and try to put some warmth back into it, but then she pulled free. "No," she said. "I don't want any of that any more. All I care about is the money."

"Isn't there anything . . ." he began, thinking of the children, ". . . to look forward to?"

"It's too late," she said. "I know what I know. All I want from everybody is to be left alone. And all I want from you is your signature."

"That's fine with me," he said, standing up. "The sooner we settle it the sooner I can leave, and the better I'll like it."

"That's your style isn't it?" she said. "We can start tomorrow. I'll call up the lawyer. The grocery chain's just waiting till they hear from me." She seemed almost to come to life. "You'll be wanting to spend the night. You can sleep on the couch."

"You sure you don't want me to sleep out on the porch or back in the shed?"

She ignored him. "Supper's at five and it don't wait."

"I won't be needing any, thanks," he said, thinking . . . might not even be back . . . and left the house. He had half a mind right then to hitch a ride out of town and leave her in whatever legal tangle she'd find herself in. He might as well prove to her—what? That he was one more man to leave her in the lurch; that the world was exactly the way she thought it was? At least he could prove to her that she should have thought twice about getting him riled. He wasn't even sure what was down there making all the boiling and bubbling now that she'd lifted the lid off the cauldron. Why had she made him come back, his mother? To humiliate him even from beyond the grave? Half the house—wanted him to have it. His inheritance . . . more stately mansions. . . . He hadn't built anything better. Not by a long shot.

He'd left his gear at the house, but there was nothing he was unwilling to part with; he was free to go on if he felt like going.

He started walking out toward the edge of town, though that didn't seem like what he wanted to do either. Then it occurred to him that if he went far enough, he'd find the cemetery. He wanted to see where she was buried. And old Avery too. He wasn't sure why. For the living to exult over the fallen dead?

It was good to walk, after the night on the bus and the half hour in the house—which had seemed far longer—good to be out in the late March weather. It was still cold, though the sky was bright and deep blue, and spring was somewhere whispering to the blood. Old snow still kept the ground, small drifts of it among the gravestones and patches of ice frozen in with brown matted grass, as though the cemetery would hold on to winter till the last.

He knew the cemetery, had sneaked off there as a boy with his buddies to smoke cigarettes, sneak a drink of whiskey. It seemed a little strange to him now that here in that fearsome privacy had begun the flirtations with the forbidden. And lovers, too, he had spied now and again, snatching at passion among the cold stones.

He entered the gate, as though into the dead center of things. No hurry. Nothing was going anywhere—all things had been delivered of their motion. And he found himself yielding to a stillness, an absence that called him beyond himself. No hurry: he wasn't going anywhere either. Everything pushed aside, suspended, he walked, without thinking about it, back to the old part of the cemetery, where the markers were so worn the names had all but disappeared into the stone. Some of his mother's people, Wagoners and Sewells, were buried there, including the one infant his grandmother had happened to bear in Salida. Her other twelve children had been born in nearly a dozen different towns around the state, while her husband had worked at one thing and another, bought and sold land, hauled rails by wagon for the D&RG. She'd scattered her children like so many seeds to the wind. She herself was buried out in California. Hadn't spent much time in any one place. Runs in the family, he thought. I come by it naturally.

A lot of little ones, he noticed. He'd read the name of a woman dead in the prime of life, and there clustered around her would be the graves of four or five of her children, infants mostly. Few of them had made it past the age of five. It must have been rough, the life on the frontier—and for some reason he thought of Callie. Hard on the women and the kids. Sickness and hunger and danger. Hard to keep the fires lit. Fodder for graves. Whatever had brought them to the West must have been pretty heady stuff. Only the strong had made it. The hardiest—or maybe the hardest. It was a question.

The dates became more recent, the old part of the cemetery merging into the new, in the continuousness of death. He found Avery first, right in his path. Ten years dead. He'd hated Avery and he'd tried to get even with him. . . . Yes, and destroyed him, a voice spoke within him. That's what his mother would have said. "There's no defense, is there?" he said. In his mind, Avery merely laughed, gave him a drunken leer. And his mother turned her back on him. He stood looking down at her grave. No explanation and no understanding . . . and no forgiveness either. How to put into words what had had no words then, what had seemed too powerful or too confused for human speech? How to speak to the dead? The power they exerted when living seemed to have grown beyond all bounds now that they were beyond him. Perhaps theirs was the final and greatest revenge now that they'd created what he had to live. No wonder she had made him come back.

"You should have left me alone, damn it all," he told her, and Avery. It struck him that that was Callie's only desire now. The trouble is, he reflected, no one is ever left alone. In a way he couldn't blame Avery. He'd won the bar; thinking how lucky he'd got, it was natural for him to go on to win the woman and the warm spot in the bed. To the victor go the spoils. Only it wasn't that simple. Avery had come around, a great bear of a man, taking off a soft suede hat and calling Jason's mother "ma'am," speaking gentle. He sat on the edge of the couch in the living room, looking ill at ease, yet uplifted in some painful but gratifying way. He couldn't find a place to fix his eyes, though he managed to keep his hands from getting away from him. The eyes, Jason had noticed, flew everywhere, landed for a moment on his mother's bosom, then leapt away, followed the back of her out of the room when she went after the coffee, met her eyes when she returned, slipped away to her neck, took a moment's rest on her bosom, shot down to the floor, followed an ankle up, landed briefly on her bosom, and flew off to rest on the picture on the opposite wall, of three horses feeding at a trough. Horses of three different colors—white, yellow, and brown—feeding devotedly at the trough—painted by a cousin under the delusion of having talent. Horses whose three eyes watched you go from one side of the room to the other. Avery's eyes met the horses'; the horses' eyes met Avery's. No doubt the horses had only a little less trouble than Jason had at the time trying to figure out why Avery was there and what he wanted.

The next time Avery came, Jason remembered, his mother had fed him supper, and Avery had reminisced about his boyhood. The meal reminded him that food was something you could relish on the way down instead of merely being fodder you threw down to your hunger to get it to leave off and lie down quiet. He'd been in the army and worked in the oil fields and had done some hauling on contract with his own truck, and in all that knocking around, he'd never cared what he put into his stomach, never really tasted it, it went down so fast. When he came around the third time, he said he didn't aim for a fine woman like her to go a-begging; it went against his principles. And didn't the Bible say somewhere to give justice to widows and orphans? He wasn't much of a Bible man, but he did remember something of the sort, and the Lord's Prayer.

It may have been that his mother's biscuits and fried rabbit had awakened some long-buried instincts. In any case, Avery said that winning that bar had made a changed man out of him. He'd never held on to a dime before, had thrown it away as fast as he made it. But now he was ready to settle down and become civilized. The next time he came he brought his traps.

"Well, boy," he'd said to Jason, and there was that great hand clapping him on the shoulder, "don't stand there gawking. I've come to be your pa. And I brought you a present. Look at that, will you?"

And there before his eyes were a pair of handmade cowboy boots and a BB gun he'd been half a year trying to wangle his mother into buying for him.

They were waiting for him. Avery was waiting for him to go wild over the gun; his mother was waiting for him to go wild over Avery; and his sister was standing there looking pleased over the new dress Avery had brought for her. Even the horses were waiting. He'd wanted a BB gun as badly as he'd ever wanted anything. They were all waiting. Before he knew what he was doing, he'd kicked Avery in the shin and run out of the room. Behind him, the horses stampeded.

His mother flew down on him like a fury. What did he mean doing that? Somebody trying to be nice and look what you do. "I ought to whale the tar out of you."

She shook him instead.

"Now listen, you're going to be nice to Avery, you hear? If your pa was half a man, he'd be here right this instant, wouldn't he?"

Shake. Shake.

"And why isn't he here?—answer me that." Shake. Shake. "Because he did us harm, that's why."

His father? Harm?

"It was him that ran away. Don't you forget that. You think he gives two hoots what happens to us? Avery's going to take care of us. Him a perfect stranger, too. That's who's going to do good for us. And you'd better treat him right, you understand? Now go in there and tell him you're sorry."

He told him. He said the words. But with his eyes he said, "Go away." His father had gone away because Avery had been his bad luck. As Jason thought about it now, it seemed that by a fantastic logic he had been part of Avery's bad luck, though Avery hadn't gone away. Sometimes he had lain in the dark, seeing before his mind's eye how it would be if his father came back and threw Avery out of the house and beat him up and broke his neck. Then things could start all over again from the beginning, fresh and new. And all his daydreams grew from the soil of that stupidity. "Go away," he said to Avery in his mind. "Go away," he said with his eyes.

It was the only thing he could say. What else was there to say to a man you'd kicked in the shins after he'd given you a BB gun? At first Avery had looked at him with puzzlement, then with a certain disgust, as though at a dog that ought to know better but that has peed on the carpet. And finally that disgust deepened and sharpened to the point where Jason was a dog he wanted to kick.

"Get out of my sight. If I see you around the next minute, you'll wish you weren't. Get." Whack. Slam. "That's right. You run. Get used to running. You're your daddy's little boy."

And whereas, before, his feelings for Avery had been only as Avery represented his father's bad luck, now he hated Avery purely for himself.

He wondered now whether Avery had been sober those times or liquored up. For having the bar made a changed man of him in more ways than one. It meant that when he poured himself a shot from the bottle, he could pour himself another, as many as he wanted, without his money wearing out ahead of his thirst. It may have been that he'd always had the susceptibility, but that having to work steady, hold on to a job, he'd never given full satisfaction to that thirst. Or maybe it had taken the bar for him to discover it at all, that fatal capacity. At the time it had made no difference to Jason, except that, sober, Avery was steadier on his feet. Avery sober would just as soon have whacked him one as Avery drunk.

But that just proved to Jason that he was right. Aha, he'd known it all along—the secret—and within his heart of hearts he rejoiced. Avery was a VILLAIN, a surefire, honest-to-God villain. And there would come a day of reckoning. That's the way it happened in the books anyway: books he read in the library all about the West and books his grandfather had collected and preserved with such loving care, all about Wild Bill Hickok. For wasn't his grandfather the natural son of Wild Bill? Or so the old man claimed in his crazy way. Hoarded away in Jason's room was the collection his grandfather had put into his keeping with tremulous hands—so much rubbish his mother called it: biographies and dime novels and yellowing, brittle newspapers and old magazines, J. W. Buell's *Heroes of the Plains* and *Wild Bill, the Pistol Deadshot* and the February 1867 issue of *Harper's Monthly Magazine.* Their pages spoke to him, created an image in his head:

". . . eyes that have pointed the way to death of hundreds of men . . ."

"Singular grace and dignity"
"He shoots to kill."
". . . eyes as gentle as a woman's . . ."
"Quiet manly face . . ."
"He shoots to kill."
"Six feet one inch tall . . . quiet manly face . . ."
"With his own hands has killed hundreds of men . . ."
". . . hundreds of men . . . shoots to kill . . ."

If Wild Bill could handle M'Kandlas and the "gang of despera-does, horse thieves, murderers, regular cut-throats who were the terror of everybody," standing up to them one lone man against ten and killing them all, then surely he, Jason, could take on one drunken bully. Next time Avery laid into him or rough-handled his mother, he'd get something he wasn't counting on. He'd show him. Prove himself. Someday they could write a book about him:

Wildcat Jason
From Boyhood to Manhood
Deeds of Daring, Scenes of Thrilling Peril, and Romantic
Incidents in the Early Life of Jason Hummer

She clung to him and he could feel her heart palpitating as she held his head against her bosom. "Oh, son, hide yourself," she cried as the tears trickled down into his face. "Save your-self against him. He is too strong for a poor child like you. And he is wild as the savages when the strong drink is on him."

"Oh, Mother, do not fear," said the boy. "When I was a babe in the arms, you were my guardian angel. Now I am a man. And I would be the most shameless coward that ever lived if I did not stand up to that brute and deliver my angel."

"Oh, son, now I see what has become of my sweet boy. He has grown up before my eyes. He will make me proud of him."

At that moment there came a violent thundering at the door, and the poor woman nearly fainted from fright. "Oh, hide yourself," she pleaded, clutching his arm. "He'll kill you."

"Begone, wretch," yelled the boy. "Venture one step over yon-der threshold and you're a dead man."

"Haw," came a voice. "You dare to stand up to me, do you, you little varmint? I'll snap you like a twig. I'll crush you like a jelly." From within, they could hear him lunging against the door.

Seizing a rifle from the wall, Jason stood, prepared to face the murderous Avery.

"Is that thing loaded?" his mother cried, growing white as a sheet.

"Quick, behind the curtain," the boy commanded, as the door burst open and Avery stood before him, a Goliath.

Young Jason fired one shot.

Fired one shot. Delivered his mother and sister and himself from a drunken bully. Dazed, he stood looking down at the dead man, finally hearing his mother's screams. "You've killed him. Oh, you've killed him. What have you done? Now what'll become of us?" He just stood there, numb all over. There was blood. They turned him over and his body flopped as though it hadn't a single bone in it. The dead man began to moan. Drunk. Falling-down drunk. Jason had shot him in the leg.

So it turned out that Avery was right after all: Jason ran off just as his father had done. And he couldn't have said then whether it was his having shot Avery that sent him off or whether it was his mother's carrying on. All he knew was that he couldn't stay there any longer. For when you've shot a man in the leg for the sake of deliverance and justice and not even your own mother approves, you are a man accurst, despised by the gods and man, and your fate is to wander, with no place to rest your head. But thinking about it now, Jason would have said that it was not they who'd sent him running but only that they had revealed to him a gigantic failure he had embraced—a failure that had been beyond his imagination.

His dream had turned to dust. The West had crumbled before his eyes: the roaring towns of the frontier, with the hardy spirits who acted for the sake of justice, against the backdrop of those simplicities of good and evil . . . gone, all of it. And what was left—only the graves in the old part of the cemetery?

All that dream and hope and enterprise and energy and daring that had led that flood of settlers and prospectors and soldiers and ruffians across the plains and over the mountains, enduring what they endured. Then you turned over the other side of the rock and there was all that greed and land hunger and vanity and blood-thirst. All the effort and all the slaughter. The slaughter of the buffalo and the slaughter of the Indian. The Texas War for Independence and the Mexican War and the cattle and sheep wars. The Alamo and Sand Creek and Little Big Horn—all of it. When the dream had died and you had to look down at the blood in the dust, what did you do then? Confess—let out all your vileness, wallow in it, maybe even smother in it? Was that the legacy from the past—the vileness and the ugliness and the guilt? A falling-down old house with the paint chipped away?

Maybe, he thought, there is nothing so false or stupid as the idea of the second chance, the fresh start. It had sent a whole people chasing across a continent—no doubt that was something. It might even be, he thought, that all those movements of history had come of having an idea stupid enough for a human to believe in. And there was Callie thinking that going to California would make some sort of difference to her. She might as well stay where she was, for all the good it would do her, he thought, as he left the cemetery. He could spare her one more disillusionment. Not that it mattered. He could leave town or he could insist on half the money or he could let her do as she pleased, and whatever it was she'd be bitter about it, see it with the same eyes.

And so, if you had no dream . . . then all you have is the ugliness, the mud at the bottom of the ditch. Either way you were damned. Either way there was something unreal, as though the human animal were doomed to carry about a certain amount of unreality with him. As for failure, life didn't seem to mind failure. It tucked all kinds of it away in the grave and went on.

He hesitated at the side of the road for a moment and turned and headed back to the house. He was going to be a rich man for a change—rich for him. What would he do with five thousand dollars? Maybe just put it in a bank somewhere and let it lie like an unplowed field. No, he'd bury it, along with the dead. Callie could do what she liked.

Sloan's Daughter

At three in the morning the phone rang: a call from Moran for him to come down to the police station. Sloan was wide awake with the first ring; nowadays he floated just under the surface of sleep, some part of him alert, waiting for Natalie to come home, or for the lapse of hours to build toward a distress sufficient to wake him. He would then get up and prowl the house. Sometimes she staggered in without a word, disheveled, lipstick smeared wide of her mouth, and took no heed of him as she headed to her room. Or she might glare at him, gesture as if to push him away. Occasionally she said, "Oh, you didn't have to wait up." Thus he knew the range of her scorn.

"Thought you'd decided not to come home," he'd said, hardly a week before.

"When that happens," she countered, "you'll know about it."

They stood locked into each other's stare, as though the next move would bring them to a space they were wary of entering. He had no idea any more what he was staring at. During her growing up he'd hoped it was simply beauty: the way the high cheekbones captured him with their curve of shadow and the eyes teased him away from what he knew of her childhood and drew him to certain depths. He had never seen such eyes, the blue held in rings of black that gave them an intensity beyond either color. In a face that held every shifting mood—pale, set off by a mane of black hair, before she'd hacked it off.

What was it now?—what new trouble beyond the mere affront to his sleep? Hastily he pulled on his trousers, grabbed his shirt from the back of the chair, slipped into his shoes, and scooped up wallet, change, and car keys from the nightstand. What sort of thing that went past doing drugs or roaring drunkenly down the back roads or sleeping with a new man every night? Which you could hardly call trouble these days, but rather a way of life.

He entered the night chill with a rising resentment. He should have kicked her out long ago. But what would happen to her, his own flesh and blood? It didn't matter what the town would think of him; one way or another they'd had plenty to gossip about over the years. He could feel it in the air whenever he walked the street. Could feel it in the very house, with its furniture and keepsakes and family history, where Manuela moved darkly silent through the battleground between father and daughter, while the two of them came and went like strangers.

She had been tearing things apart since the day she was born, happy only when her toys were in pieces. She tore flowers apart and tormented animals. And when she was older, turned loose on the town, she courted mayhem, painting obscenities on walls and sidewalks, breaking streetlights, taking other people's cars for joyrides. It was a huge joke to her, this streak of anarchy, getting herself and other kids in trouble. She had stood by watching Sloan pick up after her, paying for the damages, trying to punish her into a better frame of mind. Watching him, he sometimes felt, with a certain triumph: she could do anything and get away with it. Theirs was the family that had set the first stakes into the territory; everything had been theirs by rights. Let her bring down the wrath of the whole town and she would laugh in their teeth.

A full moon shed its light on the Mesa and on the sweeping slope of Eagle Tail and the peak of Tenaja to the southwest. Since his grandfather had got himself a great swath of this land and planted some of the richest timothy grass anywhere in the world and raised horses and the devil, they'd always been here commanding a large view of the distant peaks. Folsom man had been discovered on that mesa. He backed the car out and took the curves that he could have driven even in his sleep, descending into the lights of the town.

The moment he entered the station, he could hear her from the cells at the back—laughter, singing, swearing, Natalie's voice above the rest. Irrepressible—caged or free, drunk or sober. He tried to see past the practiced indifference of the men at their desks.

"Daddy's coming," she sang out. "Don't you worry. When Daddy's here, the world's a pearl. Hey guys, get this one—"

Moran was in his office, a large man with a head like an eggplant, narrow skull and heavy jowls. A small pink mouth under a precise mustache gave him a serious expression. He stood up with a creak of leather and came forward. Sloan wondered irrelevantly how fat men ordered their gun belts.

"What's the trouble, Sammy?" The two of them had cracked jokes in the locker room when they'd played football in high school. Moran, too, came from one of the oldest families in town, though he'd grown up in the section called Stringtown, where only some of the streets were paved but the younger generation spoke English in the streets instead of Spanish. During those years when a Mexican had the choice of being a janitor or joining the army, Moran had begun working his way up. Now he was chief of police, and he kept a clean town.

He virtually lived at the station or in his patrol car, eating his lunch behind the wheel or sending out for a pizza from his desk. How he managed to sleep or spend time with his family Sloan found a source of wonder. Moran had four or five kids. But perhaps that was what it took to earn the grudging respect of the town. Standing in front of him, Sloan had to face him stripped of moral advantage. Not even the three previous generations of his family could bolster him.

"Sorry to drag you out this time of night," Moran said, as though his sympathy perhaps went deeper. "But they were down in the cemetery breaking up the headstones."

The cemetery, for God's sake. He wanted to seize his daughter by the hair—what was left of it—yank her outside and shake her until something came loose or broke. "They? Who's they?"

"Five of them," Moran said. "Not from around here. Said they came up from Texas—Laredo. They were clean, but I'll bet they ditched a stash somewhere. Have a feeling they were heading out to sell it in California. You can hear them in there," he said, with a jerk of his thumb in their direction.

Moran didn't have to make a show of his contempt. You could read it from his eyes, from the way he stood in his shoes, held his spine. Law. Everything spoke it, his every gesture: law on his side, the town's side. And at least by proxy, Sloan was breaking it. He could see it: five of them and his daughter. A whang-bang, drunken orgy down the cemetery. Tearing across Texas and New Mexico hell-bent for wherever speed, booze, dope, and their dicks could take them. Now here to waken the dead.

"Looked like some kind of ritual," Moran said. "Stones in a ring. Something burning. You wouldn't believe the smell." His revulsion came perhaps from the same source of motive that made him prowl the town at night.

And Sloan could hardly keep down what rose within him, the desire to shake or twist something out of her. So that he would know, finally understand what went beyond all reason. He went off to summon his lawyer, to do the things impelled. If that could include getting down on his knees and uttering some apology or promise that would wipe away the past, he'd gladly have done it.

"I want to know what you were doing," he demanded of his daughter when they were finally out of the station, on their way home. At first she had resisted being released without her friends.

"What is all this? Stones in a ring. Things burning. You didn't kill anything, did you?"

"Oh," she said in a burst of rage. "Oh." Then her hands were over her ears as though to shut him out or forestall an explosion in her head. "It was nothing, nothing. Oh," she said, as if she couldn't believe. "We were drinking some beer. Dancing. Greg built a fire and we started dancing."

"In the cemetery?"

"It was a clear space. Why not?—nothing to bother anybody there. Except the fuzz. We weren't doing anything. Just having some fun. You know—fun. You don't know anything about it."

"Knocking over tombstones isn't exactly my idea of fun, as you call it. Desecrating—"

"Desecrating that fucking cop. He was lying there in wait, ready to pounce. We didn't break anything. It was like that when we got there."

"Told me it looked like somebody had taken a sledgehammer—"

"Sure, I carry one around all the time. And all the guys have them strapped to their handlebars. Regular issue."

"Don't get smart."

"I'll bet the cops did it themselves so they could pin it on us. You know what Moran does?"

He knew what Moran did.

"He goes down to the whorehouse and gets any girl he likes. Then he takes her up to the city building, and she has to do anything he wants. Otherwise they'd be out of this town."

He had to hand it to her—she knew how to slip out from under. "It doesn't change the fact."

"And once he came up to Angie Manzini parked out with her date and made her get out of the car and when he took her home—"

"All right, you've made your point. It's a dirty job and the pay stinks and nobody else wants it." And everybody liked having a clean town, if that was what it took. And more. Anybody the cops picked up who aroused their suspicions got such a working over he made a wide circle of the town ever after. Even the sheriff's office wouldn't take some of the prisoners once they'd landed in the local jail. That's the way the world went.

"Suppose it was me. You wouldn't care, would you?"

"Not care? How could you possibly say that?"

"But not about somebody else?"

"Of course I care." Though from her, he thought bitterly, no one would ever have to take anything by force.

"No you don't," she said, turning away. "Not about me or anybody else."

"What am I doing now?" he demanded. "Do you think I came down here for my entertainment? And I'm entitled to know what the hell you were doing."

"Yes," she said. "Entitled. Well, if you insist—nothing."

"Don't tell me. Something was burning."

"A dead possum—it was this guy's idea of joke. He found it on the highway. He put it on the fire."

Don't lie, he wanted to say. Don't lie. "Just tell me the truth," he said. "I'll stand by you no matter what."

She gave a shriek of laughter. "You'd stand by the devil—isn't that what you're saying?"

The car lurched as he reached over and slapped her.

"Watch out," she said. "You don't want to smash your car." Then she sat there as though inviting him to slap her again, harder this time. He was rigid. No matter what he did, she had

the better of him. They climbed to the top of the Mesa. Behind
Eagle Tail and Tenaja the sky was a brilliant red.

In his office later in the morning, Sloan sat bleary-eyed, bol-
stering himself with coffee while he tried to make sense of the
figures on the sheet in front of him. The longer he stared at them,
the more they seemed to elude him, to scatter in fragments. How
was it that some children came into the world? What had he
done or failed to do? Given her too much, too little? Did some
fault lie in her making? The figures drew him into a maddening
dance, shifting, coming together wrong on the calculator.

"Paul Moore here to see you," the voice of his secretary
announced on the intercom.

"Show him in." He was grateful for the interruption.

He hadn't seen Moore for a goodly while, it occurred to him—
had waved to him in town, but that was about it. Moore was part
of the fabric of things again, his life settled back into its former
patterns. He'd gone off to Vietnam in the early days of the war
and come back before public feeling had turned against it, something of a hero in local terms. He'd had his troubles though, had
been in and out of a rehabilitation center a couple of times.

He came in, a tall man who walked with a stiff leg, in the company of a younger copy who had to be his son and had grown
up while Sloan wasn't looking. He was a shade taller than the
father, more broadly built. They had the same faces, broad
brows and strong cheekbones, the same manly reserve. They
shook hands.

"Good to see you, Paul," Sloan said, motioning them to chairs.
"And your boy—I forgot he'd be grown up by now."

"Paul, Junior," the older said, saving Sloan the awkwardness
of having to ask his name.

"Good to see you both." He looked from one to the other. The
boy still had the look of enjoying being young—nights in town,
out with the girls. "What can I do for you?"

"We've come to see you about a loan. There's a piece of land
come up for sale over by Tenaja. Ten thousand acres. Not the best
land around, but I figure it's something to get the boy started on.
He's one of those who's got ranching in his blood."

You could see he was proud of him. A lot of the boys had no interest in continuing the tradition. It was hard work, especially if you wanted to do it the old way, rounding up the cattle with horses and spending days in the saddle, nights on hard ground, getting up at the crack of dawn. They'd been ranching ever since the days of the Maxwell land grant, through good times and bad. And Paul put him in mind of how Sloan's father had carried them through the years of the drought some years back. They talked about land prices and rainfall and grass and the prospects for the future. Despite all the hazards of ranching—the uncertainties of the market and the rainfall, and those things that fell under the label of sheer bad luck, the boy would go on with it. He'd probably been sat on a horse's back by the time he was a year or two old and would very likely ride over his own land as though he were joined to the animal.

Sloan sent for coffee, and, their business done, they sat companionably till the bottom of the cup.

"So you're past all that Vietnam business," Sloan said. He was curious.

"As much as I'll ever be," Paul said. "I never did get my sleep patterns back. I still wake up every couple of hours."

Sloan gave a little murmur.

"I don't have nightmares any more, thank goodness. Just broken sleep."

"I guess we count our blessings," Sloan said.

The two men rose to leave. "Fortunately I didn't do anything I had to be ashamed of," Paul said. He paused a moment. "But I think it was the land that saved me."

After he'd left, Sloan felt a burning to know what he'd done or hadn't done: simply followed orders in the conviction of right action or somehow hadn't killed anyone. And the land? Moore had stood at the crux of a national dilemma, its shame, and somehow emerged. He'd gone back to what he'd come from, and it held him up. Sloan was less clear about himself. It seemed he'd always been somewhere in the outlands, where the territory was far more ambiguous, and it was difficult to seize hold of purpose. He sat at his desk, following without thinking the sweep of Eagle Tail, the cone of Tenaja. He was so accustomed to the way they shaped the landscape, their tawny slopes like the flanks of horses, that he hardly saw them, though his father had bought and sold nearly all the land around them, as well as great parcels along the Mesa.

All there to be bought and sold, as it had once been there to conquer. Part of the family lore was the stories of how, on the way to that conquest, his great-grandfather, a boy of fourteen, had been captured by the Apaches. They'd taught him to ride bareback and shoot a bow and arrow, and sent him out to hunt rabbits and deer with the other boys and young braves. Then he'd served as apprentice to the medicine man and accompanied him in search of herbs, learned their properties, and helped prepare them for the ceremonies. A fascinating figure to Sloan, this boy gone Indian, speaking their language, riding over the land, ridge upon ridge, knowing it the way an animal might, as sight and smell and a feel of things, as instinct made it out; then recaptured and taken back to be a white man and help to track the Indians. For he knew all their tricks firsthand to use against them. In the company of General Crook, he'd chased Geronimo all over northern Mexico.

His grandfather had moved into more settled times, something of a conqueror as well. For he'd wooed a woman to win the land he got. Her father was the biggest landowner in the northern part of the state, and she persuaded him to deed over a stretch of the Mesa to his future son-in-law. But right before the wedding, the deed safely in hand, this Sloan decamped and married a waiting cousin from Indiana. No one knew what happened to his intended. But as Sloan's father put it, "Wouldn't any of us have been here otherwise." No one could argue with that.

On this foundation, his father had turned toward the town to build the family fortune. He'd taken over the town's bank just after the Depression, bought and sold land till the landholding company he set up controlled a large acreage. Then he'd sold it all and gone into politics. Sloan had been the one to recover all that had been lost in that fruitless venture.

Though he usually designated Sundays for his visits to his father in the nursing home, he decided to go that afternoon. He was no good for anything in the office. At least he could go where his insufficiency would go unnoticed. There were times now when Sloan's father didn't recognize him, but even when the old man knew him for his son, Sloan always left feeling deeply troubled. As though he still expected something, like a code to decipher some unintelligible document. Even on those occasions when he received no sign his father knew he was there, Sloan lingered for a time as though something might emerge from even the failure of lucidity: perhaps some word issuing unbidden from the depths to give expression to what was resistless and urgent within him. It was strange now how the feeling came to him, powerful enough to be called a longing. Something was owing to him, some debt unpaid—why did he feel that? Something that went beyond anything they'd known with one another and that might have made a difference. His father stood as though defending a threshold that Sloan had never been able to pass, and his death would only seal the doorway. Let him pluck something out before it was too late.

His father didn't give him much to go on. For the most part, the old man lay folded within himself like some ancient, molting, heavy-lidded raptor, and if there were some word within him that would strike sparks, he hoarded it to himself.

On this afternoon, though, he seemed alert, even lively, leaping through the past like a jackrabbit zigzagging through a great stretch of territory suddenly reduced to a single jumbled patch.

"Wants me to run booze into Oklahoma. A regular liquor business. Tell old man Manzini I'm in. We'll make a killing—just the two of us. Put his man Welton on the state liquor board. A patsy—does everything he's told."

Only his father hadn't run booze illegally into Oklahoma back in the fifties when he was given the chance. He'd been too clever for them. Sloan could pinpoint the exact year, the summer he'd come back home, right after his graduation from Dartmouth. Turned down the offer. To his surprise.

"I don't mind breaking a law," he'd said almost truculently, "and it's a stupid law, but I do mind getting caught for something where you don't have a leg to stand on. That's your first lesson in banking or politics."

Apparently his father didn't have then the larger instinct to know who might be bought off and for how much. He didn't trust Manzini, but Manzini had made out like the bandit he was.

Instead his father had put his trust into "slippage," as he called it, and prided himself on being sharp, canny—in the right place at the right time. Let a man look sharp and things fell into his lap. Burrow under the outer layers of fact and into the knots of hidden activity and you emerged knowing where the new high school or federal project would be located. Then you slipped in and bought the land. Keep your eye peeled on certain ranchers who expanded beyond their prospects or gambled in futures or pissed away their money in Las Vegas. Gauge the right moment—that was part of the game. You slipped one way when things slipped another. He was not a man to take the bread out of any man's mouth. No sir, he was as fair-minded as the next fellow. But when the moment arrived—inevitably in the nature of things—and what had held slipped away, spun out of control owing to a failure of nerve or judgment, that was his signal to move in. A lucky son-of-a-bitch, people called him—till he made a few wrong moves himself.

Still ruddy-faced in spite of his time indoors, the old man sat in his lounging robe as though he were about to give audience, make a pronouncement. He leaned confidentially toward his son. "Get in on it, my boy. Make your own luck. And remember the drought's on your side. They've borrowed to the hilt and they can't hold out. Take it—it's yours."

That was ten years later, when Sloan was a vice president himself, and he remembered the ranchers flooding into the bank, old men, men in their prime, even a few young ones, trying for the loan that would take them through more bad times. And some emerged still able to hold on, while others seemed beaten, swallowed up. And the old man ruling in the office: this one, not that one—like the hand of fate.

Now the old man sat humming to himself, as though letting out the sound of his inner machinery. And Sloan, impatient, broke in. "That's all done with, Dad. We've taken care of it. What about now? What about the future?"

The old man's face darkened with conviction. "Everything I got, I got myself." He rapped his chest vigorously. "I took the risks, I leapt into the ring. The politics in this state—they stink like puke. But that didn't stop me. I kept going. I went ahead."

And never got anywhere. "But Dad," Sloan protested in spite of himself. "Remember. Remember—how you got the chance." For there was a moment that troubled him still. A crux perhaps where he'd been caught. A doorway he'd never entered. He couldn't think about it.

"I could have had this state in my pocket," the old man insisted. "Governor. The Senate. All the way to Washington." He looked around, as though the room were filled with threat. "Treachery everywhere."

Everything addled in the brain, turned inside out, all the losses put down as gains. He was still taking the tally, but the figures came out skewed. He'd never even made it to the statehouse—in spite of all it had taken to try to get him there. The election was lost before it ever took place, in truth because the boys in the statehouse didn't want him. Whatever face they put on for him. The harder Sloan looked, the more things reeled and shifted before his eyes. Where was there ground to stand on? "Dad," he insisted. "Listen to me." There had to be something to hold on to. "Believe me, there was a sacrifice."

An expression Sloan couldn't read crossed the old man's face. And then his vision settled like the surface waters of an incredibly clear lake. Nothing to be seen but one's own reflection, as though the old man had slipped away entirely unmarked by experience. He leaned forward again. "It's those Mexicans—you can't trust any of them. Don't let them get hold of this state," he said, hammering his hand against his thigh. And then as though speaking a prophecy, "The spoilers," he said, gesturing beyond him. "They'll take all. Turn the land to dust. The cattle will die and the children starve. Beware of the spoilers." With that, he sank back as though the effort had taken all he had.

Sloan stood over his bed. If he died now, it wouldn't make any difference. A vast loneliness seized him. "Dad," he said. "Dad, I'm leaving now." The old man opened his eyes at the sound of the voice but gave no sign of recognition.

Fortunately for his state of mind, he wouldn't be going home for several hours. If he weren't meeting Beverly, he'd have called up some friend who was loose for the evening and gone to sit in a bar somewhere. He couldn't face Natalie's hostile silence over the dinner table or else an absence meant to provoke him. Either would have driven him frantic. And he didn't trust himself to be alone. He'd never liked being alone, especially when he was down. At the moment, he couldn't think straight. He needed someone there even just to look at.

He was picking Beverly up after school, and they were going down to the Westward Ho! for drinks and a long, hopefully casual, conversation that would lead them into a dinner of filet mignon. They too had gone to high school together, though long periods had intervened when they didn't see one another. But recently she'd divorced her husband and gone back to teaching English at the high school. She was an attractive woman, who kept herself trim and who dressed well, and she had a quick eye and a ready humor. She needed all the humor she could get, as she put it—to face those kids. Sloan liked her company. She'd once been a rodeo queen and still had a passion for horses. Sometimes she came up to the Mesa to take out one of Sloan's, a particular gelding she liked.

He waited for her in the high school parking lot for over half an hour. Just as he was about to go in and look for her, she came rushing out.

"Sorry I'm late," she said, getting into the car. "I had this little girl in my office—pregnant."

It wasn't exactly the opening he'd hoped for. Things like that seemed to be happening all the time. "I suppose she's got her parents to face." Parents.

"The parents know about it," she said. "She's been living with this boy for nearly a year. And they've encouraged her to have the baby—"

"That's pretty open-minded." He was getting them down the hill, back into town, watching out for the homeward bound traffic.

"Only the two of them have been doing drugs, and they don't dare have the child. That means an abortion—only she's had one before."

"Good grief."

"And she's scared to death."

On the edge, walking into the future with all the wrong moves. Like Natalie. Still young. But knowing too much. Drugs and abortions and abuses and every kind of sex. Too much of things turned wrong—twisted out of shape. They drove in their separate silences down to the hotel bar. "Do forgive me," she said, as they settled themselves at one of the low tables. "I didn't mean to set the trademark for the evening."

"What'll it be?" he said, as the waitress came up.

"Those kids just get to me. Awful, isn't it?"

He agreed.

"Sometimes when I look my son in the eyes, I think, who is this kid and where did he come from? But at least he's got a job now and he's out of my hair."

"Natalie's in trouble again," he ventured, and, as he told her the latest, he had, for the first time that day, hold of something known and solid. "Not that you won't have a chance to read about it in your local paper," he added.

"Oh," she said, reaching over and touching his hand. "I'm so sorry."

He'd have liked to enter her sympathy, sink down and let go. But everything was prickling around his head, like thorns left to goad him. "It makes me feel like a jackass," he said. "Like I've done it all wrong."

"I know what you mean," she said. "Only you can't let yourself think that way."

"I should never have come back here."

"Whatever gave you that idea?"

"I don't know. When I was in school I thought of being an actor—going off to the city and trying it out. I loved the theater."

"That's what's known as being young."

"But there are those who make it. Or I could have come back and raised cattle—maybe horses." He was thinking of the Moores, of his own family.

"What's that got to do with anything?" she said. "You always hated those 4-H projects, those calves you were supposed to be so vitally interested in. I remember how ticked off you were baby-sitting that heifer at the State Fair when we were going off to Santa Fe to raise hell."

He laughed, caught out. "I was the kid that escaped to the Ivy League. So I wouldn't have to look at another cow. Only sometimes I think it was only so my father could brag on it, brag about how much money he was spending on me."

She shrugged. "Listen, I've got kids that don't have a prayer, who'll spend the rest of their lives earning minimum wage—if they don't end up in jail or something worse."

Her common sense might have been balm to his spirits, if he hadn't wanted something more than common sense.

"That's just it," he said. "With all those advantages, there must have been something I should have done."

"Like what?" she said. "You've got the bank, you're well respected in the town, known in the state. You've had a hand in town politics. And you have a future, other things to do. I'll bet there are some in the wind right now."

He gave a little start: what she was saying was almost uncanny.

"So what else should you have done?"

"Married you," he said, surprised at himself.

"Come on," she said, not taking him seriously. "But you can still do that," she added. "If the love bug starts biting."

He drove up to the Mesa with that slow somewhat diffused caution that ran with the suggestion that if Moran stopped him now, he'd have reason to give him a night in the drunk tank. Two drinks before dinner, and then the wine. But the wine had eased him, and he'd ordered another bottle. By the time they left the restaurant, a certain warmth suffused and momentarily lifted him. As he left the lights of the town and took the curved road, certain phrases of the evening teased him: *married you— if the love bug starts biting—married you. Something in the wind.*

It was an idea he hadn't even entertained, marrying again. For there had been that moment, enshrined now, that could never be duplicated, that moment that had beckoned him beyond anything he knew. It was like a room he never opened, but had kept, as after a death, just the way it had always been. There were two moments he never visited, one that had promised everything of light; the other that held all that could be suggested of darkness. Whatever had come from these he tried not to dwell upon.

Marrying again. Would even the thought rob him of what had been sacred, inviolate, even though everything it led to and promised was gone?

When he arrived at the house, he found himself this time happily alone. Manuela had gone to bed, and Natalie—who knew where she was? He went to the sideboard and poured himself a generous brandy for a nightcap. He wasn't sure where he wanted to drink it, not in his father's study—still kept as though he might somehow return—not even in the living room. Finally he went to the small sunporch where his mother used to brood over her cactus garden, and his wife used to look out at the mountains at sunset. He sat in the dark looking out at the indigo night. There were stars everywhere.

One moment, that one moment he had seized and could never let go of. Seized the pearl from the muck. The muck being one of those parties in Santa Fe given by a big contractor who'd wanted to impress his political friends. Sloan's father had been off in Denver, and his mother, fading out of the picture, couldn't go, but had sent him as a proxy. The contractor's wife, Ellie, heavy with perfume and sexual interest, had introduced him all around, kept drinks in his hand, and taken him in tow for the evening.

A heady experience, all the attention from his father's cronies, along with the pressure of Ellie's hip and leg against his side, the touch of her fingertips along his arm. He knew clearly what she wanted of him, and he saw no reason not to comply. He'd caught a glimpse of that exquisite point where lust and power come together and everything is possible. At that moment, though he'd always a enjoyed a certain contempt for him, he understood his father. He felt a sudden urge to seize his hostess, throw her to the floor, mount her, climb to the peak of dizzying sensation, and leap into space. He was ready to swoon.

His hostess left him for a moment to greet other guests, and he leaned on the wall of the patio, closed his eyes, and tried to collect himself. When he opened his eyes again, he saw a young girl he hadn't seen before: a slender girl with her dark hair tied back with a red ribbon and falling in a lustrous coil down her back. The way she laughed and gestured toward those she was chatting with struck chills down his spine. He waited for her to turn toward him, and when she did, as though she'd known all the time he was there, he started toward her. Everything else faded into insignificance.

Spellbound, he lingered just beyond her group. He'd never felt such emotion, not with any woman he'd ever met. The curve of her forehead. A light shone from it. And now she was moving away, just as Ellie pounced on him again. "Here, we've got to get you something to eat." "No, please—I've got to—" And he lurched away in the direction of the apparition. But she was no longer there.

She wasn't in the big living room, nor in the others he circled through, impatient at the knots of people impeding his way. He looked about wildly trying to find her. In a panic he ran out the front door. There he saw her, just about to enter a car.

"Wait," he cried.

She turned, puzzled, then her face broke into a dazzling smile.

"You're not leaving," he said, running breathlessly up to the car. "You can't possibly do that."

"Of course I can," she said. "Tomorrow I'm leaving for California."

"But you're the only person I came here to see," he said, grasping at the words that might somehow detain her. Outside, the air felt good; he could breathe, and the liquor in his head, the noise and body heat that had all but suffocated him, fell away.

She laughed. "You don't even know me."

"Then tell me who you are."

"If you don't know that, why did you come to see me?"

"I know now that's why I came."

"I didn't come here to meet you," she said, as if the idea amused her.

"My name is Tom Sloan," he said, though even his name didn't seem to matter. "If I never see you again, you must know you've broken my heart. There—you've met me, so you must have come to do that."

She laughed again, like silver. She was moonlight and air and sun glinting on a waterfall. "My name is Natasha."

"Natasha," he repeated. A thrilling name. "And you must let me know where to reach you and when you're coming back."

The words tumbled out. "And if you don't come back, I'll follow you—to California."

"Ah," she said, as if the idea tickled her. She reached into her purse, took out a slender gold pen and a notebook. She wrote her name in it, and tore the page out carefully and handed it to him. Then she leaned over and kissed him lightly on the cheek—a kiss of good-humored amusement. Then she got into the car and drove away.

He was struck dumb: he had found his life.

Now, it appeared, he had finally to cut his losses, if that was possible, to clear a path and push forward.

"Isn't it time," Sloan said to his daughter, several days after their previous encounter, "you thought about your future?"

"What should I think about it?" she said calmly. "It's going to happen, isn't it?" Her thick dark hair, dyed a rusty orange, flopped over her forehead, then shot down the sides of her head like inverted flames. She knew how much he loved her hair when it was long.

He meant business, and there was no point beating around the bush. "Look," he said, "I've bailed you out for the last time. We've got to get a few things settled."

He'd sat down at the table with her on one of those rare mornings she actually ate breakfast. A half-eaten bowl of granola soggy with milk sat in front of her. She was now peeling an orange. Her long nails were painted a reddish black that set his teeth on edge. Her makeup was a thick mask, the blue eye shadow overdone. She made herself look like a whore—deliberately, he thought.

"Listen, I've got a job—I can earn my own way. You're trying to get rid of me—fine. I can move out any minute."

"Hold on," he said. "That's not what I'm talking about. You're three years out of high school. Can't you give a little thought to what you're going to do?"

"That's my business, isn't it? My life."

Her life—the claim by which she could detonate the lives of everybody around her. The tilt of her chin reminded him of her mother when she was teasing; only with Natasha there was laughter behind it. If only the mother had gone on living in the daughter, quickening her with the same brilliant impulse—wild, full of grace. Everything Natasha did she put into the service of playing with the world. How glad he'd have been to spend his life simply as a spectator of that brilliance, held in thrall. Only this was important to her: to be able to pick up one thing, take what it had to offer, and move on. She wouldn't be pinned down; she was always leaping beyond him. . . . This one too—but in a deadly game.

"Okay, it's your life. I'm not arguing that. But it doesn't mean sitting there while—"

"And what are you doing? Do you ever do anything but sit?"

"Look—"

"Okay, so we're talking about me. Who gives a damn about me?"

The answers he could offer would only bring on her sneer: the family, the town, himself. Those she'd always pitted herself against, raging out from her own field of force.

"You could go to college."

"What for? I had all that crap in high school. It's just four more years of looking at some dumb fuckface who doesn't know his asshole from the pencil sharpener."

"I appreciate the delicacy of your feelings," he said, "but you've got brains and talent. You really want to spend the rest of your life on your feet running drinks to tables, being pawed by guys from the gas station?"

"Not good enough for you?" She looked at him, then smiled as with a dawning idea. "You could give me a job."

He tried to read her expression. "You want one?"

"Afraid I'll make off with all your green stuff?"

"Sure," he said lightly. "The very first day you'd bring a potato sack and clear out the vault."

"You think I could stand behind your desk some day pulling all the strings?"

"Why not?" he said. "If you want to work into it the way I did. . . . If you're serious."

She sat for a moment, gave a little shrug of amusement. "It would bore me," she said. "And I hate math."

She'd been stringing him along, as he might have known. "Sometime," he suggested, "you might want to settle down, start a family."

She gave a hoot of laughter. "So you can sit with all your grandchildren around your knee while I cook Sunday dinner. No thanks," she said. "There are enough starved brats in the world."

"There are worse things," he persisted.

"I'd puke," she said. "I'd suffocate and die. I'd be like you."

Once again he had to resist the urge to slap her—she was goading him into it. By instinct she always knew exactly where to hook the dagger. With the same exquisite agony he felt when, as a baby, she used to pull his chest hairs, she jerked him breathless and staggering over a rocky and hostile territory toward some irresistible logic. He wondered if she herself could withstand the momentum that had driven her into the world and toward the breach of chaos. She seemed to blame him for her origins, her history. She seemed to blame him for bringing her into the world.

"Well, at least I foot the bills and pay the bail," he said nastily. "And those guys you picked up have records."

She didn't blink. "Kevin told me about it. How the fuzz just stopped them, frisked them, and hauled them in. They were out-of-state, so they were fair game. Told them they'd let them off if they hauled ass and left their money."

"Possession, theft, malicious mischief. Resisting arrest."

She shrugged.

You're only hurting yourself, he wanted to say. So much for trying to kick her into the future. "Have it your way," he said.

"Time for work," she said, getting up from the table. "I do work—think of that." And she snatched up her purse from the mahogany table, gave a quick glance at the grandfather clock that had ticked in the family for three generations, and was gone.

She had left behind the dark force of her energy, a mad cease-less rush, a maelstrom. The house was caught in the high wind of it, and Sloan was sucked in as well. He wandered restlessly through the living room and back, trying to steady himself in the gaze of his great-grandfather and mother, whose eyes seemed to follow their descendants across the room from the gilt frames of eternity. Looking no doubt askance at his clumsy efforts. How was he to measure himself against them? He walked out to the sunporch to stand a moment before Eagletail and Tenaja, cloaked with cloud shadow at their peaks, their slopes awash with light. Nothing offered. He turned back into the living room.

He felt a sudden impulse to enter his father's library, which now sat unused, the repository of memorabilia and family history. Only Manuela entered, to keep the dust from his father's desk and the bookshelves of family albums, the collection of maps and papers and diaries and ledgers, the leather-bound volumes of histories of the area, and the cases of artifacts: arrowheads and axes and adzes, ore-bearing rock and vials that had been used to carry gold dust, the odd pocket knife or talisman, bits of lace, and even a music box from Bavaria. Relics, given their place.

By contrast, everything had been stirred up around him and hung in the air: things were being asked of him. There was a letter he'd been carrying in his pocket for days, a couple of phone calls on its heels, meant to prod him toward a decision. What with the business with Natalie, he hadn't been able to think. But at odd moments, it had been on his mind, embedded in the resentment he felt toward her. *What do you ever do but sit? . . . To be like you? I'd suffocate and die.*

It didn't occur to her that she was the reason he stayed put: to take care of her, bring her up, be both father and mother. Perhaps she visited upon him her rage for a mother who had abandoned her: he at least had the consolation of memory. She had only the photographs of a stranger, Nastasha's pictures wherever she looked, gay or meditative, but closed off in another world. God knows he'd tried to make up to her for it, as though it were somehow his fault that she'd left. Her rage created a kind of perpetual penance for him: he'd never marry again and he'd never get really involved in politics. Now he'd been asked to manage the campaign for the aspiring Democratic candidate for governor, a man he'd come to know over the years.

He paced back and forth along the hall, back into the living room, past the door of his father's inner sanctum: where the elder Sloan had done all his paperwork and talked with visitors about politics or business, seated on black leather couches around the wagon-wheel coffee table. Where they drank scotch or martinis or pitchers of margaritas and exchanged the latest gossip from around the state.

As a child he'd been afraid to enter that room, for it was filled with voices: the war cries of Indians, groans of wounded men, the dying shrieks of horses. He had looked into the faces of Kit Carson and General Crook, whose portraits hung on the wall in gilt frames, and they had stared back out of an ambiguity so unsettling he felt defeated in anything he might try for, even with his father's hand on his shoulder patting in the assurance, "They're part of our family, son." *To have been alive then. All on that open frontier. Just looking for your fortune and clinging there in your saddle and letting the old horse go.* The man had had that strain of romance.

He'd heard, too, the sobbing of women, who'd lost their husbands or children crossing the prairies; husbands bemoaning their wives, and the strangled words of the woman his grandfather seduced into giving him her land. And his grandfather saying, *That deed was every whit she had to offer of beauty—and all her virtue. I'd rather married a grizzly bear.*

But long since he'd put off the childish things that had kept him out of that room. A kind of modesty perhaps had kept him from it. His own picture wasn't even on the wall. A question from another night was still unsettled, a moonlit night when he'd entered the doorway of that room . . .

But now he simply opened the door and stepped inside. Despite Manuela's efforts and the airings she gave it, the room had the smell of being perpetually closed up, the mingled smell of dust and old bindings and leather and exhausted sentiment. It was at the north side of the house, and such light as entered made little progress against the walnut paneling, but merely left a little pool under each window.

His father still occupied the room. Behind and above his desk was a portrait of him painted by a Santa Fe artist when he decided to run for the state senate. The lines of the shoulders as they moved toward the craggy face suggested a mountain, though his father, a thin, medium sort, had always struck him as a man trying to be bigger than he was. On the wall at least, he took up larger dimensions. *The way I think about family is this: in every generation you ought to have somebody who can raise things a notch, adapt to the times, seize the advantage.* That was his father all right. *I came along at the right moment. Now I can*

*get down to that legislature and get hold of the reins and make
sure things go along the right track and the power stays with those
who ought to have it.*

He'd lost by sixty votes. More heat than light. More bluff than
substance.

A photograph of Natasha he'd had enlarged for the sake of
continuity seemed more immediate. Her eyes still beckoned
from some unknown region: *Let's leave this house, let's find
something of our own.* As she spoke then, her eyes flashed. He
thought of how, to his surprise, her stepfather had taken him
aside before the wedding. She was coming to him with a port-
folio of stocks, and would he be able to manage them? She
cared nothing for them. To her, it was only fertilizer for the
ground. She herself was magic and fire. She wanted to change
the world. Her cobalt eyes came from the Russian sailor who'd
come over to Alaska and down the coast to Monterey. From the
great-grandmother who'd disgraced herself by marrying him
came her spirit. *Let's go up into the mountains, live there, start a
school, a center. The children are dying of tuberculosis.*

Is that what you want?

Maybe—But then maybe something more?

What then?

*Something new for the eye. A different way to walk into the
world.*

Something out of the blue?

Who knows? Maybe that.

You make me want to swirl you around.

Do it then. Let's celebrate—let's run out under the stars.

His mother's long last illness had yoked them there, at least as
he saw it, till he could see his way around. *You're so good to me,
child.* As though it were the first time she might say that of anyone. Natasha was devoted to her. *I always wanted a daughter.*
His mother so nearly forgotten while she was still alive that her
fading away seemed only a natural part of the process. Sloan
studied her portrait. Beside his father, his mother was a little
gray hill. Whatever she'd been had faded even out of her
portrait. He could scarcely remember what she'd been like,
could find nothing of her in himself.

His father's desk, with paperweight and calendar, changed every year by Manuela, suggested that someone, gone for a brief moment, would be back to occupy the chair. Papers and notebooks, whatever they were, left just as they'd been, were ordered neatly on the top.

This is such a dark room; maybe it could be turned into a nursery. Natasha had been only halfway serious. But even if she had meant it, no infant cries had come to disturb the household. Not until Natalie's arrival years later, followed by her mother's departure.

What are you looking at?

Just the stars. Suppose I spent my whole life counting them. And my neck had grown crooked and my eyes dim. Done only that. Probably I'd turn into an owl and go off hooting into the night.

She said things like that. And he'd been caught up by something mystical and rapturous, though at times somber and mysterious, that appealed to his younger self. Some dim recollection she brought from another time and place and that fitted but ill where she'd landed. She haunted him still. He was caught up now and again in little flurries of sentiment. And left exactly where?

Beverly was a dynamo. Sloan had to marvel every time he saw her, all the things she took on, took in. She'd sent him out of the kitchen after he'd put together the salad, and he'd been taken into the depths of the comfortable but sunken couch she'd saved from her marriage, along with the few family heirlooms she moved around with her, for the sake of some notion of family. A chest belonging to her grandmother stood in the living room, its marble top hidden by a stack of papers, and in the bedroom Beverly took her nightly exhaustion into a hand-carved bed. But these were out of place in the surroundings she'd chosen for herself. She lived in the rooms above a store on the town's decaying main street. It was cheap, she had debts to pay off. And a son and an ex-husband who regularly put the bite on her. Anyway, she was holing up, trying to hack her way out of past mistakes—her rotten marriage, for one. Sloan surveyed the walls, grim with old paint.

"Find something to amuse yourself," she yelled from the kitchen. "You can turn on the TV."

"Don't worry about me," he said, getting up. "I'll just stand in the doorway and talk to you—if that won't distract you."

"Fine in a minute," she said. "I've got to run this blender."

He picked up an article from her desk that had to do with the effects of uranium poisoning on the Indians who'd worked the ore; another on pulmonary disease in the Four Corners from the burning of low-grade coal in the power plant. Literature on saving the desert, on pollution, on alcoholism and drug abuse. She had to take the whole world on her back. Plus papers to grade. A stack of them were piled to one side, some with grades on them. He leafed idly through them. "When I get out of this dump," he read, "I want to join the army." He wondered what Natalie had written on her papers: when I get out of school, I want to screw every man in town.

Beverly came to him with a bottle of wine to open. She glanced down at the paper. "He's just trying to hold out till he can scram. I'm not sure the army'll take him"

"Natalie could have done something," he said. Occasionally she'd surprised him with good grades if she liked a certain teacher. It was a miracle she graduated.

"I'm sure. She's smart."

"All that waste."

She shrugged. "She's a big girl now."

Maybe it was something in the blood. Something he couldn't help after all.

He opened the wine.

"Come," she said. "It's ready."

He moved over to the drop-leaf table that had been set up in the center of the room and covered with a bright Mexican table-cloth. He poured the wine as she brought in the pasta she had cooked, and the salad. As she turned down the light and lit the candles, he caught a suggestion of how she'd been when they were both in high school together. Not all that different. She was right there, taking up one thing after another to try to straighten it out. There were things needing doing, and she threw herself into them like a dog digging up a bone. Trying to fix things. And if it couldn't be fixed, you threw it away and started something else.

"I've been asked to run the governor's campaign for Miles," he told her.

She stopped, looked at him. "That's wonderful. Oh, how very exciting."

"I haven't made up my mind yet."

"What do you mean? Of course you'll do it."

"What makes you think I should? God knows there's enough here to keep me occupied."

"Come on," she said. "Your abilities. Your experience. You've got to look forward. Maybe, like your father—"

"He was just full of himself—he bought his way in. He was a little fish." He said it more bitterly than he intended.

"But that doesn't say anything about you," she insisted. "Give yourself a chance."

Once again he was looking through a doorway, and the figure beckoning to him this time was Beverly, down-to-earth, the voice of common sense.

"You've convinced me," he said. "Great pasta."

"Nonsense," she said. "I just told you what you wanted to do all along."

He smiled. Maybe he'd marry her after all.

The moon that night was full, leaving Eagletail and Tenaja in a silvered imprint against the sky, shining into the window of Sloan's bedroom. He rose up in bed. Perhaps the light summoned him or some slight noise had woken him. The room was gauzy with light, and a pool of it lay on the floor. Everything lay in a hush as though to draw him into heightened listening. It was as though he expected to hear Natasha's voice, expected her to be in the bed beside him. Once again he had woken to find it empty, as he had that night so long ago. The empty place beside him. Natasha wasn't there, and where had she gone? Into what dream? He rose and moved toward the balcony where she sometimes stood. Eagletail and Tenaja lay bathed in the light. Should he seek her again? Follow her down the stairs into the dark house.

He slipped on a robe and went downstairs. The light was on in his father's library, and when he looked through one of small

glass panels, he saw that both were there, his father in one of
the leather chairs, Natasha sitting on the arm, leaning toward
him slightly. His father was holding her hand, patting it now and
again, gesturing at times, always talking, his eyes steadily on
her. What was he asking? What did he want? It was all being
re-created for him in the moonlight, that night when he looked
through the small glass panes of the door.

The light came from the glow of a small desk lamp. Beyond
them, from the shadows, Kit Carson and General Crook looked
down on the scene without rendering any judgment. The bookshelves and the glass cases holding the past were dark rectangles on which the surfaces lay like dark mirrors.

Her pose was in no way seductive, and yet his father's voice
seemed to wind through and around her, as she sat unmoving,
perhaps hesitant to offer whatever he was importuning from
her. He saw her withdraw her hand, stand up, and move away.
She stood for a moment with her back to him, then sat down on
the edge of another chair, her face turned away from the light.
A sense of shame seemed to hang between them. Sloan saw his
father bend forward, put his hands up to his forehead as if to
hold intact what lay between his temples. Then he said, "If it
weren't just rotten luck . . ."

The words came back as clearly as when they first were spoken, over twenty years ago. Whatever had passed between his
father and Natasha he was looking at the afterimage. What he
saw now was almost as painfully unclear as then. He pulled the
door open, rattling the panes of glass, and went inside. Natasha
smiled as though grateful for his coming. "I couldn't sleep," she
said. "Papa couldn't either. We ran into each other in the kitchen."

"Want a brandy?" his father said eagerly, as though he'd come
at the right moment. "We've been talking."

"No," Sloan said. "I'm afraid it'll wreck me for tomorrow."

There was an awkward pause, as Sloan felt the pulse of conflicting desires and something unspoken in the air. Then his father
said, "I was having a little sour mash. You could pour me another."

He put himself into the service of that request, though he was
moved to take himself out of that den and back upstairs and
fling himself back into sleep.

"I'm glad you've come down," his father said, taking the glass from his hand. He had drunk a good deal, Sloan could tell, though one could never tell from his speech. Under the influence he kept a single-minded clarity of purpose. Always had. "I was talking to Natasha—we have a little problem," he said, almost jocularly. "No, nothing we can't get around. Nothing serious."

The phrase wrung so false Sloan suddenly knew what he'd been feeling in his bones for some time. Some of the loans that had been given in the interest of getting the state to deposit funds in their bank—they had to be clinkers. His father had handled them all—he'd not been in on it.

"I'm going to announce for the primary," his father said. "For the Senate. Wait a minute—I know what you're going to say—" He waved away the objections. True, he hadn't made it to the statehouse. But there were people behind him, people who'd support him in a big way if he won. And he'd go on to win the election, because the odds were for the Democrats. The Republicans were in the backwoods. He'd put up a real fight and by God win the race. "But right now I can't draw on our assets." There were reasons for this—it was all on the level, he could assure them. But he had to put some people on the payroll to help raise funds, do the publicity. Other expenses. "Everything'll get paid back, I assure you."

For the Senate. Sloan was thunderstruck. His father didn't have a chance in a snowstorm. Somehow he caught the flash of balked ambition, of impulsive grabs at the toys of power, those hot, juggling coals. Reaching, snatching at them. And now, finally, putting his head down like a bull in his last charge through the arena . . .

"What I'm saying—" he heard through the buzz in his head, "— if I could use some of Nat's money here to keep things square . . ."

Nat's money. There was something more. Her money—to keep himself from slipping away. There was something else. There had to be. Favors promised, exchanges for what?

"You want her money?" He felt choked. He tried to see into her face. He caught a gleam in her eye, sharp as lightning. She wasn't saying anything. If he entered the vacuum of her silence and what lay beyond it. . . . Even now, if he tried . . .

"You can't do that," he managed. "It's hers."

The air softened around her. It was hers, and she was beckoning to that place, that doorway that led out of the house and into the future.

"There are friends I could go to," his father said. "But the position it would put me in—" There was something angry in his pleading. "I've got to get to them later for support. And when I'm on the way," he was assuring himself, "there will be solid strength." He brought down his clenched hand to the arm of the chair. "Solid," he said. "You can believe in that. Not some moonshine, but solid strength—action. Moving things forward."

Sloan wanted to hit him, just to keep him from talking. He was being harried; his father always came at him from all sides.

"And since it would be for a short time—a year, no longer . . ."

"But you can't—"

"Later on, after things get rolling, then it's simple, you see. They've got the confidence, they put things your way. The party, all the people who want you in there doing things their way . . ."

He had to stop him before his voice overpowered him. "It's her money. How can I say what she's supposed to do with it?"

His father turned to her, held out his palms as though, once again, it had all passed to her. But even now he could feel what had trapped him then. His father was all in his voice, a voice low and seductive, and with it, a gesture as of placing his life in her hands. And Sloan knew that he was pleading to be saved from disgrace. Without Nat's money, he'd be embarrassed, perhaps publicly. He'd be finished. He'd taken one step too far and couldn't draw back.

Natasha was looking at him, standing at the edge of that territory she always seemed to be looking toward. "Is it all right, Tom?"

She was putting him to it. "What do you say? Is it?"

He hung there. A moment that would make a difference, whereby something would happen or fail to happen, and things would shift their balance. He looked at what was before him, his father's disgrace, real and actual, and the undefined reaches behind Natasha's question.

"It's all right," he said. He breathed out the moment and watched it slip away into the next.

"Wonderful," his father said, coming over and hugging each in turn. "This calls for a celebration." Somewhat unsteadily he went over to the cupboard and did the honors. "I knew I could count on you. That's what family's for." He was triumphant as he handed them the drinks they didn't touch. "There are great things in store for all of us," he said, raising his glass. "And Tom, I want her to work for me—I told her that before—that she'd be great at it."

To his surprise, she said. "I'd like that. I've got all my old connections." And she gave him a look that could have been triumph as well: as though she had always known what would happen.

Now it seemed to him she'd drawn a sudden inspiration even from his failure. Her life took a different direction, for a time. No, she would never lack for an idea. It was he who'd been left behind to carry the burden. For she'd left him that bit of life suddenly engendered after so many childless years. As though Natalie, too, had been born in that moment.

For once she went to Santa Fe and threw her energy into that ill-fated election, she never really came back except to have the child, put her into Manuela's care, and disappear, this time to California. She took her pregnancy as a stroke of bad luck, hardly spared Natalie a look. Apparently she hadn't remarried, for she'd never gone to the trouble of filing for divorce. Nor had Sloan She'd never answered his letters, and he'd never seen her since.

And now on this moonlit night as he stood in the library, his study now, he was ready to close that chapter of his life. He sat down in the chair behind his father's desk, took all that remained on its surface, and shoved it in the wastebasket. Nor did he want to look at Natasha any longer: in the morning he would take her picture down from the wall.

He wanted to settle the matter as quickly as possible and wash his hands of it. Sloan paid for the damages to the cemetery, and the five young man, warned they'd better never show their faces around those parts again, were freed after ninety days in the county jail. Sloan's domestic life had settled somewhat since the initial upheaval. He no longer tried to prod his daughter into doing things differently: let her go on waiting tables, hustling drinks if she was bent on throwing herself away. He was of a mind, however, to leave room for the best possible sequel. Sometimes one's offspring came to their senses, married, and bore children like the rest of their kind and, willy-nilly, carried on the business of living. It was only reasonable.

So he let go of her, no longer asked where she went or what she did. And on her part, she would, on occasion, let him know, with a careless gesture, as if tossing a bit of bread to the birds, who she was going with now or that she had been at a dance in Cimmaron and seen so-and-so whom they knew, or that she had visited friends over in Trinidad. He took these as confidences—of a trifling sort, but confidences nonetheless. He felt more hopeful. She was on her good behavior; perhaps she realized that, for once, she'd pushed him too far.

He was busy with his own affairs, in and out of town, spending a good deal of time in Santa Fe. The campaign required him to travel around the state, talking with local officials, keeping in touch with party workers, attending banquets and barbecues. He was rather enjoying these forays beyond his own limited sphere. He hadn't kept entirely out of local politics—he'd been a delegate to various state conventions, but that had been more or less required of him. Now he was on the road a good deal of the time, meeting people all over the state.

They had their work cut out if they won this election. The ranchers were having a tough time these days what with the higher costs of renting government lands, lagging rainfall, and uncertain markets. The Indians, the Hispanics were a presence to be reckoned with, making their various demands for education and economic opportunity. Mining interests and cattle interests; real estate and tourism. The environment. Preservation and development. All those realities that had emerged out of the territory, vying with one another in the variegated landscape.

The land. Virgin territory once. Unknown, unexplored, where his forebears had come to carve out their destiny: trapping and prospecting, buying land and running cattle, surviving past the grizzly bear and the Indian. To put him in a land settled, divided by fences and ownership, with towns and cities. And what could be done with it now? He tried to imagine what still lay under the soil, in veins in the mountains, what still could be mined and put to use. Tried to imagine what the desert might yet yield. Beverly must have caught wind of something: he could see himself helping to shape all that, part of it. It was a heady thought.

After the election—the polls indicated an easy victory for the Democrats now that the excesses of the previous administration had been exposed—and during the lull before the new administration took office, he intended to put his own affairs in order. For a man who liked things under his control, he'd left his personal affairs in disarray. Since Natasha had left him, he'd never made any effort to end her claims on him, though in fact she had made none.

But, as his lawyer advised, half his wealth was hers at his death, and he'd made no real provision for what he now had charge of. He held power of attorney over all the family properties and funds, now that his father's mind had failed, and these would become his entirely. He'd been waiting to see what he would do about Natalie, whose extravagance was in keeping with everything else that flowed from her nature. He'd thought of settling a large sum on her if she married decently. But even if it did happen, it wasn't likely to be soon.

As it stood now, he gave her sums of money now and then, perhaps determined by how well she behaved herself, though he tried not to think of it this way. He didn't want her counting on anything. His only weapon against her was unpredictability. As far as he was concerned, she threw money away. Maybe that was why she was behaving herself: she liked nice things, and a waitress's salary didn't provide them. So far she hadn't been blessed with any rich boyfriends. With money, at least, he'd drawn the line. Otherwise she'd have run through it like wildfire, sweeping away all his efforts. But if he set up a trust fund with certain stipulations, perhaps a fund for her children . . .

All of these notions had been occupying him since that evening with Beverly. He was thinking seriously now that he might marry again. There'd been a few brief affairs after Natasha left, but they'd been casual—he'd seen to that. Natasha had ruined him, left a vacuum not to be filled and a reluctance to make the effort. It was Beverly who'd reminded him of what might be enjoyed in the company of women, their physical presence, their interest. His own life had worn ever thinner—the bouts with his daughter had left him emotionally dry.

Yet women were drawn to him, he knew that. Almost everywhere he went he'd met women who would have been glad to see more of him. And a few had. He didn't expect to be dazzled a second time. No illusions there. But the right woman could spice things up considerably. He wished Beverly were younger; he liked her as well as anybody. But if he married someone young enough to have children, a new generation . . . wealth and status to trade for youth and fertility. Something for the future.

He was in Santa Fe for the final rally, where he'd remain for the election and watch the returns at party headquarters. A big champagne party was going to be held afterward, with the victory speeches and all the rest. After the rally, he returned to the La Fonda, where he was staying. At the desk he found a message; opening it up, he found himself summoned once again by Moran. Urgent, he read.

He studied the words on the paper, his chest tight. It was late, nearly two in the morning. The message had come not half an hour before. Sick at heart, he tried calling the chief, but he was out, could not be reached. He left a message, then went up to his room.

He couldn't sleep. It had to do with Natalie, he was certain: his mind wouldn't move beyond that conviction. Anything to do with his father would have come from the nursing home. Perhaps they didn't know his whereabouts, had contacted Moran. It was impossible to convince himself. Natalie? To what end? She knew where he stood; she liked her little luxuries. But even as he pushed away the possibility, he was overtaken by rage: he didn't want to think about her. He'd had his fill of her. He wanted his life.

He tried calling. Then again. Finally he got hold of Moran.

"I'm afraid there's bad news," Moran told him. "At your place. There's been—quite a bit of damage."

"Natalie?" he asked. "Manuela?"

"Both gone."

"Gone?" He was mystified. "Gone where?"

"We're still trying to find them."

"Let me get this straight," he said. "What happened?"

"Looks like a party that went too far. I guess you'll have to see for yourself."

Quickly he sent off messages to those who depended on him. He threw his clothes together, settled his bill, had his car brought, and left immediately. It was just starting to get light. He could hardly think. Alcohol, fatigue, anxiety, and lack of sleep had made hot wires of his nerves. Damage to the house and the two women gone. Unthinkable.

He'd hoped to arrive that morning, but the carburetor gave him trouble near Springer, and by the time they had gotten hold of the replacement and managed to install it, he was looking at the paling light of late afternoon. When he stopped by the police station, the cop at the desk put in a call to Moran and the two of them arranged to meet up on the Mesa. As he came up the road to the house, he saw that Moran had arrived before him and two patrol cars were parked in front of the house. He looked past them to a gaping hole. The front door had been ripped off its hinges and the wood was blackened around it. Moran walked up to meet him.

"They did a real job on it," Moran said.

"Who?"

"Those punks that were through here before."

"They came back?" He shook his head. "I thought we scared the shit out of them."

Moran shrugged. "Looks like it didn't stick. We've got a warrant out."

Sloan walked inside, Moran behind him. The place was a shambles. Furniture had been smashed or hacked apart. The mahogany sideboard that had been shipped from England and then brought by train for the sake of his grandmother's English china stood with its doors ripped off, the top hacked and split. The dining room table lay wrenched apart into various pieces, the chairs thrown over, kicked in. In the living room the bro-caded sofa leaked stuffing from the seats and cushions. And the rocker where his grandmother had nursed his father and the two other sons who'd died of diphtheria lay in pieces. The keys of the piano had been systematically pried loose, and the strings cut apart.

Among the wreckage were a number of beer cans, empty and half full, the contents spilled out on the parqueted floor, dried pools of liquid that held the crystal splinters from the chandelier above. In the study, the furniture for some reason had been left intact, though the books had been thrown to various parts of the room, as though in some hilarious contest, the glass cases shattered, and the various portraits slashed, their canvases hanging down in white pieces from the frames.

It was like an earthquake. He couldn't believe it. Something inhuman in its sheer wantonness. Had she hated him that much? One final orgy of destruction and then out of there. It was not the abandon of a party got out of hand. No, he wouldn't fool himself into believing that. And Manuela?—she'd been there too.

They'd tied her up in the bedroom, Moran told him. They'd found her in a state of shock and taken her to the hospital. Moran shook his head. "Only now she's gone too." Somehow she'd managed to get out of the building and had simply disappeared. They'd searched everywhere for her and hadn't been able to find her.

There was nothing more to be done at the moment. "We'll find them, don't worry," Moran assured him. "They've been in trouble before. So there are pictures, fingerprints."

Find them—what for? Sloan wondered. They stood for a moment outside while Moran and the other officer speculated as to the direction taken by the vandals, the measures for their apprehension. Then they left him.

For some reason they hadn't touched the upstairs bedrooms. But he had no desire to sleep in the desecrated house. He wondered if he would ever want to sleep there again. He would go down and spend the night in a hotel, then find a crew to come and clean up the wreckage. Even though every pane of glass was broken and the chill November air had no let or hindrance, the place still reeked of beer. He wondered why they'd stopped short of setting the house afire. Perhaps they'd made one brief halfhearted attempt at the doorway. He leaned against the porch, not wanting to move, though it was getting colder. The afterglow was deepening on the slopes of the mountains.

He felt shaky, as though his knees might buckle. What did he have anymore?

He was back at the beginning, only it wasn't a beginning. His great-grandfather could walk into an unknown territory and take a gamble at the hazard of his life. Cunning and skill pitted against the wilderness. And survive, create a line, those who'd track down the Apaches, clear a way for settlers, make their fortunes, even as there'd been those casualties for history. Challenges, the tasks clear. And his grandfather and father, who'd taken what they wanted.

"You've destroyed this family," he said to Natalie, to her back as she went fleeing from the chaos she'd created. Where had the seeds of destruction been planted? He searched his mind.

As he stood in his confusion, something bolted against him in the dimming light, a dark wind that seemed to blow his ancestors around like shadows. He could see them. Briefly they danced on the stage of his inner eye. Until they were gone and his daughter took a turn, dancing in front of him as the world became a playground of forces and upheavals. He tried to shake off the vision, to pin his gaze on those props of the landscape that had endured for so long, shaping what he knew: Eagletail and Tenaja, brightening under the bent rays of the sun, silent and impenetrable. There she had brought him—to that last measure of agony, to that nightmare where things lay without connection, waiting for what hand to put them together? As he looked out at the peaks that in some lost time had been given their shape by powers that had heaved up the earth, it was as though they spoke: Your time here is very brief. There is nothing you possess. Nothing at all.

The Chasm

Old Man Beaudry and Lester Crump had come finally in Lester's truck, roaring down the dirt road in a cloud of dust; and Buddy was there, so that, with his father, there would be four men in all. From up in the fork of the cottonwood, where he had been on the lookout for them, David said, "Howdy, Mr. Beaudry. Howdy, Lester." And when the old man said, "Where's your pa, boy?" he slid down to go hunt him up.

First they sat around the kitchen table drinking coffee and talking basketball and county politics; then they stood around the corral matching the prospects of the year's grass against the rainfall and joshing his father about his cattle. His older brother, Buddy, who, despite his being tall and muscular and strong as any of them, could be shy as a girl, stood quiet, leaning against the chute of the cattle pen, listening. And since no one was paying him any mind, David mostly climbed up and down the sides of the corral.

"See you got more of them black ones, Murl," the old man said. "You must be partial to the color." He was making a joke of it, but from the way he said "black ones" it was easy to catch his drift. He might as well have come out and said they were a blot on the landscape.

"It's all the same meat," he heard his father say. "I buy 'em three cents a pound cheaper than you fellas and sell 'em for the same price you get. I'm satisfied if you are." Then he laughed, magnanimously, like a man who can afford to be good-natured over a mere difference of opinion when the cash is on his side. "Go ahead and raise your Herefords."

"Well, it's always been the custom around here," the old man said, "and it doesn't hurt anybody, s'far as I can tell."

"You're just like my old woman," his father said, "natural-born stubborn and can't understand simple arithmetic. Don't you know it's all on account of you fellas that I can buy Black Angus three cents a pound cheaper."

The old man smiled. "That just means you'll be getting rich quicker'n me. And since I'm getting older'n I care to admit, you'll probably get there and I probably won't."

Then his father shaded down his humor, saying, "Well, I don't like to see a man done out of what he's labored for and what's his by all that's fair."

"Well, in that case, boys, you'd better give some thought to the color of your cattle." Then he added, "And never listen to an old man any more'n you can help."

"Seems to me, Beaudry," his father said, with a perfectly straight face, "you ought to give me back that calf I gave you, now you've got him in shape. You wouldn't want him contaminating your herd."

"Murl, you old sinner."

From where he sat, astraddle the top post of the corral, David looked down to see the old wind-beaten face break into wrinkles with his laugh. He liked the way the old man laughed, as though he had drawn his humor from somewhere deep and gotten rich off it.

"The only reason you give that calf in the first place was 'cause you were sure it was dead on its feet."

"The one he give me didn't last the night," Lester said, for the sake of truth. "Sorriest animal I ever laid eyes on."

Even Buddy chipped in. "Pa was cussin' because there was two bum ones in the lot. But then he says, 'I got an idea. I'll have my money's worth out of them yet.'"

"Listen, lemme tell you what he done," Lester said, waving Buddy off, as though he alone could do it justice. And he went ahead, putting up his own rather reedy voice in imitation of the booming voice of David's father, with so ludicrous an effect that David had to clap his hand over his mouth and nearly lost his balance. "So now here comes Murl. 'Lookee here, Lester,' he says, 'being as how you're such a good friend and neighbor I brought y' over a little present.' 'Well now, Murl,' I says, 'that's right kind.' And he says, 'Come over here to the window so's I can show you.' So I come over and look out. And there it is. You couldn't hardly call it a calf," Lester said, not angry, yet not showing any amusement over it either. "Looked like it was going to keel over any second."

His father threw back his head and roared. Lester tried to say something else, but by then they were all laughing. He could no longer keep up a straight face but turned red as fire, broke up, and joined them.

"Well, I see we done a good job of tickling that little chap over there," the old man said, drawing their attention to David, who was so pleased he forced his laughter beyond the point of having anything to laugh at but the sound he was making.

"And what really tickles me," Old Man Beaudry said, shaking his head, "is mine lived, and here I've got one of his black cows."

"I'll do you the favor of taking him back, seeing as how he don't match with the rest of your herd."

"Just you never mind," the old man said, "I can collect the sale price off him same as you."

"You watch out there, Beaudry. Next thing you know you'll be having a whole herd of Black Angus."

But with just a flicker of expression, the old man indicated it wasn't likely.

"Hadn't we better get started?" Lester said. "I got chores waiting."

"Davey boy," his father said to him, "fetch me that bucket in the shed and that length of rope hanging on the door. Damn," he said, with sudden memory, "I've come off without my knife."

"This here'll do," the old man said, taking a jackknife from his pocket. "I done it lots of times with a jackknife."

When Buddy had taken the rope from him and he'd set the bucket within reach, David climbed back to the top of the corral to watch. It was a simple operation, painless to the animal, done in a matter of seconds. His father, having taken a pole and climbed into the pen, was urging the calves into a chute one at a time. Lester and Buddy stood somewhat apart to wrestle them as they came through, and the old man both worked the gate and did the cutting.

"This one's a she," the old man said, letting out the first. "Get along there." And he sent her trotting off. "Okay, get ready for the next."

When he let it out, Lester threw it to the ground and Buddy bound its legs. Then the old man knelt down and took his knife and severed the testicles. The blade caught the sun for a second and shot out a flash of brilliance; and it was all done.

"There," the old man said, after they'd untied the rope and the calf had leapt to its feet, "that'll change your mind about a few things." And he gave it a smart slap across the rump to send it to the other side of the corral.

There was really nothing for him to do. He could climb into the pen with his father, where he would only be in the way. He could work the gate, but he could tell that the old man wanted to do it. For a time he watched. He watched Lester, who was getting red in the face from the exertion, and Buddy, who wasn't, as they tackled the calves and tied them up. Though Lester was built heavier, Buddy was as strong, and lighter and quicker on his feet. You couldn't tell his strength just to look at him, but it was there for all his being so slender and easy in his gait. It was something he shared with all the men, even Old Man Beaudry, who'd been old as long as David could remember, but who was solid as a rock and could ride and hunt and shoot as well as any man alive. It was as though Buddy had got his growth and gone to live in a different world, where he was somebody separate and distinct. And David couldn't tell how Buddy'd gone or how he'd got there or whether he'd ever get there himself across the nine years' gulf that lay between them.

Not only that. When they looked at David, they all said, "This boy's got his mother's eyes"—and he wasn't sure whether it made the slightest difference. Sometimes when he was wrestling Buddy and got him pinned to the floor, he couldn't be sure whether he'd done it himself or whether it was Buddy letting him do it. And they said nobody could ride like Buddy. He could ride like he'd been born in the saddle.

Last year Buddy had taken the prize money for riding the Brahmans at the State Fair rodeo and had gone off to the regional. And if he hadn't got his leg hurt the first day, there was no telling what he might have done. He'd wanted to go ahead and ride the next day anyway, but his mother wouldn't let him. He was strong. He was on his way to becoming a star.

"You ought to leave this one alone, Murl," the old man was saying, as a calf stood there uncertainly, ready to bolt. "He'll make you a fine bull."

"Well," his father said, "I don't need another bull."

"You ought to keep him anyway. He's a fine animal."

"You ought to, Murl," Lester insisted with some warmth. "It'd be a shame."

He shrugged. "Okay, boys, you talked me into it."

David could recognize the tone his father took when he was being agreeable against his will. They were his neighbors, they'd come from their own work to help him with his, and it was too much to make them alter an animal they felt admiration for. Besides, when Old Man Beaudry said something, people generally listened to him. They looked up to him, but not just because he was old: he seemed to have an instinct for the right thing to do.

David could see what they were talking about. It was not simply a matter of size; it was as though the calf were made to possess something that wasn't there yet but would be in time. He could almost see how it would be then, and it seemed to him that when it was full-grown the something that would take hold of it would make him stand back and admire and would maybe scare him to get too close to. They sent the calf trotting over to the other end of the corral, and he was able to distinguish it among the others. Then they continued without pause, and he left, for he had thought of something he wanted to do.

When the hills took on their first tinge of green, he was seized with a restlessness that nearly drove him crazy. It was like wanting to sneeze and not being able either to do it or to drive away the feeling. Late in March, there came a few days of warmth that made the sap rise and the damson plum blossom in the side yard. Then just when you were getting used to the feel of spring and were running around in your shirtsleeves, there was a blizzard. His mother would stand in the window fretting over the plum tree, afraid that the freeze had done for the fruit that year; and sometimes it had. Right after the storm the sun would take over again, for this was the last snow of the winter and didn't amount to much. Its sole purpose in coming seemed to be to rob his mother of fruit for jam.

First the high mountain meadows turned green. At the beginning when you looked off into the distance you couldn't be sure it was green you were seeing or not. But that first trace of color was a promise made good almost before you were aware.

Though it was hard to tell from one day to the next whether the hills were any greener, suddenly one day you were looking at the richness of grass-filled meadows in the hollows and valleys. Now, as he turned his horse into the hills, he could see where the grass was coming up through the last year's brown stubble. Near the peaks there were still patches of snow that would linger until the end of June.

Several days before, when he was riding fence with Buddy, he saw what appeared to be a cave opening from the rocks near the head of a canyon. He'd ridden that way dozens of times and maybe had looked straight at it without noticing it, and maybe he'd have gone past it again if his glance had not been caught at the moment by a motion overhead. Suddenly his vision was taken up by two eagles ascending with a great sweep of wings, then leveling off and sailing through a curve of distance so smooth and sharp and sweet it made him whistle. And Buddy said, "I never seen two of them together like that." When they dropped down behind the crags, he looked down to see where they might have come from, and there was the shadow among the rocks, darker than the shadow made by a boulder.

He hadn't told anybody about the cave, not even Buddy, because he wasn't sure of Buddy anymore. He might have joined in with the general run of grown-ups who told you it was fool-hardy and dangerous to go off exploring caves by yourself and made you promise you'd never do it under any circumstances. For if they had a reason for anything you were supposed to do or weren't to do, it was usually nothing better than that it was for your own good. But since he hadn't told, he had been spared from making any promises of the sort that, having been wrung out of you under duress when you hadn't any real conviction about keeping them, filled you with a great deal of uneasiness when you went back on them. At the time, he'd simply marked the cave the way a dog buries a bone to come back to. Remembering it, he had gone round to the enclosure to put a bridle on Wingfoot, the sorrel mare his mother kept for riding.

It was a cave. For a time even after he could see it, he wasn't sure about it and could only say over to himself, "Let it be a real cave." For often there were only little shallow depressions in the sides of the hills the wind had hollowed out, leaving a shadow like the shadow of a real cave; but once you got up close you saw it never got out of the daylight and you were cheated out of your hopes.

But this one was a cave, a source of astonishment. The wonder he had felt on first perceiving it when he had not expected it grew as he approached. He hadn't thought it would be nearly so hard to reach, for from the distance it looked as though he could simply climb the hill to where it was. But as he came round a boulder, he saw that it opened from a shelf above a steep, rocky chasm. He came round the boulder in time to catch a flock of wild goats in various motions of surprise, cavorting in a kind of frenzy among the rocks, leaping to and fro over the chasm, making strange cries. Yet they seemed to pay him no heed at all. He left the mare tied to a bush beside a great white rock at the base of the chasm and began climbing the rocks to the mouth of the cave. Then the goats scattered and fled.

It was a deep cave, so dark he could not tell how far it tunneled into the hill. He got down on his hands and knees so that he could crawl in, but he did not go far. A breath of wind that seemed to come from the depths of the earth touched his face, and he was afraid to enter further into the darkness lest he fall into an abyss dropping away beneath him.

Once he was outside and stood up, he felt strangely giddy and extraordinarily excited, and on a sudden impulse he went leaping and hollering among the rocks like one more goat. Yelling, waving his arms, he hardly knew what he was doing. When he sat down finally, panting and run out, his head was still in a whirl. And the thoughts that chased one another through his brain seemed to come from nowhere at all, but were more compelling than a dream.

He was seeing his brother perform in a rodeo, finishing a spectacular ride that defied death itself. But what Buddy did next was perfectly astonishing: he went over to the great sleek black bull that stood pawing the earth at the side of the pen and lifted it up upon his shoulders and carried it all around the arena, to the roar of the enthusiastic crowd. In honor of the occasion, they slaughtered the bull and roasted it on a spit over the fire, and Buddy devoured the whole animal himself in the space of a single day. Then, from somewhere, a voice speaking in the tones belonging to deference and honor told him that Buddy would die and become a star.

When he found himself on the mare's back headed home, he had the sensation of knowing something he hadn't known before, as though he had suddenly been gifted with prophecy and could foretell the future. But he could not have said what he knew.

During the rodeo he lived in a fever of excitement. The things he saw and heard and ate and smelled created such a welter inside him it was touch-and-go whether he would laugh or holler from sheer excess of feeling. He liked the crowd, the way everybody milled around and stirred up the dust and laughed and talked and sweated and breathed beer fumes and made a human heat and a human smell that, beneath the July sun, mingled with the smells of hay and manure and the effluvia of animals—the skittery calves, the quick and restless broncos, the momentous bulls. And if there was one thing he could pick out and follow to its source, it was the smell of roasted peanuts that went tearing down to the pit of his appetite, so that the last thing he did before starting time was to buy some with his own money, along with a Coke to chase away the thirst afterward. He wished he could be back of the chutes with Buddy, but even if he could have been, he would have wished just as strongly to be out in front where he had a clear view. He did have the satisfaction of being able to say to a perfect stranger who had asked him if he liked rodeos, "My brother's in it," and thought to have made a great impression.

They got settled in their places in the bleachers; on one side of him, his father, feeling good with a couple under his belt to celebrate the sale of a piece of land that had brought him a good price; and on the other side, his mother, wearing a new silver and turquoise pin the shape of a thunderbird, the sign of good luck, and telling him to quit fidgeting and to hurry up and finish his Coke so he wouldn't spill it down the back of somebody's neck. Overhead the sky was brilliant, with only two little bits of cloud in it that seemed to have been left behind. The announcer was welcoming the crowd, getting into his stride; he told about a couple he knew, the husband so bowlegged and his old woman so knock-kneed that when they stood together, they spelled "ox." There was a ripple of laughter from the crowd. David drank his Coke down to the ice and sat impatient.

But then began the whole magnificent motion of things in the brilliant openness of the day, as the horses came dashing in for the Grand Entry parade. Everybody stood as the band played and the officials came riding in carrying the colors, followed by the queen candidates and the trick riders and ropers in scarlet and blue and yellow and lavender, and men in western shirts on horses with fancy rigs that glittered silver in the sun. In a moment the arena was filled with men and horses, circling it, then snaking into a graceful curve from the center. It was just men and horses, the same as he saw every day of his life; but as he watched them in the parade, the men dressed in their fancy outfits and the horses stepping to the music, everything he knew of men and horses seemed more real to him, more vivid. Something touched him at the top of the backbone and sent a shiver down the rest of it and made him feel that he stood on the brink of a great event.

For the rest was the contest, and it was the contest that now caught him up and held him. When they let out a bronco, it was as though they had turned loose a charge of energy and no one could tell what direction it would take. He liked the way the broncos hid their heads and kicked the lid off, as they say, and the way the riders bounced up and down, their legs coming up so high at times it seemed they would roll backward off the horses. And he yelled himself hoarse because it was beautiful to see—the springs into the air, the pitches and kicks, and the rider holding on for all he was worth.

The sun beat down, drenching the arena with light, so that at moments the air seemed to turn to liquid and waver before his eyes. He had gotten thirsty again, but he wouldn't let himself think about it; he wanted to concentrate on what was happening.

Beside him, his father said, "Wait'll Buddy comes. Then they'll see some riding."

He realized that he had very nearly forgotten about Buddy, and for the rest of the time, all during the calf roping and the steer wrestling, he had the sense of waiting for Buddy, as though all the rodeo up till now had been for the sake of Buddy, an introduction to what Buddy would do.

"Stop wiggling so much," his mother said, on the other side of him.

He glanced up at her with brief wonder. Generally, she didn't pick on him unless she had something on her mind.

"It's almost time," his father said.

For now it was the Brahmans. When the first one roared into the arena, he had the sensation of something dark coming into the day, as though the sun had suddenly gone behind a cloud. In fact, he looked to see. But there was only the sheer dazzle; even the two small fleecy clouds had traveled on. Still the dark blotch remained before his vision. Tensely, he watched the rider. Then it was in his mind—he might get killed; he might get killed doing that. And he knew what had darkened in the day. It was terrifying to look upon, the bull, with its upthrusting horns and humped shoulders and hanging dewlap and great haunches that seemed to move with a dull, vengeful purpose. He thought that if he could see into it, the eye would have the look of wanting to gore or trample a man. When the rider fell, he wanted him out of there in a hurry and watched anxiously as the clown did a little dance and dodge in front of the maddened animal to draw the bull away, to clown him away before something happened.

But nothing happened. Even though David held his breath when the second rider came out, nothing happened. He just fell off as soon as the bull cleared the chute. He picked himself up and went after his hat and stalked out. You could tell he was mad, getting pitched off before he'd had a chance to show his stuff. Buddy always said he hoped that would never happen to him. "I'd hate that. Being out there in front of all that crowd and making a bad show and then not qualifying for the prize money." It seemed to be the only thing he was scared of. "Sometimes I'm so scared I won't ride well," he had said once, "I get hollow in the stomach. But mostly I don't think about it. I just let 'er rip."

The next three didn't come to much. One was disqualified because he failed to spur the bull as he left the chute. The other two, who got off to a good start, grabbed hold of the rope with the hand they should have kept free. Then came a fellow who knew how to ride. Up and down he stayed with the bull, and just when you thought he'd go the limit, he was off. He had ridden through several troublesome humps, and when he fell, you wondered why it was then and not before. But the contest wasn't over. The moment he was on the ground, the bull turned and started for him, and he had to roll over quick to avoid the hooves. The clown flashed in front, took off running with the bull behind him, and dived into a barrel in the nick of time. The crowd ate it up.

"They always come to see the clown chased into that barrel at least once before it's over," his father said. Then he added, "That fellow'll be one for Buddy to beat."

Then the chute opened and there was Buddy. The bull charged out like a whirlwind, with Buddy precariously on top. One hand held on to the rope from the surcingle, and the free hand was flung up and out. He couldn't see Buddy's face; but as he rode the arching bull, it seemed that if he leapt only a little higher he would escape from his body and become joyous and free as air. He was up there for an eternity upon the back of that mad motion arching and plunging. Then David saw the bull twist its neck and throw back his head, and in the next second something happened that made him close his eyes even before it had quite happened, though he knew what it was from the roar of the crowd that came first like a great burst of excitement but then trailed off in a groan. When he opened his eyes, he found himself jerked to his feet and Buddy lying on the ground and the clown drawing away the bull and people running up from all sides. He didn't know whether Buddy had been gored or trampled or both, but he was sure in his own mind that he was dead.

The dark blotch grew before his eyes and dizzied and sickened him. He had the sensation of being wrenched away from himself. He was not himself and the things that had happened were not happening, but rather everything was whirling about him at a dizzying pitch, with no connection with himself yet threatening to carry him along. He felt terribly fragile, as though he might break any second and must therefore treat himself with great tenderness and care. He kept going back to the moment and back again, saying to himself in a precise adult way, "Now let me see . . ." And as vividly as though he were living it again, he saw Buddy poised there one moment on the back of the bull and then lying flung out on the ground. Over and over—the way he kept feeling with his tongue in the empty place when he lost a tooth. And each time his brain halted and reeled and he felt sick.

After the funeral they sat in the living room around the fact of Buddy's death. Outside, the afternoon lay hot and heavy and still, and within, the heat and stillness seemed the greater for the weight of grief. "Wish it would rain about now," Glen Simpson, whose ranch was down the road a few miles, said. "The grass is all drying up," Lester said. "There's supposed to be rain," one of the women said. And the subject was abandoned. David watched a fly buzz in the window and wished it would rain and that the afternoon would turn over and roll away. It was like a great rock in the middle of the room, dull and dumb and heavy, and if you could only bulge it . . .

Did they believe it? he wondered, looking at one and another. His father sat on the couch hunched forward, heavy and motionless, as though he would never again move and nothing would ever again matter. And his mother's face was set stiff as a mask. But she had something to do. She went out to the kitchen and brought back a pitcher of iced tea and some of the cake one of the neighbors had brought. For they had come with plates of food; they could not give them enough of it. And as they came, one by one, they seemed to belong to a solemn procession that not only brought food for the living but came offering a tribute to the dead.

"Now listen, Jeannie," Venita Crump said, "there's no reason for you going to all this trouble." But his mother waved away her objection, and in the end, Venita and his Aunt Ella, who had come from Las Cruces, and young Judy Beaudry, who kept house for her father and was the only one still at home, all got up and went back to the kitchen to help her. And when they had all been served with iced tea and cake and the women had sat down again, they ate and drank. No one said much. David drank his iced tea and tried to keep the ice from clinking in his glass. Any sound seemed an affront. Every time he heard the fly buzz in the window, he wanted to get up and kill it. He still could not believe it.

He hadn't been able to believe it when they stood out in the cemetery, though he knew what he had known before: that there was nothing you could do with any dead thing. You couldn't take it home with you or keep it around; or if you had it, you couldn't be easy in your mind or go on with whatever you needed to do until you were rid of it. It was beyond any human keeping. You had to put whatever it was that was dead back into the earth. And there was the awful grief—but even the grief wouldn't let you forget you must give it back to the earth. But what if you couldn't let go of it? What if there had to be something to keep back?

One by one, people were taking their leave. "Bye, Jeannie, Murl, take care now." Still sitting next to him, Old Man Beaudry had his arm loosely, affectionately, around his back, and now and again his hand made a gentle irrelevant little tap against his shoulder. He looked down at the hand, gnarled, the veins standing up, the fingers folded slightly, like the claw of a hawk, and a shudder went through him. He did not want the old man to touch him.

The old man, too, got up to leave. "Well, I've lived too long," he said, with a shake of his head. "It's a bad business, the old folks living to bury the young." He picked up his hat, fiddled with it a moment, but did not put it on. "I'm heartily sorry, Murl," he said, touching his father on the arm. "He was a good boy."

Soon they were all gone, and the three of them sat till it was nearly dark, when his mother began putting together a supper they barely tasted and that mostly went to feed the dog. She went about the kitchen with the sort of clocklike precision that might come from her having to tell herself to do everything she did. And as much as he wanted her to talk to him, to tell him something that would give him ease, he couldn't bring himself to ask her.

After supper, he went outside and kicked at stones and blew the fluff off dandelions and went down and fooled around the horses for a while. Then he just stood leaning against the fence. The big cottonwood was all slicked up with moonlight so that the trunk made a silver path up into the dark hanging leaves. And the stars were thick. He wondered how the earth could be so calm and the insects go on humming in the grass roots and the sky be so deep and the stars so beautiful when all the time Buddy was dead. For it seemed to him that because Buddy had been, it was impossible for him not to be, that to take away Buddy, who was like no one else that lived, should be such a shock to the whole universe it would shatter like an egg into a million million fragments. Yet there was the fact. Buddy was dead before he'd even had time to become a star: the newspapers had hardly had a chance to get hold of him. It made no sense, no sense at all. . . . Then, remembering, he thought about how Buddy was supposed to die and become a star, and that seemed a strange way of putting it and made no sense either. Nothing about Buddy made any sense. He had known all along, yet he hadn't known a thing; and he didn't know what he was supposed to do about Buddy or how he was to think about anything without Buddy. But as he stood there remembering, he touched a point of stillness. All he could do, he thought, would be to look for his brother in the midnight sky.

Gate of Ivory, Gate of Horn

I.

Rachel's father died when he discovered Becker was stealing from him. He perished slowly from a single idea—a sense of justice. It smoldered in his stomach and singed his brain; it blinded him with fury until his eyes dimmed and his vision went dark, and his heart tore against his chest and finally his dreams rose up against him. It went on till it was clear that Becker had taken everything, even though, by that time, Becker was dead. During those years Rachel watched in silence, without knowledge, and listened to her mother, who fed on bitterness. It required her every waking moment, for no matter how she moaned and wrung out her portion of grievance from the daily routine, it was never enough. Each day it had to begin afresh.

The three rooms they lived in were already blackened with sentiment: it rose up from the cookstove and coated the walls and sheathed the lightbulb in sticky dust where the flies sometimes settled and were trapped forever. It yellowed the flowers in the living-room wallpaper and made a permanent groan in the mattress springs in the bedroom. What little light found its way inside was swallowed up by surfaces and beaten into dust.

"Things just walk out of the store," her father said, in one of those hushed, inconclusive adult conversations Rachel wasn't supposed to hear.

She could picture it: pieces from the herd of furniture that stood at either side of the aisle, slipping out one at a time on their little straight legs or curved feet, disappearing most likely in the deep of night. Perhaps Becker had a secret whistle to summon the chairs and set the tables scampering, the lamps tittering along on their little brass knobs. This time Max had taken a radio, a shortwave radio reached by countries all over the globe. Rachel would have liked such a radio herself. A whole world would have danced along the airwaves, all the foreign

76

cities spoken to her. But when she asked if they could have one, her mother said it was much too expensive. Something only Becker would take for himself, she said, drawing her mouth into a little tight bow. But when her father had confronted him, Max simply shrugged. He'd needed a radio and, according to him, Sam Goldman had told him he could take whatever he wanted whenever he wanted it, for wholesale. As for the payment, he hadn't gotten around to it. The man had no shame.

During the day the furniture sat, heavy with waiting while time sank down around it and expired: the cowhide-covered couches with brands burned into them that were to appeal to the instincts of ranchers civilizing themselves; the velour living-room sets, complete with coffee tables, two end tables, and a gilt-framed mirror, priced for the aspirations of Mexican miners. The bedroom sets with their accompanying dressers and bureaus, the mattresses and box springs. The stoves and refrigerators. They all waited. Into their midst walked the occasional customer, into that atmosphere of burdened expectation, where everything hung suspended on the prospect of a sale. "I had a bite on a refrigerator," her father might report at lunch on a Saturday, and Rachel could see the customer circling it with maddening indecision like a fish near a hook. With a sale came a sudden flurry of activity. Louie, who spoke Spanish to the Mexican customers, and one of the delivery boys at the back would unbend themselves from where they'd been sitting like moss on the steps to the second floor, stir into motion to haul down the piece in question, set it inside the truck, and take off in a cloud of dust.

Sometimes when Rachel entered the store she found her father making work for himself: adding up the payments for the day, looking back into the files, or, if nothing else offered, reading the *Furniture Retailer.* Alone in the place, Becker used these lulls to go out to the drugstore to drink coffee with his cronies from the Elks club and the Chamber of Commerce. Creates goodwill—good for the business. He'd been in the town for a long time, even before Sam Goldman had picked him up out of the slough of his shiftless life and given him a job. Before that, as her father put it, Becker didn't have a pot to pee in. Now he was everybody's pal and acted like he could give away the store. Creating goodwill.

Somehow she never thought of Becker as waiting. If he was in the store, he usually stood in the window, nodding and smiling and giving a wave of the hand to people he knew passing in the street. He was a large florid man with a mane of white hair he must have been proud of and a prominent nose. His mouth was a wide thin line that opened to a thick laugh and uneven yellow teeth. He would stand in the window, his leg thrust forward, his hand on his hip, as though he meant more to the world than simply being a former manager of a furniture store. He was there to be looked at, admired in his checkered suit with the gray silk vest, watch chain linked across. He watched the world and the world recognized him and returned his attention: waves, nods, smiles. In one hand, he held a cigarette in a black cigarette holder, and when he took a puff, the diamond ring he wore gave little ejaculations of light on the path to his pleasure.

It was not what they had expected. It was to have been the realization of a dream. Where do dreams come from? She could ask that now. From dream seeds like those that send up the strange little plants that spring forth for a brief no-time. She'd marveled over them as a child: See, watch it climb the side of the glass. Exotic little forms suddenly existing from out of a little red pellet dropped into a glass of water. Living briefly on air.

In that childhood moment when the dreams of her sleep moved unbidden across the screen of the mind, where they came from she could not fathom—no, not the dreams of her sleep nor the ones that leapt across her waking mind, for they came then too—in that moment her father went off in the pursuit of one. Yes, he said once, after he was sick and broken, "Yes, I had my dreams too." Yes, he said, when all he could do was wait uselessly for the curtain to drop. As though it were a bad business all around.

He had never gone away before. It was still the war, still the time when they drew the shades at night and kept just enough light to guide them through the darkened house, where the fear of German submarines and German planes reached toward the Atlantic, the great arena of sea and sky. Every week her father went off to serve as an air raid warden. And in the hours before his return who knew what might break in upon them and dash their lives to smithereens. It was against such peril that Rachel knitted uneven green squares with the others of her Girl Scout troop, toward the comfort of some hapless GI wounded in battle, and collected scrap metal for the drive at school and spent her allowance for the stamps that would end in a war bond and pasted them in her book. All this was being patriotic. And now her father had taken a train West, as though it were possible to make plans and travel toward something else besides the war.

They waited for him to return with the news that would change their lives. Waited in the antebellum house with the white columns and the drafty rooms on an elm-shaded street in the little Delaware town where the DuPont plant had opened up not long before the war to make nylon for stockings and then for parachutes and to bring the town into the twentieth century: a small town that stood in the midst of a flat spot of green given to truck farming. They were city people originally, from immigrant families whose dreams had sent them trekking across Europe and finally to the Lower East Side before the turn of the century: where her grandmother had raised seven children and never learned to read and write. Now in this generation they were to carry the dream to New Mexico, the Land of Enchantment.

Opportunity had knocked and beckoned, and her father went out to look things over: another branch of the family had left behind their failures in the East and gone out and opened a furniture store. Now Sam Goldman owned three, and he needed a manager for one of his stores—he didn't like the way things were being run. "Too much time off drinking coffee with his pals," he said of his manager, Max Becker. Jabbing the air with an unlit cigar to prove his point. "Leaves Louis in the store by himself. Looks bad—bad for the business."

The evening her father came back from his journey it was turning toward fall. The house with its high ceilings and uninsulated walls and rooms long empty of a past was already full of drafts. But when he opened the door, he brought in with him a gust of air from an unknown place. It excited Rachel like the approach of an electrical storm, and she danced around the living room unable to contain herself. After he'd taken his suitcase upstairs and had a chance to wash up, he laid out on the table a handful of Mexican coins, among them a shining silver peso. "They took me up to the town and showed me around. It's about this size, maybe a little bigger. High in the mountains."

On the back of the peso was a great eagle. Mexico—one of the countries represented in her stamp album, and she wanted to go there, and to Dahomey and Ecuador, because they had stamps that most took her eye.

"Right in the area is the second largest open-pit copper mine in the world. They have train tracks going down to the bottom," he said to convey a notion of the size.

High in the mountains, deep in the earth. These suggestions were almost too large to take in. It was the piece of colored rock he laid on the table, striated with layers of red and orange, veins of blue running through it, that immediately struck her thought. Imagine living in a place where the earth gave way to a great bowl. A place of red and orange rocks. She'd never seen anything like it. Beside them he laid down a fossil shell. "Just think," he said. "Those mountains were once under the sea." She picked up the fossil and the rock and the peso by turns. Mountains that once had been under the sea stood a mile high above the town. The colored rocks had been dug from deep in the earth. And the peso, as big as a silver dollar, had come from Mexico. It was enough to convince her to strike out for the place at once.

Her father wanted to go as well. It was a great location, so Sam Goldman had said. But the store needed somebody with brains. Sam tapped the side of his forehead. "Max is no manager. He doesn't think ahead. Lets inventories get low; loses sales when he doesn't have the stock."

Push Max aside—but keep him on the floor—put Nathan in, and the place was a gold mine. And it would give him a place of his own. His own business, the chance to be his own boss. His investment would make him an equal, there to split the profits at the end of the year. Becker had no money in the store; he was merely an employee, someone who had to be watched, and Sam hadn't been able to keep a careful eye on him. This was Nathan's chance. And though he'd done well selling insurance, even in wartime, when he'd had to beg and borrow gasoline coupons, he didn't like knocking on other people's doors. But your own business was something else. You could invest yourself, build it up with your own hands, make a place in the world. And the town would look up to you.

"Well, what do you think?" her father said. They would talk until late at night, long after Rachel had gone to bed.

"There's nothing here," her mother said. Nothing in the twelve years they'd lived there in the large, drafty house. Nothing in her Sundays with the Conoways, who were fuddy-duds of the first order. Or the Sunday bridge club, with the Dunns, Miss Gwen, the high school teacher, who wore plunging necklines, and her Ed, the dentist with the soft southern face, the little teasing dimple in his chin; Bill Mueller, the taciturn German you could never kid about anything, a bachelor, who collected butterflies—a queer hobby for a grown man; Homer Benson, the optometrist, who walked with a limp but provided a good living, and Elizabeth who knew how to spend it (she should only have it so good); and the others. Nothing on the long Sunday afternoons when they went for a drive in the country for want of anything better to do. Nothing in the ladies' nights at the Kiwanis club or the afternoon bridge club, where she sat on her handkerchief for luck. A dozen years with nothing to show for them except a parcel of slights and disappointments.

It was a town high in the mountains they came to—isolated, clinging to its nest at the foot of the slopes, up for grabs by mud and dust. When it rained, and the water roared down from the mountains, it filled the ditch back behind the rear doors of the businesses on the main street and made a flood of the streets as well. The brick and stuccoed houses rode up one set of hills, the unstuccoed adobes of the Mexicans up the other. Reba Lerner had never seen anything like it. Seaford, Delaware, had been at the bottom of the heap socially—full of small-town people. Backward. Whoever even looked at a *New York Times?* She'd never found her real niche. Yet she'd wept as they drove out of town.

"Do you want to go back?" Nathan said.

She did not want to go back. Now she found herself in a pit. People without any upbringing whatsoever, who came to drink your liquor and tell off-color jokes, and weave drunkenly home in the wee hours. Who couldn't carry on a decent conversation. Beneath contempt. There, all in one prospect, was the promise of an eternity of disappointment.

Hardly had they been there a week when one of the region's well-known flash floods visited the town. The rain swept down from the mountains, and half an hour later the streets were a river running between the high sidewalks. Two days afterward when Rachel and her mother could go downtown and cross the street, where, even so, the unpaved side streets still ran with water, Becker took them out back to show them the ditch in full flood. Still the water rushed past, having snatched up everything in its path—sticks and tree branches, and pieces of fence and the odd scrap of lumber. A child's ball went bobbing past.

"Get caught in one of these, and it'll carry away a car," Max said, with a great sweeping gesture to orchestrate the show.

Reba Lerner felt one thing and another break loose and slide away like pieces of flotsam in the flood. By then she'd heard about rattlesnakes and scorpions and centipedes, and wherever she turned, she was affronted by a landscape brown and dry with thorny twisted things that stabbed the air and struggled for water. The grass was poor thin stuff compared with what she knew—a single cow needed a square mile in which to forage, just imagine! The trees were stunted things, scrub cedar and scrub oak that could hardly raise themselves above the ground, and in town the random acacia or boxwood elder stood with its dusty leaves like tongues panting for water. She tried to picture beyond the muddy flow that crossed her vision something that would take the place of real grass and trees and the yard where mock orange and lilacs had filled the air with fragrance and the roses climbed the trellis and wisteria hung over the porch, humming with wasps and bees. Instead the mountains rose up before her, alien and formidable. Each day she found them blocking the way to promise, shutting out all escape.

"Would you look at that," Reba Lerner said to Nathan, almost as an accusation, while the muddy water rushed past. Ugliness.

The town could have invented it. Why hadn't they told her, why hadn't she been warned? Didn't Nathan have eyes? Surely her stupid sister could have said a word. To pick up stakes and come here. To try to fit her eleven rooms of furniture into a miserable three-room duplex. The town with its unpaved streets and shabby storefronts, its one department store with what passed for the latest fashions.

"That used to be the main street," Max said, indicating the ditch. "Honest. I'm not kidding you," taking Reba's dismay, Nathan's irritable silence, for simple incredulity.

"The water came down just like that"—another sweep of the hand, glitter of the diamond—"and left the ditch. Thirty feet deep."

It was beyond anything she could imagine. Back east she'd seen the tail end of a hurricane once and woken from a night where the wind had gone mad to a morning of broken trees littering the street. And she had read of terrible things in the newspaper. There at least they weren't happening to you, though God forbid they should happen to anybody. But here you came upon nature in the raw, everything in the raw, including the people.

And Max standing there as if he were a showman, a regular magician revealing all the sights, with Nathan looking on against his will. He'd been interrupted from what he'd been doing, and the empty store was clamoring at his back. "Listen," he said, "someone could come and walk off with the whole place." Nathan turned and left them.

"Come on, Rachel, we're going," Reba said. Her loyalty had been called upon whether she felt like staying or not.

"The merchants just opened their back doors," Max went on, oblivious, "and that became the main street."

He was planted solidly in his wing-tip shoes, without hurry, with no pressing business to move him, and he could have stood there all day. Nathan worked like a slave, always had, and Reba had to weigh her chances about what condition his stomach would be in when he got home and what she could think of he'd be willing to put into it. Sometimes she had to rack her brain. And whether she should even venture to suggest a movie. She was cooped up in the house day in, day out, but most nights it was impossible to coax him from his chair after dinner. He was like an old man.

"It's not like Jersey," Max said, following her so as not to lose his audience. "Here you go down a highway, sun in the sky, dry as a bone, only some streaks off on in the distance. And suddenly here's a wall of water coming down one of those arroyos."

"Think of that," she murmured, heading into the back door.

"Max, will you come here a minute," Nathan said, summoning him like a schoolboy. "You've added wrong."

Max put on his glasses, gold-rimmed hexagons, the light playing across the lenses in little flicks of fire. Reba gave a sigh, the mark of her exasperation, to which she sometimes added, "I don't know how I stand it." This was her diversion, coming to the store to sit of an afternoon, to wait, but for what? To find Nathan at his figures and Max on display in the window, and his dowdy wife, with her dark clothes and thick black hair, looking like she just stepped off the boat. She gave you a smile, let her grant that, but you couldn't say two words to her to make an adult conversation. This town, these people: she'd been brought here like a hostage to live among savages.

Henrietta Becker, known as Henny. The moment Rachel saw her, she had the queer feeling that this woman had been waiting for her, perhaps for a long time. She was made shy by a sense of strangeness. But the smile was gentle, even tentative, as though to cover a restrained excitement. "Come here," Henny said, in a voice that struck her as foreign, for its slight trace of an accent and for a quality in it that thrilled her, "and let me see you." The next thing she noticed was how big Henny's hands were, like a man's, with their broad palms and long fingers. But the touch on her shoulder was light, a gesture that made her forget for a moment everything but the sensation. And when Rachel looked into her eyes, a velvety blackness, she forgot everything in a sudden attraction, the sense of a doorway opening and her looking into a new place. Henny's eyes were a shining darkness that drew and held her and for some reason made her tremble.

"You've come here," Henny said. "I hope it will be a good place for you."

Rachel could only stare.

"You going to hang around here all day?" Max's voice broke in, and Rachel started guiltily as though she'd been caught doing something wrong. Henny did not turn around.

"Your supper will be on the table," she said.

"I have a meeting tonight. Come on, come on. Get going. Make it snappy."

Henny turned to Rachel's mother. "I'm going to take this child home with me," she said, with a deference that still carried a certain authority, "if you don't mind. I made some cookies this afternoon . . ."

"You'll spoil her appetite," Max interrupted.

The sides had been drawn up, and Rachel experienced an irrational longing to go with this woman she had only just met, as though wherever Henny might take her, it would be exactly the place she wanted to go. She looked to her mother and saw the afternoon moving dully toward supper, toward the moment when her father would walk through the door, give her mother a perfunctory kiss, wash his hands, and sit at the kitchen table. The radio was on the side of the table next to the wall, and each night he turned it on for the voice of H. V. Kaltenborn, with its stiff intensity hammering out the news, to be taken in with the flavors of the pot roast and the tints of the evening sky darkening outside the window just above Mrs. Pennington's roof, as though the three of them were gathered there for that rite alone, listening and silently chewing. Only when the news was over and the radio switched off was there room for her mother to say, "Well, how was your day?"

"She will have one or two and take the rest home," Henny promised. "She will keep her appetite and her health. She will do proper justice to her mother's cooking."

In a way new to Rachel, this tall woman seemed to concede nothing, but to preserve something of her own with a certain stubbornness, with even a brightness of expression. And Rachel was in collusion, a rocky ground for her timid footing. Her mother and Max had become allies in the name of what was good for her. Which was altogether distinct from something else they were unable to recognize and that Rachel could barely glimpse herself, let alone define.

She looked to her mother for permission or denial, not hopeful, so much depended on what was ravaging her at the moment, but saw in her expression a willingness to give in provided Rachel not be late to set the table, provided she go easy on the cookies.

Rachel was assured that the evening meal was the one reality that waited in the flux of possibilities. It waited in a setting in which the six o'clock news, which no one must interrupt, and not spoiling an appetite with sweets shared the same moral space and density. And something was being exacted from her for which she'd be called to account in the future. It was owing in the balance for this leniency.

"Have it your way," Max said with a shrug. It was too inconsequential to bother with.

"Which way shall we go home?" Henny asked her. "Sometimes I go one way, sometimes another." There was more than one way; other prospects could turn something up, cracks across the surface of the ordinary: some bit of desert poppy or thistle poking up on the edge of the unpaved street, some Mexican child with tender eyes or an old man with a face older than time, some wandering dog busy with smells or a cat stalking, or an occasional rabbit, all to be taken in, these bits and pieces, perhaps something to be found among them, one never knew. These remained to be discovered. She was not yet ready to determine what one might find that would make any difference. She was too new and her eye didn't know what to land on. She knew no one and must wait for school to start to find friends. She had not yet learned of the light cast on things by longing or by disappointment or love, the way the ordinary shifted and was changing by dreaming.

"We can go by way of the Chinese grocery, the bowling alley, the Catholic church. But that way we have to walk up the hill. The long way around we can go by the old house with the pillars. Have you been in the Chinese grocery?"

She wanted to go to the Chinese grocery, but she wanted to see the old house as well.

"That's another way," Henny said. "A new way made out of pieces of the other two. I have not tried it."

In Ying Lee's Market, they found Mrs. Lee standing behind the counter, a small woman with gray hair pulled back in a bun. It formed a frame for a face whose cheeks rose full above the angular slant of her jaw, above a small pointed chin.

"I stole this child," Henny said. Mrs. Lee looked at Rachel—they were nearly the same height and gave her serious inspection. "Ah," she said. "A good face."

"I stole her for my own."

"You have stolen her. Maybe if I see her first . . ." She gave Rachel a little smile, as if in complicity.

Rachel was being invited to enter the story Henny was making up, she saw that immediately. It both pleased her and made her shy. She had become something other than she was, shaken loose from all she knew of herself to play another part. Like when she'd played dress-ups in the old house. In the room where her mother shed all her cast off clothes and hats. How she loved to go into that room smelling of dust and disuse. It was occupied too by an old Edison phonograph her father had bought in a second-hand shop, its horn like a morning-glory trumpet. She had heard Caruso sing once while she tromped about in high heels. But now she was in this strange town, where her sense of reality stumbled against stuccoed adobe houses and dark-skinned people speaking a language she couldn't understand. And the things that grew around her carried their own warning, the spiny leaves of thistles and desert poppies, the needles of the cacti. *Don't touch,* they commanded, as they held out their weapons, *or you'll be sorry.* She had wandered far from kinder flowers. Even the roses seemed much kindlier with their pure colors and rich scents in a green setting, and all the rest, snowballs and azaleas and hydrangeas blooming in the lazy humidity, generous to excess.

Already she was afraid, looking at this world, a stranger without welcome, not belonging to it, not in possession of key or talisman. How was one to enter? Would she always be among strangers?

But Henny threw it all into the air again, let nothing settle. And the old Chinese woman was part of the conspiracy, with only a glance between them. It was delicious. Rachel forgot herself entirely, and wanted to know only where the make-believe would take her.

"I stole her. I will leave another in her place, and no one will know the difference."

The old woman gave a smile that brought wrinkles to her face, yet there was in her expression an almost childlike glee. "I give her a treat. Because this the first time she come in. Maybe she come back." She moved from behind the counter to where two wooden boxes were set beside bunches of scallions and carrots and heads of lettuce, in which the fruit nested in pale yellow papers. She lifted one out, came round in front of Rachel, and held out a pear. "Very lovely color," she said, asking her to admire the speckled yellow. "It remind me of different place."

"Your son?" Henny asked.

"Still in very great trouble," Mrs. Lee said. "Sometime I do not know. I visit him in the hospital. Very hard."

Henny nodded. They did not say more. She bought garlic and carrots and mushrooms. "Let me pick," Mrs. Lee said, inspecting the mushrooms one by one until she'd found the whitest, the most nearly perfect, putting them one by one into a little bag.

The sun was a brilliant glare as they walked toward the brick house with the great round pillars supporting the porch. "A grand place once," Henny said. "They used to have dances in the ballroom, and musicians would come to play." Rachel could see ladies in long dresses and hear the strains of music that animated the dance, just as in *Gone with the Wind*.

She could almost forget that it was now a boardinghouse and the paint on the pillars was crazed and cracking away in places. The windowsills were worn down to the bare wood. "This house belonged to a judge," Henny told her. "A man prominent in the town. He was scalped by the Indians. His wife, too, as they rode to Lordsburg in their carriage. And his little son was carried away." They turned the corner into a rutted, unpaved street, and then climbed a hill where the houses sat behind iron fences enclosing varying pretenses of a yard, some with clumps of prickly pear, others with scanty patches of grass going brown under the sun.

"And here we are." It was a brick house painted white, with high windows, set back from the street. Ivy clung to one side. Inside it was cool and dark, and coming in from the bright light, Rachel had to blink to make anything out. She stood there uncertainly, waiting to know how to act. The furnishings were nothing she recognized as belonging to the store. Almost before she registered the difference, she noticed a picture on the wall and recognized a fox, its black eyes directed by quick assessment. Then next to it, a lion, all superior majesty, but with a wrinkled brow as though it knew too much; then a crow who knew how to put its wits to use with flattery, and a bear who knew that sheer bulk and force would win its way; a jackal clever in the ways of discrimination, digging up its food at the precise moment. She moved from one to the other, each present with a certain kind of knowledge inviting her to enter a particular doorway. Henrietta left her there to go into the kitchen, and she was in the room alone, listening to see if the room was friendly to her.

The blinds were drawn against the afternoon sun, except for a band of light streaking in at the bottom and falling in a beam of dancing motes to the floor. It was a room that belonged to another time and place, for she recognized old things in it that perhaps had belonged in the family. Dark varnished surfaces that smelled of furniture polish and gave off gleams of highlighted grain, and tall cabinets with glass fronts. She wanted to run her hand over the dark varnished wood of the long table and stare inside the beveled panes to where the cut glass stood, its incised patterns of leaves and flowers catching glints of light, and to consider the surfaces of the smaller tables that held embroidered runners. And from the decanters of wine and fruit brandy on the sideboard came the ruby gleams of liquid that took one's taste to something deeper than everyday. She had been allowed once to taste a maraschino cherry that had been steeping in a glass of brandy and knew about it. This room was different too, and the dining room beyond it with its dark, carved furniture, and to the side a room lined with bookcases. She moved toward the doorway. A clock chimed on the mantel, and as she watched, an old man with a scythe appeared, followed by an old woman with an hourglass. Time was old here.

She walked through the light-filled doorway of the kitchen, past a cow ruminating over a meadow full of flowers, as though each one presented an object for contemplation. Henrietta had poured a glass of apple juice for her, which stood next to a plate with two cookies. The kitchen still held the odors of baking, the smell of cinnamon and nutmeg and cloves. On the windowsill among the plants a large, striped, yellow cat, both alert and self-absorbed, sat cleaning a paw.

"Animals must know a lot," Rachel said, while she watched the cat. They seemed always to know what to do and not to have to apologize for it. What was it that told them what to do? She hadn't really thought about it before, but they appeared to have an advantage.

"This cat always knows what kind of person comes into a room," Henny said, "whether it should stay or not." Rachel hoped it would allow her to stay, though she didn't try to pet it. When she had sat down at the kitchen table, Henny took out the pear Mrs. Lee had given her and set it next to the plate. She turned it around in her hand. A beautiful color. Rachel ate the pear and two of the spice cookies, nibbling little pieces from around the edge to make the taste last longer. Meanwhile Henny talked to her as she peeled potatoes and sliced carrots and mushrooms. She moved slowly, Rachel noticed, not like her mother, who expected people to move fast and told Rachel she was a dreamer and to get her head out of the clouds and watch what she was doing.

But Henny handled carrot and potato, onion and lettuce leaf, each with attention. Rachel watched the way her hands moved, the large fingers, arranging, peeling, working as though separate from her in their own knowledge, while Henny sat on her stool and told Rachel about her grandmother, who made the children hide under the bed when she was sure the witches were roaming the village and named all the cows in the shed after the constellations.

She was still talking to Henny after she'd licked a finger to pick up the last crumbs of the cookies, hoping Henny hadn't noticed such a breach of manners—fortunately a little package of cookies lay wrapped and waiting for her to take home—when she heard the clock strike again. She ran into the den in time to see the hands at the half hour. The old man with the sickle and the old woman with the hourglass wouldn't come round this time, but she had to leave. She would barely make it home before it was time to turn on the news.

She ran down the hill to the duplex where they lived next door to the nuisance boy on one side and, on the other, the old woman who played hymns on her wheezy organ every evening and spoke of tuning into Jesus. Hopefully, her father suggested, Jesus had a tin ear. When Rachel came through the front gate, she was still panting. The hill had helped her home, though it very nearly sent the ground spinning out from under her and up into her face as she flew past herself. If she could only fly, she could always be home on time; she could enter the air, so light and fast. . . . She came onto the porch and past the green metal chairs that stood sentinel with a certain grim determination, let the screen door clatter shut behind her—something she was continually scolded for—and threw open the front door. "Henny sent these," she said, catching her breath, presenting her bribe.

"Where have you been? I had to set the table myself." The cookies had not appeased her. "I hope you didn't spoil your supper," her mother said, still intent. They were having liver that night, and she'd prepared it with bacon and onions. There were so few things she could get Nathan to eat—the same things over and over—and then usually some complaint about his stomach. Or something didn't suit him. "Go and wash your hands before your father gets home."

Light had already ebbed away from the dark kitchen with its smell of frying onions, and the day was moving toward the war news and supper, dishes to be done afterward. Against the backdrop of those certainties, it was now all right, her being late. It was only one more thing to be held against her in the long and inevitably growing list, to be held against whatever she was becoming. Whoever it was she didn't know and couldn't fathom, this someone who didn't seem to have arrived yet but had to be put up with in spite of herself. Someone who very likely would never get anything right. For a spear's point kept pressing against everything she knew, dividing her mind against itself, getting her into trouble. It sent her heart pounding and turned her subversive. It came on more strongly every time she opened the door into the living room, where the tired furniture sat, brought all the way from Delaware, and the antique figurines, shepherd and shepherdess, simpered coyly at one another across the reach of the revolving bookcase table. Or when she entered the kitchen with its stained sink and docile table and chairs and the nightly ritual of setting round the silverware for the evening meal. She said nothing about where she had been, for nothing had been asked. *I have stolen this child and put another in her place.*

At the supper table she subsided into the silence her father expected and that always held sway over the evening meal. For now he had come home and taken his place and turned on the radio: "There's good news tonight." It was never good news that she could see. Never anything that changed the voices, not even of H. V. Kaltenborn himself. Or made a difference. Nothing changed, except perhaps the smells that moved from one meal to the next, from liver to pot roast to stewed chicken, that hung in the stale air, while outside the day went down and there was nothing to show for it. Things fried or baked or broiled in the sauce of sour expectation and set on her father's plate. To placate him for his day, offer a reward for the long hours that offered no riches, gave no hum of future prospects. From the other side of the duplex came the thunder of the nuisance boy running up and down bouncing his ball.

"You can't even hear yourself think," her father said.

"Not only that, but eight o'clock in the morning—all morning long. I don't know how I stand it." The reminder of what her mother had to contend with. "Well, and how was your day?"

Though she expected to see Henny again in the store, it was a while before she came in again. Max said she'd been sick, so Rachel had to wait to visit her. But there were others who came into the store, who had been coming very likely before she was born. If she came downtown, she was almost certain to find Fred and Josephine established in the overstuffed or occasional chairs that lined the aisle. Josephine: a squat, dumpy woman with business in her walk, and the look of a sharp-eyed bird, as though she'd spotted a grub on the sidewalk and would beat everyone else away with her wings if they tried for it. Behind her Fred, thin as famine, moved as if in a slow leak toward extinction, with only a few small splinters of light from his eyeglasses to mark his progress. Rachel saw a skeleton, with clothes to dissemble—a purely temporary arrangement. "Vell, vat's news?" he would say inevitably, when he first came in, and present both uppers and lowers of his grinning teeth. And then, as though he'd made a joke, Heh heh heh heh.

Every afternoon they came to sit. Though they never bought anything they couldn't get wholesale, they acted like the store's privileged customers: they knew Sam Goldman; they knew Max and Henny (though Henny, God forbid, was a little off and had always been, and they'd said as much to Max). They knew everybody, knew the things nobody would want told, all the secret things about which they said, "This you won't believe." These they told with the saliva of pure relish in their mouths, things not to anyone's credit and usually to someone's bane. Things they'd seen with their very eyes, they assured you. Heard with their own ears. Ears more sensitive than any antennae, that could hear through walls, pick out of the air groans in the dark, the whispers of illicit passion, words spoken in dirty deals. All the sounds that hung in the air that no one else could hear. Ears that grew on stems; eyes like telescopes.

After thirty-five years in the town they knew all the inside scoop at Kennecott and the Veterans Hospital and City Hall. He who has ears, let him hear. They trafficked in rumor and gossip, entertained themselves with surmise—*Let me tell you what I think*—that made Josephine put a finger to her nose and nod her head and look at one sharp as a razor.

Every morning over the telephone Josephine picked and plucked from this one and that the latest bits of her store of news. And then she made another round of calls sharing these in the primacy of first knowledge. Sometimes even before Rachel left for school the telephone rang over some choice tidbit that could not wait until she came down to the store that afternoon. Meanwhile Fred, taking his slow way downtown to the bank, to City Hall, to Simon in the men's store, to the Wassermans, who could not be counted on for much, culled whatever crumbs he could find.

Even on Saturday, when it was sometimes busy, they came and sat and watched who came in to make their payments and who might be looking to buy.

"You have to be polite," Nathan said. And he sat down with them if there was a lull. For they were friends of Sam Goldman's; they went back to him with everything that went on in the store. With chagrin Nathan knew they were telling Sam how few customers were in the store and how slow business was. Josephine was the quick one: nothing was lost on her. Fred, with his thick accent and slow speech, was there to register the precise degree to which any piece of news was to be gloated over or deplored. "Yes, vell. . . ." In either case he would conclude with his little laugh, heh heh heh heh.

Then there was their own story: "Yes, vell . . . a tregedy. And to think, we could have been millionaires."

When this enormity had had a chance to register, Josephine would say, "If Fred had only waited another year. . . ." For then the mining company came in and began exploring again. A shrug: what can you do?

"The ting is. . . ." And Fred would point a bony finger. "They made me an offer. So I think, the mine is worthless, it's a few hundred dollars, vy not?" The silver mine on the edge of town that had brought so much wealth in the early days had fallen into their hands in payment for a debt. The silver had been mined out long before and the shafts abandoned for years. Right after Fred had sold it, another vein of silver was discovered. A rich vein. And for the years now that the mine had been operating the lucky owners had been making a fortune.

"Millionaires." And visions of silver teased and mocked them.

For Reba Lerner, Fred and Josephine were proof that some people had all the luck and never had to spend a dime. She knew things about them, too. For all their pissing and moaning, they were rich: they owned houses and property all over town. And Josephine, who made the rounds collecting the rents, descended on her tenants like a scourge. Nothing escaped her eye: not a scratch on the door, a spot on the rug. She kept count. She opened their cupboards and snooped in their bedrooms and lifted the lids of the pots on their stoves. She scolded their children and harried their dogs and once had called the dogcatcher on a beast that had snarled at her.

In those shacks. If ever she bought anything, it was for "the rental houses," and was either cheap or secondhand. And when did she ever freshen the walls with a coat of paint? A cheap-skate to end all cheapskates. Leave it to her to sniff out a bar-gain—anywhere. She drove ten miles away to save two cents a pound on a chicken. And then told you about it. Spend ten cents worth of gas to save one lousy dime. And once she brought back a bottle of aspirins to the drugstore when she found them cheap-er elsewhere. The druggist took the trouble to count: three were missing. They all knew her, they all had her number. Stories about her, about them, all over town. They added insult to injury. Fred had sold scrap metal to the Japanese even after Pearl Harbor.

Which all went to show, as Reba Lerner put it, that if you were rich and without shame you could get away with murder. "I'd just like to have money," she often said to Rachel, as she looked around at the three crummy rooms that contained her life and her prospects. "If you have money, you can tell people to go to hell." Oh, the things she had to contend with instead. Max, for instance, who would make anybody poor. While Josephine plopped her fat backside into their chairs, bragged about her bar-gains, told you what you already knew, and got under your skin.

"I used to tell Sam," Josephine said, "here I was coming into the store, and only the Mexican fellow there. Nobody to watch the cash register. Where was Max? Nobody knew. Off with his cronies." She looked around, as though expecting an avenging angel. "It cries to heaven."

"The big shot," Fred said. "He likes to play the big shot. Heh Heh. A big shot."

"And still the big shot," Nathan said. Let it get back to Sam Goldman that the guy was not only a loser but a total loss. "He takes home the best Zenith because he needs a radio. He still hasn't paid for it." He was in charge after all; Max was simply an employee. It has him upset even when he isn't thinking about it.

"They think he's the cock of the walk. At night, he's never home. The Elks Club. Out at the Dix. Henny always by herself. She's a little off, but what can you expect with that for family life?"

"You can't make conversation with her," Reba said. Then to be on the safe side. "A sweet face—"

"It's like saying she has nice teeth," Nathan said.

"No, I think she has a sweet face," Reba insisted.

"Very bad luck with the children," Fred says. "A tregedy."
When Rachel found herself in the midst of these conversations,
her impulse was to retreat. And she never stayed longer than it
took to be polite. But this time she had come into the store with
a definite purpose. She had seen Max on the street.

"Max told me that Henny was feeling better," she said as she
came up to the four of them sitting on the aisle. "Could I go over
and see her?"

"Say hello," her mother said. Then— "Not yet. I don't think she
wants to be bothered."

"She told me I could come anytime," Rachel insisted.

"Another time," her mother said. "I have things for you to do
around the house."

"What things?" she objected.

"Don't talk back," her father said.

"We'll be going in a minute."

Rachel hung about irritably at the edge of the adult conversation, knowing she couldn't present her case with the hope of
any sympathy. A long stretch of summer boredom lay open
before her. There was little to do except wander up behind the
courthouse, where one side of the hill had been torn away in the
interests of something valuable. There remained a pile of shale
to clamber up and a bed of clay below. Some of this she had
brought home and fashioned into animals and left to dry in the
sun until Reba made her clean up the mess. Besides her books
and an occasional afternoon at the swimming pool at St. Mary's
Academy, there was little to do.

"The daughter ran off," Fred said. "The son got in with bad company. A great tregedy when kids don't behave—heh heh heh heh."

"The son took up with Mexicans," Josephine continued. "The
worst elements. At nights they went out and stole hubcaps.
Sometimes he played hookey while he was in high school and
used to hang around the pool hall."

"Fortunately he was drafted. He got killed in Italy."

"But the daughter was nothing but. . . ." She looked around,
gave Rachel a glance that made her flinch, and let go the rest of
the sentence. "And Max with all his gallivanting around—never
home. What kind of father? You can understand it.

"'And Henny. I said to him, Max, it's not good to leave her so much. She's strange enough already. God forbid something should happen to her. But you're the one making her crazy in the head. . . .'"

Rachel hated their talk, slicing off pieces of people's lives like meat. It made her stomach churn. She knocked into a floor lamp and caught it before it rocked over.

"Will you be careful," her father said. "If you break something, it'll come out of your allowance. I've never seen a child who could be so careless."

Reba stood up to leave. She couldn't get a moment's peace.

"Mex, I tell him, you have a wife, you have a fembley, vat is dis? And he says right in front of her—dat cow?" Fred gazed around him with his palms extended, the light flashing from his spectacles.

That cow, that cow, that cow—Rachel heard it in her ears all the way home.

Fortunately, at least in this case, Rachel's mother was a stickler in matters of social decorum. Even though Henny had been presented to her as a little off the beam, suggesting that Rachel had no business near her, still she was Max's wife and she had sent over an offering of cookies: a neighborly thing to do, not to be discounted or ignored even in the face of suspected insanity. In truth, she couldn't believe Henny was anything more than a little dense, one of those people who didn't know how to talk, probably with an inferiority complex because she had no taste, no more sophistication than a tree stump.

For that matter, Josephine, who prided herself on how smart she was, could only be described as coarse by comparison. She didn't know the first thing about those social niceties that immediately reveal a person for what they are. Even before she opened her mouth, she put her foot in it. She must have come from the lowest class of people, Reba guessed, the scum of the earth. Her father was probably a pushcart peddler or a tailor. Henny might not know from nothing, with her old country ways and clothes twenty years out of style, but at least she knew how to make a nice gesture. Reba owed her. One never returned a plate empty, even though, in this case, there was no plate to return. Besides which, Reba Lerner prided herself on her baking, and frequently when she made a cake, she sent pieces of it around to neighbors she was on good terms with or to someone who had done her a favor. She lived for those compliments about her cakes, those appreciative comments that allowed her to feel she knew about the small but important things of life.

Whereas she might have refused Rachel's request to visit Henny simply because she wanted to go, she sent her there with a piece of cake as a matter of duty, even though Nathan had been so upset about Max the previous evening he had been evil to live with.

Rachel was buoyant with expectation. She had been released after the usual tedium of Saturday routines, of having her hair washed in the basin in the sink, of scrubbing the floor and cleaning the bathroom and helping with the ironing, all of which she hated, and allowed to go to Henny's, then to the Saturday matinee. She went in the performance of social ritual, carrying the gift that would allow her entry. She suspected, though, it made no difference. Henny wasn't like other people she knew, and even her house, in which she so entirely belonged, gave her a curious sense of difference. It had drawn Rachel with the sense of unexplored possibilities, haunted her with a desire to go back.

The night before she had a curious dream about Henny, if that was who was in it. She had come to the edge of a lake and seen a figure in the water, a great head, huge breasts and belly, surfacing like separate islands, but all belonging to the same great figure. Her dark hair streamed on the water. And beyond the lake, all in marble, was a statue of the same woman elevated on a pedestal. In the dream Rachel did not know if she felt the greater awe for seeing Henny naked in the water or elevated in marble.

When she knocked on the door, Henny met her with an expression of welcome. "I am very glad you came," she said. "I have been hoping. . . ."

Rachel was flattered. Although she had a constant itch to go somewhere, it didn't occur to her that she might be anticipated. She held out the cake and said shyly, "My mother thought you might like some cake."

"Chocolate," Henny said, appreciatively. "Do you like chocolate as well as I do? But come in. I'm about to have tea."

She appeared happy, not at all sick, and it was very exciting to be welcomed into the kitchen where Henny filled the pot with water and, as she waited for the tea to steep, poured out a glass of ginger ale for Rachel. They did not remain in the kitchen this time. Henny put a cup and saucer and the teapot and two slices of cake on plates on a tray, and together they went into the room Rachel had only looked into before. Before she poured the tea, Henny took a round disc from a little drawer in a large oak music box with pictures of birds painted on the sides and set the disc in motion.

Rachel didn't know the tune, though it teased her with instant familiarity, tinkling music that was unlike any she had ever heard. Fairy music

"You like that?" Henny said. "It belonged to my mother, the only thing of hers I brought with me when I got married. I had to have the music box and one thing more."

Rachel admired her first choice: she would have chosen the same way. "And what was the other?"

"This," Henny said, showing her a large stuffed clown that sat in one corner of a chair by the window. Dressed in motley, it surveyed the room with an expression that hung somewhere between laughter and tears, its peaked hat falling to one side.

Rachel stood in front of it. A curious clown with its downturned mouth and wide eyes, as though what it saw was far more than it could take in. "I never liked dolls," she confessed. "My aunt sent me dolls all the time—she worked in a doll factory, but I never played with them." With their wooden expressions and painted smiles, they sat there stupidly in their little lace-edged dresses. They were never her babies; she'd already concluded that babies were a nuisance, though she had enjoyed dressing up her dog and kittens in doll clothes and pushing them about in a baby carriage. She was too old for that now. The clown intrigued her.

Henny stood just behind her. "When my son was a very small boy, he would stand in front of this clown and say, 'When I am older, I want him to come and live with me. We will tell each other stories.'"

Then Rachel noticed that the shelf behind him was full of children's books. "You can look at them," Henny told her. And Rachel pulled them out one after the other and looked at the colored illustrations of animals and princes and wicked stepmothers. She had to handle the books carefully, for some of the bindings were loose and the covers ragged. She could tell that some of them had been favorite books because the pages had been turned again and again, until they bore the marks of the hands that had turned them. "David loved to read," Henny said. "But he liked me to read to him too. He would memorize the stories."

"What stories did he like best?"

"He liked the stories of the old heroes like Achilles and Jason and the Golden Fleece."

Rachel had never read those. She had always loved fairy tales, and the stories from the Arabian Nights and Old Testament stories. She loved reading about Sinbad the Sailor and David and Goliath and stories about dogs, and horses, like Black Beauty. Sometimes she wondered why she was so unlucky as not to have a horse or a dog with special talents, like Lassie. She wished that it were really possible to find a lamp with a genie in it that could be summoned to build a palace in a single night or to discover a cave full of thieves' gold like Ali Baba's. It seemed terrible to live in a world that didn't have those things that were all so interesting.

"I like stories," she said, as though admitting to a weakness such as an inordinate fondness for chocolate candy. They were childhood things, to be put aside until you couldn't think of a single other useful thing to take up your time.

"I thought so," Henny said. "I thought you would. If you'd like to choose a book to take home with you. . . ."

Did she dare? Perhaps if she was very careful. She was a little old for fairy tales now that she was almost eleven. There waited for her books on science and history that would make her more intelligent, books like her father sometimes read, but never her mother. Now that they had come to this strange town, she felt a shock as of the ground shifting beneath her. Everything was changed. Her childhood could no longer be counted upon. Even the air she breathed was no longer the same: the yard with the mock orange tree and snowball bush and Muscovy ducks and chickens her mother kept there, the dusky nights on the front porch with the smell of summer and the glimmer of fireflies, Rehobeth Beach, where they used to go on Sunday, were now only a memory. She had never experienced before the way certain things got cut off and became the past. Things she didn't know had been slipping away from her. But now she was alone. Not even her parents could be counted on to tell her what doorway she was entering; they too were in a strange place.

She had the sense that she was growing up past the unreal things in storybooks to what went on in the world: the furniture store where time sank into waiting, the stretch of days where only unpleasant things waited to be done and bills had to be paid. The stretch of days that became life: where one had to save every nickel and not waste anything, or get spots on one's clothes, where one had to be constantly looking out for germs, especially on toilet seats, to be careful around boys and gentiles. All finished by the six o'clock news.

At least there were the movies, and she really ought to be going, to be on time for the matinee. Yet she found it hard to tear herself away. She pulled out a book about the knights of the Round Table. She tried to imagine Henny's son being grown up and leaving his books behind. "Where is your son now?" she asked.

"He was killed in the war," Henny said.

Rachel had never known anyone who'd lost a son in the war. She looked at Henny, thinking she had asked the wrong question. But Henny did not push the subject away.

"He was very eager to go and fight in the war," Henny said sadly. "He would not have been happy otherwise."

Rachel did not understand that. "Where did he die?"

"In the campaign in Italy," she said. "They couldn't find him afterward. I will show you."

While Rachel ate her cake, Henny took out a collection of coins her son had collected in North Africa and Italy and laid them out in front of her. One by one Rachel picked them up just as she had looked at the coins her father had brought back from Juárez. There was strange writing on some of the coins that Henny told her was Arabic. Rachel studied the marks and curves. How many places she had never been. It was exciting to think of someone being where the coins came from, but then she had to remember that he was now gone, that he'd left behind his childhood forever in the shelf full of books.

"I'm hoping he'll come back," Henny said. "And tell me the rest of the story."

Rachel looked at her curiously. "I have many stories," Henny said. "Every day when I wake I have more. People come to me in the night and tell me their stories. When I wake up, I have them in my head."

"How does that happen?" Rachel asked, and caught her breath. She was almost afraid to hear. Perhaps dreams were stories, but then where did they come from? Joseph had been there to tell the Pharaoh the meaning of his dreams and save the Egyptians from famine. They'd let him out of prison to become the Pharaoh's right hand, and she quite admired the picture of him driving his chariot, looking important. It was one of her favorite stories, even though it had happened so long ago, so far beyond anything that might happen in her life. When her mother called her a dreamer, she always said she wasn't, because it was a criticism. But so often she found her mind somewhere else. She didn't mean for it to stray; it just wandered off in spite of her. And often when the insistent voices of the ordinary brought her back, it was as though she'd been startled awake. And she felt ashamed.

But Henny's dreams were stories, and her voice drew her into listening, into letting time slip past. If she stayed longer, she would miss the matinee altogether. That was like a dream too, but it was okay to watch because there were movie stars in it and when you went out of the theater you yawned and went home and set the table.

"There are fifty people in my family," Henny said. "Nearly all of them are gone now. Sometimes they come and tell me how they died, so that I will know. Or they come and tell me things they don't want forgotten. Last night my little nephew Mateus, my brother's child, came to me. He was a tall boy for his age—I have his picture—with such curly hair. Last night he came to me and told me they had to run away into the forest, he and his mother, so they wouldn't be captured. They lived on berries and nuts and sometimes they would go to a village and ask for food. But when winter came, they had nowhere to go, and one day Golde dropped in the snow and wouldn't wake up."

"What happened to him?"

"He tried to find help but he was already sick. He had a bad fever and died of pneumonia."

"And all the people come like that?" Rachel said.

"Many of them come. But they tell me other things. Lots of things. My cousin Abel came to tell me how he fell in love when he was hiding out in one of the villages. In Poland just before the end. He had been smuggled out of Warsaw. Every day a young girl, Elsbeta, brought him food. And when she gave him the dish she smiled in a way to make him dream. During the day he helped mend harness and do other chores and he would think of her smile. He wanted to marry her. The girl had lost her parents, and he had no one either. Every night he came to tell me about his love. Yes, they were smuggled out of the country just as the Allies came. I hope they have many children."

As Rachel watched her, Henny herself was caught in a curious light, not quite real. The ordinary world sank beyond the drawn blinds, the hot street under the light full of Saturday dust and effort. It was the sensation she got inside the movie theater. There when the lights went down and the screen lit up, a magic descended and she forgot everything else. And for the time in that darkness, even though other kids squirmed in the seats, she was filled with something more real than anything she knew on the street. Even though it was all false and couldn't really happen. And Henny had become that, even more—something as vast to her as the figure in the lake, taking in all her family, all their stories.

"And your son?" Rachel said.

"He has not come yet," Henny said. "I pray for him to come. If he came, it would be such joy. . . . It is the only thing I'm waiting for," she said softly.

Reba had not seen her sister and brother-in-law since they had left Las Cruces in July. When they first came to New Mexico, they had stayed in Gertrude and Joe's house until Nathan could get the hang of the business. Every day he got up and went to the store with Joe or else took instruction from Sam Goldman, who, in fact, owned both stores. Sam's wife was Joe's sister, and now both his partners were in some way family connections. After two months the Lerners had moved up to Silver. Now they were going down to Las Cruces to visit overnight. Though Reba didn't dare say anything, she had a bone to pick with her sister: Gertie had not only encouraged her to come to such a godforsaken place; she'd abandoned them after they got there. That dismal little town in the mountains wasn't Las Cruces, where Gertie had it so good, and where Reba's worthless brother-in-law had finally lucked out. Nathan had no use for him either: he had no real head for business. He was Sam Goldman's errand boy. All he thought about was going fishing over in Arizona or up to Elephant Butte Dam. That was his speed. It had been difficult to persuade Nathan to sacrifice a valuable Sunday to take this trip and spend his time with them. They had to leave early Sunday morning and drive a hundred miles, then come back that evening, tired and dissatisfied. Reba could almost see ahead to the ill humor of the return trip. But she needed to get away.

Rachel was eager to go. Though she knew it was unlikely, she wished her Uncle Joe would take her fishing. But perhaps she would see her cousin Mervin, who was fifteen and in high school. He had been voted Laziest Boy in School by his classmates the previous spring, a designation he somehow regarded as an honor. Reba thought it was nothing to be proud of, and said so. But it intrigued Rachel that anyone would dare to be lazy, it was so unlike anything she was allowed to do. She had to get good grades and was paid fifty cents for every A. She liked her cousin, a tall youth, with a long jaw and large eyes, whose arms and legs seemed to get in his way. She liked to tickle him, and sometimes while she'd been there they'd had tickling games, scrambling under the covers of her bed, grabbing at one another, trapping and tickling and squealing with laughter.

Her mother had made a cake to take for the Sunday dinner Gertie was preparing for them, and Rachel was its guardian in the back seat. The road curved up out of the town and continued in a series of hairpin turns, through two little towns piled along the road like so much scrap and refuse no one had bothered to pick up and cart away; past the turnoff to Santa Rita and the big mine. They had driven out to see it when they first got to town, the great pit in the earth, and Rachel had been astonished. Tracks along the sides, the various levels spiraling to the bottom, for the cars of ore bearing rock. It was so deep, so wide, Rachel imagined the whole town could fit into the great pit with its exposed veins of red- and ocher- and ash-colored earth: momentous.

Then the smelter at Hurley with its stack against the sky and the band of smoke that poured out from it, alongside the heap of white slag like a geological formation that kept growing year by year.

"They waited long enough to invite us," Reba said. "It's just like Gertie. She was never one to put herself out. She acts like she doesn't know we're alive."

"So what are we rushing down there for?" Nathan wanted to know. "I don't know why you wanted to come."

Rachel wished her mother hadn't said anything. She held her breath lest her father turn the car around and go back. It was like him to do that.

"It's nice to get away," Reba said with a sigh. She was going to visit her sister because weekends lay like stretches of desert at the end of the week. She should have known better, should have known what to expect of Gertie. She hoped for the best from people, but they let her down. Gertrude had always been stupid, and selfish. She'd cost their folks a fortune. Joe was the one she had to have, even though he didn't want to marry her. She had eyes for no one but him. And he had to be talked into it. Their father had bought him finally—that's all you could say— and he proved to be a loser. Three times her father had set him up in business, and three times he'd gone bust. He'd gone out West with his tail between his legs. And that was not the last of him. He'd forged their father's name to a check—for a thousand dollars. Gertie didn't know about it—they'd never told her. She didn't know how the rest of the family had struggled to pay it off. Reba held that against her too.

"Oh, look," Rachel said. She'd been keeping an eye out for it. The familiar landmark, the Kneeling Nun. It was a story. A girl had loved a soldier, loved and lost, and taken her grief into a convent. Finally, in her grieving she'd been changed into rock, immortalized. She knelt atop the mountain, with the wind and rain for company, maintaining her solitary vigil over the stretch of desert.

They all looked at the figure of local sentiment. Nathan gave a cursory glance and turned his eyes back to the road. He had already taken in the various geological features. This rock provided a landmark to remind him how far they still had to go. At least, Reba thought, it was only a rock. It could just stand there looking out over the desert. Mile after mile of it, to Deming, visited by dust storms, out in the middle of nowhere. And the nowhere continued to Las Cruces.

They had not parted on the best of terms, Reba and her sister. Those two months of living together had been a real strain. Naturally, Reba tried to do her share. But Gertie was no housekeeper; even when they were girls together she'd always been the sloppiest one. She managed always to do things the hard way and could never take the smallest suggestion. But that didn't give her the right to make accusations. Reba still couldn't get over that. She'd merely been trying to clean out the desk, straighten up a bunch of papers. There was a letter from Sonia, their older sister, nothing to speak of. She'd glanced at it—nothing anyone would want to keep—and tossed it out. Gertie was furious. She had accused her of spying. Imagine saying something like that when she was only trying to straighten, avoid clutter. It was none of her business, Gertie said.

She was not really taking the cake as a peace offering; she just wanted to do her share, not be beholden. And she'd have liked to tell Gertie a thing or two about bringing them out there in the first place. She would have been glad to put the blame where it belonged. But she couldn't say anything. Gertie would just yell at her and have a fit; it wasn't worth it. "And whatever you do," she turned to Rachel, "you're not to get in one of those games with Mervin."

"What games?"

"You know what I mean."

"What's wrong with it?"

"It's not nice."

Rachel didn't know why it should be *not nice.* Something hung in the air that she didn't know about and couldn't pin down.

"Boys and girls don't touch each other like that," her mother said.

Once she'd laughed so hard she'd almost wet her pants, and had escaped breathlessly, embarrassed. It seemed she'd always blunder into things, bat against them blindly because she didn't know any better, know what she was supposed to know. She turned back to her comic book.

When they got there, her uncle hadn't yet gotten back from his fishing.

"He went out at four this morning," Gertie said, as though she couldn't understand why anybody would be up at such an hour. "He doesn't get home till after seven on Saturday, but it doesn't faze him. He's still up before dawn."

"You'd think he'd want to sleep late," Reba said, before Nathan said anything that could be taken the wrong way. She could see he was annoyed.

"Not when it comes to fishing."

Mervin was still in bed. "He can sleep like the dead," Gertie said, as though both husband and son kept her at a loss. At the sound of their voices, he got up and finally emerged sleepy-eyed, hair unkempt.

"Did you wash?" his mother said. "Go wash this instant And make your bed. I don't want to have to clean up after you. Kids—I tell you. . . ."

Reba went off to the kitchen with Gertie, while Nathan sat in the living room with a cup of coffee and the Sunday paper. He didn't like Joe's company all that much—no intelligence to speak of—and Gertie he could barely tolerate. His newspaper he could have read at home. He was worried, somehow afraid he'd made a mistake. Perhaps it was too early to tell, but the intuition fretted him, troubled his digestion. He burrowed into the news, batted the paper into place.

Rachel wandered out on the back porch in search of one of the numerous cats that lived outside. One of them was about to have kittens just before she left. But her aunt told her the kittens were wild. While she hunted for them, her uncle drove up in his truck.

"Did you catch any fish?" she greeted him.

"Sure did," and he showed her two large catfish he'd caught, along with several crappies, all from the Rio Grande. He filled a tub full of water and put in the fish to keep fresh until he could clean them. She squatted down while he cut off their heads and slit them open and pulled out their intestines. The cats appeared and hunkered down at a safe waiting distance.

"I wish I could have gone," she said.

"It's too muddy out there," he said. "You'd get all dirty." She'd always wanted to go, all the time they'd been there, wanted to go with a fierce longing. Why, she didn't know. But he always said the same thing. Even when she protested that she didn't care if she got dirty.

"You're back," Gertie said, at the screen door. "We're eating in half an hour. You'll have to get Mervin out of the tub."

But he was already out and dressed in shirt and jeans, though he didn't have his shoes on. He seemed taller than when Rachel had last seen him, gawkier. She looked at him, not quite certain if he was the same person, and knew she wouldn't ever try to tickle him any more or let him tickle her. She asked him about high school, what subjects he was taking and whether he liked his teachers. "It's okay," he told her, with a shrug. "The usual stuff, history and math and English. It's all boring."

It seemed too bad he felt that way.

"Hey," he said, in a low voice. "I got something to show you."

She felt pleased he was taking her into his confidence. "What is it?"

"Ssh, not so loud. Come on back."

She followed him back to his bedroom, where two single beds occupied the room. A desk with a gooseneck lamp for the purposes of homework sat in one corner with a bookshelf along the side. Rachel had slept in that room while they were living there. He pulled out a copy of the Old Testament from the shelf, an odd thing for him to be interested in. But when he opened it, she saw that the insides of the pages had all been carefully cut away with a razor, leaving an inch margin around a hollow inside. He took out some pictures.

"Look," he said, with obvious pride, showing her one, then another.

She looked at them without comprehension. They didn't seem turned the right way. She turned them upside down. But that view left her none the wiser. Various parts of the body appeared to be occupying various unusual positions. "What is it?" she asked him.

"Don't you know?" he said. "Don't you know anything?"

A sudden noise made him glance up. Hastily he replaced the pictures and put the book back in the bookcase.

"It's time to wash your hands," Rachel's mother said, an edge of suspicion to her voice. "What have you been doing?"

"Nothing," Rachel said. "Mervin was showing me a book." For reasons she didn't understand her loyalty was to her cousin.

She had been caught, as usual, doing something wrong. But it was a worse moment than usual. She had made a discovery, not one she'd wanted to make: for the rest of her life she was doomed to tell lies, and to feel wretched because of it.

Not long after the visit, which had left them as unreconciled to their circumstances as they were before, there came a day on which things shifted on their axis, teetered for a moment, and fell into their allotted place. That day, when her father came home from the store, he looked more gloomy, more irritable than usual. And Rachel knew enough to keep out of his way. After the news was over, he picked at the stewed chicken on the plate in front of him, and after a few bites pushed the plate away.

"You don't like it—it isn't good?" It was a reproach for the hours Reba spent in the kitchen, where the single lightbulb gave off its dim light against the grease-stained ceiling. A reproach for having been uprooted and brought to this town far from everything she knew, where they were supposed to be making a killing. And where was this wonderful life she was to have stepped into?

"My stomach is off."

Go and please him. If she made anything different, he pushed the plate away. If she cooked what he liked, his stomach was off. She could see that something was wrong. Lately Sam had been unloading a lot of junk on him—things he couldn't sell in the Las Cruces store. And the loss would come out of Nathan's pocket. This was the gold mine they'd come to. And a strike was threatening at Kennecott, now that the war was over and the Communists had taken over the union. Everybody was talking about it. The miners would be out on the dole, and nobody would have any money. These were the things that made Nathan get up in the middle of the night and sit up for hours brooding at the kitchen table. It was the same when he left the shirt business—with what that rotten brother of his had pulled on him. Pretending to close the business and then selling on the black market. They found out after they left Delaware. Nathan was too honest for him. Too honest to make a killing. She held it against him. Who else had his scruples? Other people were just as well pleased not to let the right hand know what the left was doing. Like his brother. But Nathan. . . . And what did it get him? A bellyache.

After dinner her father sat and read the paper while Rachel did her homework. School had started. She didn't like her teacher very well, an old woman with a crooked jaw and a mouth that reminded her of a great fish, with a streak of blue in her gray hair. When Rachel told her she was from Delaware, she said, "What are you doing here?" As though Rachel had no right to come and sit in her classroom.

It was hard to find someone who would be her friend. All the girls had been in school together last year and already had best friends and names of boys to write on their notebooks. She didn't fit.

Nor at home, where she could only be useful if she did what she was told. Even her mother and father fit into their lives better. Every night they played gin rummy on the card table and listened to the radio in the living room while she lay on the floor under the lamp doing homework. They sat up and talked after her bedtime, as though they were waiting for her not to be around. That night it was the same.

Rachel didn't know how she heard it. It could have been her father's voice muttering in the space between wakefulness and sleep, for she slept on the back porch and they sat late at the kitchen table while her father took a late-night snack to make up for what he refused at dinner. But once the words were uttered, they moved through the air, and went repeating themselves through the three rooms. The message must have run along the walls, and the tall secretary desk caught it first and whispered it all around. It was taken in by the chairs, the over-stuffed chair where her father sat and which had taken his shape, and the sofa that stood against the far wall, with its hard proper cushions and curved back. It was there like the news, exchanged back and forth by the bisque shepherd and shep-herdess, who gazed at one another across the surface of the table, wooed but never won, but stood together with the milk-glass hands spread for the calling cards of now antique and forgotten callers, and the smirking majolica cat that took in all secrets and gave none away. *I'm sure Max is stealing.*

And then the news spread to the kitchen, where it found a cockroach running among the crumbs and a chorus of dying flies. The refrigerator, stove, and sink sat in their workaday indifference. But the news seemed to fill the three rooms, to become part of the space closed round by the fading wallpaper and the aging carpet in the living room, by the grease-stained kitchen, by the regions of the bedroom. Whenever she came inside, Rachel was startled by it, for once things had become infested with knowledge it was impossible to take it back. It reverberated back and forth. It hung over the bed where her mother and father lay.

That night Rachel lay in the dark, her eyes wide open.

"This whole business—I don't like it. The whole thing smells bad. We didn't take in three hundred today."

Across from him, Reba sat in a quandary. What did it mean, what did he want to do?

"I don't like the way Sam talks. Promises—a lot of wind. There's no business now. Who has any money? And things aren't handled right."

So why couldn't he have figured all that out beforehand? Reba could have asked. He was supposed to be so smart. The night pressed down on her.

"And Max. I don't know how long he's been taking, but I'm sure."

"How do you know?"

"Nothing I can show. Only an instinct. The other day I came up with a discrepancy in the figures. I checked back at the end of the day, and it came out all right. It struck me funny. But today when I was upstairs with a customer, I looked out over the balcony and saw Mrs. Morales come in to make a payment. Twenty-five dollars. But afterward when I looked in the box—no receipt. I took out her card. It was marked on her card, but no receipt. And the end of the day the register was twenty-five dollars short."

There was a long pause as they both sat in the dark.

"What do you think?"

The question struck her like a blow. What was she supposed to say? Most of the time he bullied her, treated her like a child, told her she was stupid if she so much as ventured an opinion. Now he was asking her what they should do. Nathan had broken a three-year contract with the insurance company where he was doing so well and where for the first time he had made some real money instead of killing himself in the shirt factory while his brother sat on his *tokhis* in New York. They had pulled up stakes, bragged to all their friends about the wonderful opportunity, been given a farewell party with everyone there, and now here they were in this wretched town. They had been there so little time, only a few months. And then what? Go back? With their tails between their legs. "Maybe it's your imagination," she said.

"I don't like it. I'd like to get out."

"But you've been here only a short time," she said. Could he know already? Maybe he hadn't given it a chance. "Maybe you should wait," she said, "at least until you're sure."

He sighed and got up to go to bed, and, with that, their fate was sealed.

The next week Sam Goldman came up to see how things were going. He was a man who carried prosperity with him in a round jowled face and a potbelly. His fat was soft, benign, and though his eye kept a certain shrewdness, there was amplitude in the smile under the gold-rimmed glasses. He had made it. His suits were well tailored, and the tie circumspect. He was proud of what had come as the fruits of his labors. A house designed by an architect in a new suburb and furnished with the best from his own store. Inhabited by a wife and children for whom he could provide. When his daughter married, a good dowry. For his sons, a place in the business. For his wife, all the conveniences. From the East he had fled, a failure. What hadn't he tried? A shoe store, a delicatessen, a window-cleaning service. Nothing panned out. And now he was living in the lap of luxury. He'd come to Las Cruces, opened the town's first furniture store, then a second. He'd given a place to a worthless brother-in-law. His bounty had extended to Max, no relation. And now to relatives of that worthless brother-in-law, may they always remember who'd done them a favor.

He came into the store with the stride of a man who knew what he was about and who had no time to waste. The eye gleaming, the scalp shining with the lubricity of the next promising deal. Rachel could see her father hated that, hated what he'd failed to become, even as he despised it. As Sam approached him with brash unconsciousness and prosperous fat, the fabric tight against his thigh, he would very likely be thinking of some way to insult him. Not directly, though he could do that too. But more likely through innuendo. The underhanded moral slap—he was good at it: spit in Sam's face and he thinks it's raining.

Sam greeted Max, looked over the sales figures for the last couple of months, checked the inventory, made a list of the items that were low and that he would ship up the next time he sent his truck, and then came home to eat lunch with Nathan.

With Rachel's help, Reba had drawn the table out into the center of the kitchen and covered it with a linen cloth from the days back East when she had entertained. Her older sister had sent a smoked turkey from New York, and of this she made sandwiches, with potato chips and pickles on the side. She made fresh coffee and was there to fill the cup.

Max was useless, Nathan told him. Twice a day he was out for coffee. And though Nathan had told him not to be gone more than twenty minutes, it was more like forty-five, sometimes an hour before he moseyed back. And his head was like a sieve. He couldn't be counted on for anything. But then Nathan brought out the clincher.

"Max is stealing from the business."

For a moment Sam's face took on a blank look and his mouth compressed. "How do you know this?"

Nathan told him about the payment, about the missing receipt. He'd counted the money in the till. Then it happened again.

Sam chewed thoughtfully and agreed to a second sandwich when Reba encouraged him to have another. Otherwise she kept quiet. He shook his head: it was unwelcome news. He didn't want to be faced with it—it got in the way of business as usual. He was not a man cut out for complex moral issues or ambivalent feelings. He did not want to acknowledge the perfidy of a man who owed him, whom he'd picked up from the street. Besides he knew something of the nature of temptation. He himself had dipped his hand here and there: the ordinary pursuits of any successful businessman if he wants a business. He had milked Uncle Sam for plenty. And perhaps because his own practices could not altogether sustain scrutiny, he had a certain reluctance to sit in judgment over one of his kind. It made him superstitious. It could be, God forbid, that he or one of his would be struck down by such self-righteousness. As it was, he was always careful to give his share to the synagogue in El Paso and to the charities in the community. He was a generous man. And though Max was useless, a real liability if Lerner was right, still what happened to a man sixty years old, who still didn't have a pot to pee in, when you threw him out on the street? That didn't sit well. But finally he had to take the word of a man who, though he had all the moral goods on his side, was hard for him to swallow. He was always there with his frown of moral superiority, insisting how honest he was, how hard he worked himself. The man had utter scorn for anyone who wasn't like himself. He'd listened to Nathan pick flaws. Hard and uncompromising. The sort of man you wanted in your place so he could work himself to death, but whom you'd just as soon avoid otherwise. He felt the need to intervene, to soften the corners.

"Maybe you made a mistake," Sam said. It was possible. And to condemn a man on the basis of it.

Nathan couldn't believe it. Sam prided himself on being a businessman. He had to question the judgment of anyone who'd hire Max in the first place and keep him on over the years. And how much had he gotten away with, walking out of the store with anything he liked, using the store like a club. And now to insult him by doubting his word. Did it take eyes to see? It was in the man's character to steal.

"Twice—it happened twice," Nathan said. "How many times does it take?"

"All right," Sam said. "But you don't have any proof. I can't fire a man and put him out in the street until you can show me the proof."

Nathan had to hold himself back. A man who was supposed to have some intelligence. Let him leave his brains with his wallet, if he loved the guy so much. Sam had already made his pot; he didn't have a worry in the world. He had it to lose. But Max wasn't robbing only Sam; he was robbing Nathan. Sam couldn't see that. Work your fingers to the bone and give it to a common thief! He wouldn't stand for it—he'd find the proof.

From that moment on her father was in the store every spare minute. He was more faithful than any lover. Everything that kept him from it filled him with a furious impatience. The day was something to get through, so that he could close the store and give himself to his one consuming idea. And when he was not going over the books and the old records, his brain seethed with figures and speculation. If her mother went downtown during the afternoon, he said to her, "I'll be late." And sometimes he did not have his dinner until seven or eight in the evening. The news was turned on as usual, and Rachel ate her meal in silence as the voice of H. V. Kaltenborn hammered through dinner and into the lessening light of the shorter days right down into the darkness.

Rachel knew her mother wasn't listening. Her eyes bore a glazed, distant look, and her mouth turned down into her grievance: this is what my life has become. She perked up for the human interest story at the end. Then her gaze shifted into focus and she said things like, "Can you imagine," when someone proved some feat of daring or came into a million dollars or miraculously escaped death. Those other people who had all the luck. On Saturday after dinner when her father went back to the store and stayed until midnight, or on Sunday afternoons when they might have gone for a drive, she would sit silently weeping, often over dinner preparations when the onions she diced invited tears or when she peeled potatoes.

Though she couldn't have put it into words then, Rachel knew why her father drove himself so mercilessly. That a man like Becker, lazy, incompetent, dishonest, should enjoy himself at his expense, be carried along in the world on his shoulders, was anathema to him. He was caught in the cleft of what he hated. Often Rachel woke up to hear him in the middle of the night. The glass pane of the back door would suddenly be illuminated by the kitchen light. She heard him first in the bathroom, then in the kitchen. The refrigerator door would open and close. She knew he was sitting at the kitchen table, eating a piece of cheese or cold meat left over from supper and reading the *Reader's Digest*. She knew better than to disturb him. Once she had blundered into the kitchen and he had started up from his solitary brooding as though he'd been caught out. "What are you doing up?" he demanded.

She could not sleep those nights he was in the kitchen. His presence hung over her as she lay in bed drifting in and out of sleep, aware that hours had gone by and the kitchen light was still burning. In the morning he frequently said, "I didn't sleep well last night." She was careful to keep out of his way. At school she worked at fractions and wrote reports on the koala bear or learned what it meant to be good citizen. Miss Williamson had her pets, and there was no way she could be one. They got to be the monitors and to work on the class newspaper. She came home from school, set the table, did the dishes afterward and then her homework. Sometimes she could go over to someone's house.

Rachel had a friend named Thora, who lived in a large house that had a garden alongside it. She loved going over to Thora's because the house had a huge living room with Oriental rugs on the floor and a baby grand piano on one side. Thora's mother could play, and Thora was taking piano lessons. Bookcases with green leather-bound sets of Dickens and Thackeray and Sir Walter Scott lined one wall, and flowering plants grew in the windows. The light was gracious inside, and filled up the kitchen as well. Thora had a room of her own with built-in shelves to display her collection of animals, made of china and colored glass and crystal, a number of which her father brought back from his travels in Germany and Switzerland. She had a bed with a duster and a vanity table with lotion and bubble bath and special soap on it. Things weren't all crowded together as in her space on the back porch. But she could go over to Thora's only when she was invited, and Thora never came over to her house. By tacit consent they knew this was how things would go.

Rachel never liked to invite anyone over; it made her nervous. The three rooms they occupied held the secret that bound them together, and it hung in the air like a bad smell. You knew it the moment you stepped inside.

She had another friend, Fanny, whose father had a horse and wagon and went around collecting bottles and odds and ends that people threw away. Rachel admired the horse and wished she could have one. Fanny sometimes climbed up on the horse's back and rode it around with only a bridle and no saddle, but she did not let Rachel do it because the horse didn't know her and might object. Fanny never came home with her either.

The rest of the time Rachel had to find things to do by herself. She lay on the old rug on the back porch and read stories of Aladdin and Ali Baba and the Fisherman and the Genie over and over again. She played elaborate games of monopoly with herself, inventing the other players, or she played war, the right hand opposing the left. Sometimes she went up the hill behind the courthouse, where the side of the mountain had been cut out, or wandered down the alley and around the neighborhood.

Her mother was making a quilt. When Rachel came home from school, she found her over the quilt frame sewing. She had a whole box of pieces she'd been sewing together for years in the flower-garden design; she had turned to it in her boredom, and over the months she had taken the flowers and sewed them all together in a white background, then put on the backing. Someone had showed her how to make a quilting frame, and now she sat for hours over the stitching. Or she knit sweaters or crocheted. It was something to do.

The days and weeks ran together; a year passed and then another. It was always the same. Behind them sat the store that took in all their effort, shaped their hopes and frustrations, defined their various kinds of waiting; so that while they sat in the chairs along the aisles, they watched the door, waiting for someone passing in the street to enter and furnish a household and change their fortunes for the day. They waited for the day to end and for Nathan to come home for supper and tell them what sort of day it had been. Most of all, they waited for Max to reveal his hand and be kicked out of the store once and for all.

The rest was mere chaff, to fill up the time. Reba was left to her domestic tasks, and Rachel to the business of growing up, while Nathan went to do battle with what loomed so large at their backs and continued out of inertia, what kept each day filled with the suspicion that Becker's hand was in the till. Rachel sensed that her presence at the dinner table prevented her father and mother from speaking of it. In the suspense of the unspoken they went through the motions of the evening meal while Mrs. Pennington belted out one of her hymns. When they got up from the table and left her to the dishes or to her homework they gave themselves the diversion of gin rummy until they could go to bed and rake over bits of incident and speculation.

Meanwhile something pushed and pulled at her, something that wouldn't fit inside the waiting. Whatever it was galled her into outbursts of ill humor and ready tears. She found ways of avoiding coming home directly after school every day. She joined the Girl Scouts so that she could go to their meetings; she went downtown and stood over the magazine rack in the confectionery and tried to interest herself in movie stars and fashions. She visited Henny under some pretext or other or went to the library and browsed endlessly among the shelves. She wanted to grow up; she wanted to go away and live some other kind of life. Only she had to wait even for that to happen.

II.

The problem was her hair. That's what it said in the slam books that got started and passed around at school during her freshman year. Under each name where reactions like ugly! or nice! were written, they wrote for her (The Brain) that she would be okay if it weren't for her hair. Someone had written, "If she'd only comb her hair—It looks like a rat's nest." And there were words like *awful* and *sloppy.* If indeed it was her hair that stood between herself and social success, something had to be done. She had discovered the secret of popularity, even as in the ads, where an unfortunate though good-looking boy was shunned by his fellows because of some unwitting social offense, but finally introduced to mouthwash or the right soap, thereby becoming the triumphant life of the party.

But even then, a little niggling thought: did people really like or not like you because of your hair? And on some level she wasn't entirely convinced that a change of hairstyle would bring to her a flock of girlfriends eager to invite her to slumber parties and boys to follow her around. Perhaps if her antennae had been more highly developed, she might have guessed that *cute* and *nice* went as deep with implication as a brassiere cup.

It was true that her hair was long and fine and a single gust of wind took it in all four directions. No matter how often Rachel brushed it back, it behaved as though a charge of electricity had been sent through it. When she looked in the mirror, she saw that she wasn't pretty. But if something could be done about her hair, she might have a chance in life, lessen the effects of wearing glasses and braces and being round-shouldered and known as a Brain.

Every fall her mother gave her a home permanent, but it never made the slightest difference: her hair was exactly the same afterward, though her mother claimed it had something called body. Rachel did not believe in home permanents: she was sure they were a make-do, something to get by with, like the clothes her mother sewed for her, taking her inspiration from the Macy's ads in the *New York Times* rather than spending good money at the local Penney's. For her hair she wanted the real thing. Across the street from their duplex was Susie's beauty shop. Susie herself used to come over and visit sometimes in the afternoon when she didn't have a customer, flouncing across the street, as Reba described it, and plumping herself right down in a chair. Susie had bought a mattress and box springs in the store, and though

Reba could barely tolerate these visits, she felt she had to be nice to her: conceivably she might buy something else. At times she spoke of redecorating. While they awaited that happy event, Susie came over to speak of her exploits.

"I was down at the Murray," Susie said on one occasion, for she liked to go out drinking and to pick up men, "and this rancher came in. Bought me two drinks and stood there with his arm around me, nuzzling me and rubbing his hand up and down my side, reaching for my tits."

"How rude," Reba said, face stiff.

"Rude?" Susie said, with her deep, throaty laugh. "Honey, when you're my age, you're just happy for a little attention. A guy comes along and he's looking for a sweet time, you don't knock it." Then she gave Reba a serious look. "You look like you could use a little fun yourself."

Reba had never been so insulted.

Susie was a big woman with grizzled hair and a horse face. She had wide-set eyes and prominent cheekbones. Her teeth were all crowded together, so that one front tooth overlapped the other, and she had a snaggletooth off to the side. Rachel was fascinated that she'd had five husbands.

"She's been around," her father said, without admiration, "and when she curls up, it's not with a good book. I hope she doesn't wear out that mattress she got."

Why not, Rachel wondered; then she could come in and buy another. But she knew better than to say so. Her mother would have called Susie a whore. Her father, who'd read some Shakespeare in his youth, was partial to *strumpet*.

It was perhaps a measure of the degree to which Rachel had made a nuisance of herself that Reba agreed to put her into such hands even for a permanent. Rachel had watched women come and go from Susie's Beauty Salon, usually older women, who left with blue-tinted hair, her regulars. But she had no thought except for herself. To cross the street would be to enter the doorway of her own expectations: her hair would be cut and curled and she would be transformed.

Her mother came with her to give a few instructions but under no condition was she to remain.

"Well, you come right in," Susie said, "and we'll do it up right. Get you a nice hairstyle."

To her surprise, Rachel saw when she entered the doorway only a single padded chair, a basin, a table, and a lone hair dryer in the corner. Under it sat an older woman reading a copy of *Glamour.* A mirror hung over all.

"My hair is awfully fine," Rachel said, with a sudden access of doubt. "I hope you can do something with it."

"Of course we can," Susie said. "Nothing to it." She leaned Rachel back over the sink to wet her hair, sat her up again, and started to comb her hair into sections, then to trim. "You got a boyfriend yet?"

"No."

"Well, you will have. Your folks let you go out on dates?"

"Not till I'm older." No one had yet asked her for a date to the show or to any of the school dances.

"Time enough. My ma wouldn't let me near a boy till I was eighteen. Thought she was protecting me." She gave a strand of Rachel's hair a little sharp tug that almost made Rachel cry out. "I couldn't have brought anybody home anyway. I tried it once, and it was a disaster."

"How come?"

"Well, because of the clutter. My mother would never throw out a blessed thing. Had to keep every scrap. Newspapers and bottles and magazines and calendars and shoe boxes and old wrapping and ribbons and all kind of stuff. She kept it, never knew but what somebody might want it. Maybe to line their coffin. Filled the whole damn house. My dad was gone by then—wasn't any room for him—he'd long ago given up making a fuss. Every once in a while she'd get a wild hair up her ass and think she was going to straighten it all up. But she'd just stir up the dust a little, pick up one pile and set it down on top of another. You had to pick your way through the mess if you wanted anything to eat, try to pull a piece of clothing out of the pile of laundry and wash it out yourself."

Swatches of her hair lay in a circle around the chair. Susie had combed it out and was now applying the solution for the permanent, setting in the clips. "Large and loose," she was saying, "Just enough for a curl."

The one time she brought a boy home to meet her mother, she continued, she was nervous. She liked him a lot and she didn't know any way around it. He'd sat in all the clutter not saying a word. It had him buffaloed all right, but she prayed he wouldn't hold it against her. She brought out some fudge she'd made. Her mother had gotten fat eating chocolate fudge. Then he asked to use their bathroom. Terror seized her. She hadn't thought about that. It was impossible to get to the bathroom unless you cleared a path, and it was so full of stockings hanging and clothes piled up and bottles empty and half empty you could hardly use the john. And the sink was crusted with twenty years of iron rust and toothpaste. No, she told him, he couldn't use the bathroom. He never again asked her for a date.

The next fellow she dated she ran off with and got married. "Divorced him when I was twenty-one," she added.

"Why did you do that?" Rachel was intrigued. She'd never known anyone who'd gone off marrying just like that, then divorcing. As if it were nothing special.

"Well, you see, honey, I didn't know from nothing. And to me sex was the big riddle you had to wait till marriage to get an answer for. Not that you do even then." She gave another laugh. "I ran off with this older guy, see, because he knew something I didn't know. A shoe salesman, how about that? And he had to teach me everything. I was just a poor dumb kid."

Again Rachel got a little yank that almost made her cry out. She knew her mother would be scandalized at what was coming into her ears, but she had to hear it, even if she got her hair pulled for it. By now half her head was covered in clips and she looked like a creature growing a strange set of appendages. But Monday morning when she went to school and went to home-room, she'd try to come in a minute or two late, so everybody'd be there to see her.

"So we were going along, me doing my best, not knowing exactly how—all new to me. I mean, hell, pardon the language, honey, when I was growing up, it was like nobody has a body. They're there, but you're not supposed to notice. Anyhow, one night he says, 'Why are you so stiff? Relax and loosen up a little. Move with me—like Melba does it.' Well, that caught the breath right out of me. Melba was a bar girl down at the tavern. 'You mean you're doing it with Melba,' I said. And burst into tears. He was supposed to love me, right? And there he was putting his poker into another set of flames. You get me? And didn't think any more about it than that magazine rack over there."

There was a pause for Rachel to take it all in.

"But I wasn't going to stand for him two-timing me. No, sir. I may have been stupid, but nothing written said I had to stay that way. So I packed up my stuff and cleared out. He couldn't get it through his head why I was sore. I didn't know what I was going to do. Wasn't going back home, that was for sure. So I got me a job and put myself through beauty school."

There were four other husbands after that: "I rummaged through the lot trying to get me a good one. A good man is so hard to find," she intoned, "you always get that other kind." There'd been one she'd really loved, the third one, Bob. But he'd died after a brief illness. After that her heart was never the same. It was his name she'd gone back to after she'd tried on all the others: Lightfoot. Suzannah Lightfoot. "That's how I keep him alive. I really loved that guy."

The clips were bristling all over her head. She was going to get her braces off in a few months and her teeth would be all straight and even, and then. . . .

"But I've had my good times, believe me. And they've not run out yet, thank goodness. Listen, kid, I've been with white men and black men and Mexican men, and under the skin there's no difference at all." She gave Rachel a little poke.

Rachel didn't know what to say. The girls she knew wouldn't dance with Mexican boys. It was all a puzzle to her: Anglos and Mexicans.

It didn't occur to her until much later to wonder whether Susie was just talking or trying to tell her something. She knew she'd never breathe a word of it at home. She'd have liked to ask about the other husbands, but her head was full of clips and rollers, and she was ready for the dryer. By the time she was cooked, as Susie said, and her hair was being combed out, two other women were waiting in the shop, and the conversation had shifted to medical problems and operations. Susie put her hair in pin curls and told her to take them out later that afternoon.

Rachel hardly knew what to do with herself until the bobby pins came out. She ate lunch and tried to read a book. Then it was two o'clock and she went into the bedroom and shut the door. Her hair had an odd new spring to it. When she pulled out a curl it snapped back up to her head. She tried to brush it out, but the bristles snagged in her hair. It was all frizz. She burst into tears. All ugly frizz. She brushed harder and harder. It would never come out. She looked like a bushman.

"Well, you see," Reba said. "You wouldn't be satisfied till you had a permanent. That's what it means to have fine hair."

"It looks terrible," Rachel cried. "I'll never be able to go outside."

"Don't be silly."

She yanked at her hair with a brush. All through the afternoon she kept at it. She felt as though she'd been scalped.

Her father didn't come home until late that night. He woke her up as he sat in the kitchen eating whatever had been left on the stove for him or what he'd foraged from the refrigerator. She lay in bed for a long time until she felt driven to go once more to the bathroom mirror to see if her hair still looked as horrible as she thought it did. She would take the risk. She opened the door to the kitchen.

He was sitting at the table, his chair turned sideways, eating a piece of bread while he read the *El Paso Times*. When the door opened, he turned in her direction. She'd barged in on him. There was no peace and quiet anywhere. The late hours belonged to him. "What are you doing up?"

"I had to go to the bathroom."

She stood there unable to move forward or go back.

"Why don't you have your bathrobe on?"

"I forgot."

"You forgot. How many times have I told you?"

She was suddenly aware of herself standing there in her nightgown, aware of her own physical presence. She hadn't thought about her father. It was different now that she wasn't a little girl anymore. She had a body that kept doing strange things without warning her beforehand. It made a difference, though she didn't understand why or what to do about it.

"Well go on. Make it snappy."

She did have to pee. Then she stood on top of the toilet seat to get close to herself in the mirror. Nothing had changed.

Her father didn't look up from his newspaper as she went back through the kitchen and out to the porch. His face was heavy with fatigue, pale with a blue shadow on it. She was careful not to bang the door.

That same year Shirley Melton, who lived on the other side of the duplex, asked her if she would baby-sit. Shirley was a large, soft, fair-skinned woman in her thirties, with hair so pale it seemed a continuation of her skin. She wore it in a big pouf that fluffed down over her forehead and fell into her eyes. Her face was round and soft with a double chin on the way, and her expression was vague and sleepy. Sometimes on Saturdays when she wasn't working she went to pass the time of day with her friend who worked at the frozen food locker on the corner. She walked out in high-heeled wedgies, wearing a low-cut filmy blouse that revealed her white shoulders, and shorts that came up high on her thighs. "I call her the Crisco kid," Nathan had commented once, "because she has fat in the can." *Slovenly* was Reba's word for her. Just a big cow.

She was the mother of the nuisance boy who ran up and down bouncing his ball, sometimes at the crack of dawn. It didn't seem to bother her. Worse, perhaps, she kept a large flop-eared mongrel named Trigger that gave his deep-throated bark to the neighborhood sometimes for hours.

She had no husband anyone knew about. But she had boyfriends. Rachel had seen her all dolled up, sleek black pumps on her feet and a gold chain on her wrist, ready to set off with the man who had come for her. Then she gave a little light, teasing laugh as she clicked the gate behind her and left a wake of scent, the mingling of her cologne and powder, as she moved into the evening.

Now when Shirley had a date, Rachel collected twenty-five cents an hour to see that Gary got to bed at eight o'clock. He was seven years old, a copy of his mother, her vague expression sharpening into something thin and steely. Rachel usually read him a story from a comic book. He liked Superman, and Batman and Robin,

and every time hero and villain clashed, he brought his fist down
on the sofa cushion with a cry of, "Wham! Bam! Give it to him."

The rest was mostly unintelligible, he was so tongue-tied, and
when he couldn't say what he wanted, his face grew red and
tight and his fists doubled up. Rachel was afraid he might break
something and she'd get blamed for it. It was a relief when she
had convinced him to go to bed and she was left to herself.

At first, she walked up and down through their rooms—four,
actually, because the back porch had been walled in for a bedroom—eager to see how their half differed from hers. It held
nothing of interest, only a davenport and a radio and a recliner
chair in the living room, some *Cosmopolitans* and the local newspapers on the coffee table. But Gary had one good book, about a
boy who ran off and joined the circus. Rachel read it in three
installments, and wished she were a boy and could travel with a
circus. She looked forward to those evenings of adventure.

But her unexpected source of revenue dwindled not long afterward when Shirley's parents came to live with her. Rachel was
called to baby-sit only on those rare occasions the three of them
went out together. Shirley herself seemed to contract in a signifi-
cant way. She didn't go out as much. Her hair seemed to lie in tamer
fashion along her forehead, the little bounce had gone out of her
walk, and her expression was both resigned and somehow furtive.
Gary didn't bounce his ball as often or as early, and though he still
continued to bark, Trigger was occasionally bullied into silence.

All of this was owing to Mrs. Kober, Shirley's mother, who had
taken charge of the household. She was a thin, sour-faced old
woman who looked with a savage eye on the recalcitrance of
matter and spirit continually presented to her. She swept the dirt
off the steps with the vigor of pure rage and hung out clothes and
stood over the ironing as though performing acts of vengeance.
She allowed no one out of her sight for long, and her voice rose
in the air like a hook to pull back husband or grandson or dog, all
of whom had taken to wandering as far out of its range as they
dared. For Gary and the dog, it was out of the yard and down the
alley. But Mr. Kober made it all the way downtown, where Rachel
sometimes saw him standing in front of City Hall with the other
old men, jawing and spitting on the sidewalk.

At lunchtime Mr. Kober, of the same bland face as his daughter, the somewhat more masculine focus sharpening the nose but losing out on the mouth and chin, leaving him with an expression both apologetic and foolish, would leave his cronies in front of City Hall and make his slow way home. He always wore the same brown suit and vest, a watch fob hanging in a loop at the pocket, a brown fedora on his head, and had the same rumpled look as though he'd slept in his clothes. He walked with a cane.

One night when she woke up, Rachel heard moaning coming from the other side of the wall.

"What's the matter? What's the matter now?"

She recognized Mrs. Kober's voice. The moaning had to be coming from Mr. Kober. Rachel could hear every word, every sound.

"I'm in such pain, such agony."

"Well, don't tell me about it. It's all your own fault."

Mr. Kober moaned again, and his wife told him to be quiet and go to sleep. After that he moaned more softly. Even after the night grew still again, Rachel lay awake in the dark for a long time, listening again for the voice. She found it hard to sleep.

Every night she heard him. Sometimes when Mr. Kober started to moan, she turned on her radio and let music from the late-night station play softly. Once her father caught her with her radio on and made her turn it off and go to sleep. She had to wait until he was asleep too. But even with the music playing, she could hear the moaning.

What could be the matter with him? Hearing him every night worried at her. It would go on, it seemed—it would not go away. She decided to ask her mother about it, though she wasn't hopeful of an answer. Even if she knew, her mother wouldn't tell her things. Lately when she came into the room, her mother paused in the midst of a flurried exchange with her father she wasn't supposed to hear. She connected it with her Aunt Sonia's weekly letters from New York that her mother pounced on and wouldn't allow herself to be disturbed in the middle of reading. Finally Rachel couldn't stand it any longer and sneaked off one of her aunt's letters.

We begged him to end it before he got in any deeper. Who would want to marry a woman like that? But now she's threatening suicide if he leaves her. I don't understand Walt, a

handsome man like him taking up with that kind of trash.
He's talking about marrying her, she's getting a divorce. It's a
scandal for the family.

So her Uncle Walter was having an affair with a married
woman. The family had told him they'd never speak to him
again if he kept on with her. After she read it, Rachel was astonished: the woman wanted him as badly as that. She'd have liked
to ask why, but she didn't dare. Perhaps she wasn't supposed to
know about Mr. Kober either. But she had to ask.

Her mother got a look Rachel recognized, as though she had
something in her mouth that tasted bad, and for a moment
Rachel thought she was going to tell her it was none of her business. Surprisingly, she said that Mr. Kober had a venereal disease
from the time he was a soldier in World War I.

"He was off doing what he shouldn't have been, and he didn't
tell anyone," Reba told her. "He thought he was being so smart.
Now he's paying for it."

Rachel knew what she was talking about. She had seen two
films down at the Gila Theater that had been advertised as important and educational. The first was about a girl who got herself
pregnant because she allowed a boy to go too far, and it was a
terrible shame to the family, but fortunately the baby died and she
didn't have to be an unwed mother. The second was about venereal disease and showed various organs of the body ravaged by it,
in stages both early and late. For a whole summer after that Rachel
lived in terror. She had used the toilet over at the Meltons' and was
mortally afraid she might have gotten the germ. She didn't dare tell
anyone. Neither could she stop thinking about it.

After that, whenever she saw Mr. Kober walking home with
his cane, she thought of what she had seen. It held a certain
shape in her mind and made her look at him as though he
weren't quite human. Her father had made up a sort of nonsense rhyme that had invaded her ear without elevating her
understanding:

Mendel, Mendel
Cock and fendel,
How does your garden grow?

She shrank from Mendel Kober's gaze, as though she shared in some unknown guilt from knowing his predicament, hearing him moan at night: some fear of contagion that lay deeper than germs. She didn't want even to speak to him if she could avoid it. She wished that she didn't know about him. She would never be able to forget it. Whether by accident or effort she kept finding things out that became secrets unbearable to keep. With Henny she was convinced it was different. She kept alive the people she knew things about; they lived and breathed again. But Rachel had no idea what to do with her knowledge.

Henny was still waiting for her son to come and tell her the story of what happened to him. It was her great dream. Once she had gone to a séance to see if the medium could bring him back, only nothing came from her contact but a series of squawks and shrieks. She would have to be patient. "Somewhere we will meet," she said. "Somehow I can't believe that anything that happens is ever really forgotten."

And even as she said it, Rachel had a sense of things lingering like an unseen color in the air. Meanwhile, from the store of all she knew, Henny told Rachel about other members of her family, so that they came to be even more real to her than her own. They came alive through the telling: presences in the room.

Rachel especially liked to hear about Henny's father, who was a man touched by curiosity. Wherever curiosity touched him, and that was in a variety of places, it left a hollow that had to be filled. He had to know everything about people: he was always eavesdropping on conversations, looking in people's windows when their curtains were open. Because he was a scribe in the village, who wrote letters and bills of sale, he knew about debts and quarrels and relatives in America. He had a passion for travel and went from one town to another on various errands and commissions.

And he always wrote down what he saw, what the houses looked like, how the people dressed and behaved. He learned languages and became a merchant and traveled to Austria and Germany and Hungary. He described different kinds of flowers and plants he found in the woods and meadows and was a great lover of mushrooms. He was always trying them out. If the little square he ate in the morning hadn't made him sick by noon, he had a plateful for dinner. He drew pictures of them, described their color and size and how they tasted. He recorded the weather every day and the direction of the wind. He filled whole journals full of things he had seen and places he had been. But he did not have a chance to write down the last things he saw. One night he'd come to Henny to tell her how they'd all been rounded up, he and her mother and her aunts and uncles, and shipped on cattle cars to a camp surrounded by barbed wire, filled with the stink of death.

"How could it happen?" Rachel wanted to know. "How could Hitler kill so many?"

"He didn't do it alone," Henny said. "It takes others to play out the great dream of force." She mused over it: "A blond-haired, blue-eyed race of giants that would rule for a thousand years. Though he was a small, dark-haired man himself."

Across the room the clown in his motley seemed to invite laughter, it was such an absurdity. What sort of dream if it left cities in ruins and millions dead? "Couldn't they see that?"

"Not if you don't want to see. Something holds you spellbound. Like a fire in the brain. And the frenzy touches everyone. Everyone babbling, running amok. Few could resist. They chose their deaths. And the rest were silent, afraid."

It had taken nearly all the years of her childhood to put it down. Her father had wanted to go. He'd been in the navy during World War I and wanted to go back to submarine school. But he was too old and they wouldn't take him. Being an air raid warden had allowed him to wear a red band on his arm and go off to spot planes, but it hadn't been enough to satisfy him.

"Sometimes there is no choice but to go and fight," Henny said. "My son had to go. I knew he would die. But think what would've happened if Hitler had won."

The clown with its downturned mouth surveyed the battleground where her son had fallen and others had perished. It surveyed a scene of bombers and tanks and cities under siege. It surveyed a scene too vast to take in. It could only dissolve into helpless laughter.

"But we won," Rachel said, trying to pick something out of the gloom. She could remember how they listened every night to the news as the troops moved closer and closer to Berlin, and from the other side the Russians coming to join the Allies.

"Yes," Henny said. "Only we have to be careful not to rejoice too much." They were silent for a moment.

"Because of all those who died," she said. The room grew dim around her. "And what will never die."

"Do you think it'll happen again?" Rachel said, with sudden fear.

"It can happen," Henny said.

"But we won," Rachel said. It would be terrible if Henny's son died only for it to happen again.

"It rises up and everywhere people fight against it. But it's only a shadow, and when the struggle is over, something remains— down below, down deep. And bombs and guns will never blast it out. They only send it deeper. And you can't tell when it will rise up again."

Rachel contemplated an amorphous, distant horror that would take no shape. It was too much to take in.

"That's scary."

"It belongs to everyone, even those who fought against it."

A great hollow was growing beneath an unanswered question that seemed to go as deep as the earth.

"Once someone tried to win over it, and he came very close, but he failed too."

"Someone in your family?"

"No, it was very long ago."

"At the beginning of the world?" They were always doing such amazing things back then. All the heroes. She'd have liked to be a hero, but the chance seemed remote.

"No, not so long ago as that, but in a time when some men could still speak to animals and birds."

The shadows of recent history receded, as a light evoked from something else remembered touched them. It was a silvery light, not the first light of things illumined in their basic text, when the syllables of existence spoke out of the great light that had been too much for gross matter. But that of the scattered sparks before they dimmed. It was a light in which things kept a certain sharpness of outline, before it became old light muddied by experience.

"Tell me," Rachel said, inviting Henny to speak out of that light.

"A very long time ago," Henny said, "lived a boy even younger than you are now, but who had eyes for the misery of the world. When he looked around he saw so much suffering, he was filled with sorrow and could think of nothing else. He couldn't run off and join the games of his friends, and he found it hard to sleep."

The boy went to ask his teacher why the world was full of suffering and was told it was because of the Evil One, who had never ceased the struggle to own the world. The boy wanted to know what could be done about it. Nothing, he was told. Nothing, nothing could be done.

But he persisted and finally, reluctantly, the old man told him that it was a task only for the most pure of heart, that he must fast and pray and pray and fast until one day he would know the right moment.

It struck Rachel as a miracle almost that anyone would know the right moment for anything.

The boy, Henny continued, did as he was told. He prayed and fasted for many years, until he was a grown man. For that is how long it took. Then he went back to his teacher, now only barely alive, who told him there was a secret place in the forest where the Evil One kept his heart. "Once you find it," the old man said, "you must squeeze it until it bursts."

So the young man found his way through the forest to where the Evil One kept his heart. And he seized it and began to squeeze. It was a very tough heart and required all his strength. Even so, it resisted. Suddenly there was a great howl that resounded through the forest, and the Evil One himself appeared.

He was very frightening to look at, as you can imagine, and it was only because of his great purity that the young man could keep his ground. But he did not flinch. The thought of all the suffering of his fellow creatures drove him on.

But the Evil One began to plead, first in one ear, then in the other; then he filled up both ears, so that there was nothing in the man's head but the pleading. But the young man heard all the voices of wailing and loss, which joined together and overcame that one voice. He continued to squeeze. The Evil One began to gasp and weaken, his voice coming in little wisps and sputters. But he spoke so piteously—

Rachel heard the front door shut and then the sound of footsteps going upstairs. Henny paused in her story and waited until, a moment later, Max stood in the doorway. He looked ruffled. "I see you have a visitor," he said, as though Rachel had no business there.

"You're home early," Henny said.

"I have a headache," he said. "Where are the aspirin?"

Henny looked at him in silence.

"Goddammit," Max said. "You think you could remember one little thing when I ask for it. Don't you keep anything in that head of yours except nonsense?"

"In the medicine cabinet."

"They aren't in the medicine cabinet. If they were in the medicine cabinet, I wouldn't be asking. Now think."

She remained silent, and a tension grew between them that Rachel thought might pull Henny away. But Max pulled away first and slammed the front door behind him. Henny sat blankly for a moment, as though trying to pick up the threads.

It was all over, Rachel knew. The clown must know it as well. But whether it was ready to laugh or weep, she could not decide. And it didn't matter, for she was sure the story was gone out of Henny's head.

But Henny drew a breath and continued. "For just an instant," she said, "the young man felt pity and let up on the pressure, and in that instant the Evil One leapt up and seized the heart and disappeared in a trail of laughter that rang through the woods."

At the time, Rachel thought she understood why the Evil One laughed, but when she thought back on it, she wasn't sure. And where did Henny think the devil had gone?

"He dived into history," Henny said, "and you can read about him in all the newspapers."

And hear about him, Rachel thought. When she was little, she was certain that when the war ended there would be no more news. She had never told anyone of her mistake. Now, she realized, the devil whispered every evening to H. V. Kaltenborn— and not even half of what he knew.

Nathan couldn't recall when it began, but sometime that summer he began having trouble with his eyes. The long hours he spent over the books in the dim light of the office had left their mark. His vision blurred, the figures swam on the page. He decided to let up a little, take things easy for a bit. Then the features of people's faces began to blur and move out of focus. Sam persuaded him to take a few days off to go to a furniture market in Los Angeles. Reluctantly—the store would be in Max's hands—he agreed to go. But driving back, he very nearly sideswiped a truck he was passing. It scared him. He went to a local doctor, who sent him to a specialist in El Paso. Though he was only fifty-one, he was developing cataracts.

They could have been caused by malnutrition in his early youth. Hard to say. They would have to be removed; only he had to wait for them to ripen. For the next few months the world around him gave the impression it was being rubbed out.

One of the delivery boys had to come to pick him up in the morning and brought him home after the store closed. Reba didn't know how to drive: he'd never let her learn. He could see just enough to wait on customers, though he had to be careful climbing stairs. And with the aid of a magnifying glass, he could write up the sales contracts and receipts. Reba came down to the store in the afternoons and sometimes waited on customers herself but mainly helped him with the paperwork. On Saturdays, Rachel came down to the store to read to him the figures on the receipts and help total up on the adding machine and make up the deposit for the bank. But Max kept the books. Though Nathan was on him all the time to give him the totals, he knew he was helpless. Max was free to steal as much as he could get away with. Steal from a blind man.

"If only we had known," Reba said, as though a messenger with the warning had stopped to tipple on the way and forgotten his mission. "This is what we have to thank my dear stupid sister for."

He felt everything slipping away from him. He would have been glad to strike out at someone, but now he could only blunder in the dark. The past two years were gone and he had eaten only the bread of frustration. During those hours he wasn't in the store, when Reba wasn't reading to him, he was free to think of how the time had gone. How he had come home, brain reeling, numbers swimming before his eyes, to meet Reba's look of reproach. Sometimes he knew she'd been crying. All he could do was launch into a tirade: Max was nothing but a common thief. God knew how much stuff he'd taken without paying for it. Sam was in for an eye-opener. Wait till he saw how much the bastard had robbed him.

It was strange how the time had fled, week swallowed by week, month by month. He scarcely knew what went on with Rachel or Reba, what they thought about, how they spent their days. When he came home from the store, he took off his coat, gave Reba a kiss, asked Rachel how school was, heard it was okay, ate supper, read the paper, and went to bed. Otherwise, he was in the store. Sometimes Reba dragged him off to a game of cards with Fred and Josephine or the two played gin rummy at home. He went through the motions, that was all.

He had gone below the surface of life, it seemed, beyond the touch of the ordinary, its pleasures or pains or any suggestions of its significance, to a depth of his own, where Max alone existed. Everything else was an interruption, a distraction. Yet what consumed him was an agony to him. The longer Max was around, the more he would steal. The thought that Max might be robbing him any time he turned his back enraged him. Now it was as though he'd been struck down only to give Max the further opportunity.

Once when he came home after a long Sunday at the adding machine, he'd caught Reba brushing tears from her eyes.

"What's the matter?" Women and children crying always got on his nerves, made him want to yell at them.

"Nothing."

He shrugged. Though she busied herself over the stove, she was a silent reproach to him. He went into the bathroom to wash his hands. When he came back into the kitchen, Reba was blowing her nose.

"For God's sake, what are you crying about?"

"Just things."

"You think I like them any better?"

"It's always so hard," she wept. "We never go out, we never do anything."

"I'm beat when I come home. What do you think I am?"

"And Sundays—it's such a long day."

"You think I do it for myself? When a man takes the bread right out of your mouth. . . ." Everything he did was for the family. For every birthday he bought each of them a savings bond; he spent a fortune on insurance, so that they'd have something if anything happened to him. He invested every extra penny. For fifteen years he hadn't thought of taking a vacation.

She didn't say anything.

"What do you want? I didn't like it at the very start. 'Oh Nathan,' he mimicked her, 'It must be your imagination.' So now what do you want?"

"You throw it all up to me. How was I to know?"

"How could you be so stupid? Now you come complaining. Just what I need—"

He looked up to see Rachel standing in the doorway. She had to stick her nose in. If she knew what was good for her. . . .

"How can you talk to me like that?"

"Talk to you? No one can talk to you. You don't think; you're worse than a child."

Rachel stood looking at him as Reba fled into the bathroom.

"You shouldn't talk to Mother like that," Rachel blurted out. "You should tell her you're sorry."

"Who asked you?" he thundered. "Who told you to put your two cents in?" Something in the nature of the female made him want to lash out. He hated their tears and whimpering. They undid him, made him mad. In a rush of noise, he jumped all over her.

Then he had two females crying—more than he could endure. That night he didn't eat any supper. Until bedtime no one spoke, and it was a good thing. If anyone had, he would have cut them to the quick. Let there be silence: the silence of the tomb.

The insult. It had been forming down in the depths, during all those weeks and months that Fred and Josephine had been coming into the store, plopping themselves down in the chairs on the aisle as though by fiat, taking in this crumb and that, no doubt saving it up to take back to Sam Goldman. Spies and tale bearers. Her father suffered them with loathing. Rachel could see into his contempt, as into seething gall. For he was a man who wanted something worthy, beyond the ordinary, who demanded intelligence and honesty and was hard on himself; a man of pride, who didn't have to take his hat off to anyone. He had no tolerance for the boobies and the inane, much less the chiselers and drones and deadbeats. He held out for the virtues of hard work and discipline and responsibility. Those who failed to come up to the mark, he met with contempt. Something churned around in that contempt until it couldn't be held down any longer.

Fred and Josephine were talking about Max and Henny, for whenever they had scraped the barrel of everything else to deplore, there were always Max and Henny. Something was happening to her: her memory was going. Rachel knew this as well. But the space left by what she forgot was filled up with stories of the people she remembered and who, she said, came to her in her dreams. Rachel wondered if they knew that.

Josephine and Fred thought it was Max's fault. "I say to him, Mex, you are never home. What is this?—the Chamber of Commerce, the Elks Club, every night out. What is this for a fembly man?"

"I go over there," Josephine said, "and she doesn't have a thing to say. The last time I fixed her lunch. Otherwise I don't think she'd have eaten."

"And you know what he said," Fred went on, pointing with a bony finger. "He said, 'Why should I come home? She isn't even a wife to me. She's forgotten how to cook.'" He held out his open palms and showed all his teeth. "Heh, heh, heh."

"The other night—get this," Josephine said, "he took her to see 'The Snake Pit.' She was terrified."

Rachel had seen the film, too, about a woman who went insane and saw herself as cast down in a pit of snakes. No wonder Henny had been frightened. Rachel could hardly bear it. But when she went to see her, Henny was glad she had come. And she told her things as usual, about the cousin with the beautiful hair, and her aunt who had once been accused of being a witch, because she lived on the edge of the village and was seldom seen. They said strange lights bobbed around her house at night. In her memory her stories burned with a brilliant glow. As Rachel watched, it was as though she'd left behind the present moment, entered a doorway, and stood on different ground, visiting some other plane. Rachel could almost see it, the place from which her voice came with the thrill of recognition. Then, as though she were looking around, Rachel could hear her say, "Where is he? Why hasn't he come yet?" And when she returned, some other piece of herself seemed to have been left behind.

Now the conversation shifted to other things. There was talk of reviving Tyrone, which had once been a thriving mining town and was now a ghost town. Fred had bought the railroad there for a dollar.

"Maybe it will be worth some money," he said, looking at Rachel's father. "And the houses." He owned some of them too.

"You'd reach up somebody's crotch to grab a nickel," Rachel's father said.

"Vhat?" Fred said, grinning around at them, not comprehending. "Vhat are you saying?"

Josephine looked furious. "We're leaving," she said, grabbing Fred, making him stand up.

"Look," Nathan said, thinking better of it. "I was only joking."

"Anything for a joke," Josephine said. "Maybe next time you can say something about my nose."

Indeed she had quite a formidable one: the better, Nathan had commented often enough, to butt into everybody's business. They hustled out of the store. A week went by, then another. Every morning Fred passed the store, back straight, looking to neither left nor right. Let Nathan see him if he would. They did not come in.

Nathan received a call from Sam Goldman. They'd come to him and told him they'd been insulted. Sam let him know he should apologize. Sam had known Fred and Josephine for years and did not want to offend them. The whole thing galled Nathan: being put in the wrong by people he despised. And for merely speaking the truth. The trouble was, the world cherished falsehood, flung up from the flimsy lattices of hypocrisy, glittering and gaudy, to disguise the truth. Only let someone tear away the cover . . .

There was no way around it: he'd been put in the wrong. Nathan called up and told Fred that he hadn't meant to offend him, that he was sorry if he had. The next day Fred and Josephine bustled into the store, "Hello, hello, vat's news?" and took their places in the chairs on the aisle as though nothing had happened. Where else did they have to go?

It was very strange. When Rachel looked into Josephine's face, she was looking beyond the moment to where something else was shaping, pointing toward the future. Coming into focus was Josephine's bedroom, though she'd never been inside her house. Fred was no longer there, no longer in the world, his absence hanging over the older woman in her isolation. An older woman sitting at her vanity table looking into the mirror, gray hair undone and hanging down her back, a brush in her hand. In the air the call that went riding through the open window to where the Mexican boy was cutting grass: *Emilio, come Emilio.* His entering the room, the sun still warm on his back, little beads of perspiration gathering beneath the fuzz on his upper lip. *Come brush my hair, Emilio. I can't raise my arm today.* A little shift of her torso, the silk robe falling open to reveal her neck. Emilio: a stocky, well-muscled boy with coppery skin and black hair jagged along his neck. He stood above her, both their expressions in the mirror, an expectancy perhaps tending toward mirth. And then from behind his back, where he'd been holding them, he lifted up a pair of grass shears, putting the points to her throat. In the mirror her expression melted into terror while his moved toward the contempt and amusement he'd been hiding like the shears. Trembling, she took up her purse, the boy snatching it away, pulling the bills from her wallet and stuffing them into his pockets, laughing as he left her. Then all merging into departure. A For Sale sign stuck in the lawn in front of the house, Josephine hastily packing her things in a single suitcase and fleeing the town where she'd lived for over half a century.

But now, the moment coalescing into the present, Josephine sat and surveyed the furniture with a glitter in her eye that looked like triumph. It was a mortification for her father to have to apologize. Rachel knew this too. It was one more thing to hedge him in, along with the store, and the threat that the mines would go out on strike and no one would have any money. And Max—who stood like a cormorant watching his chance.

There was nothing to do but wait. As the summer twilight deepened and the cicadas ground away in the trees, her parents sat in the two green metal chairs on the screened porch, picking over the bones of the day. After she finished the dishes, Rachel had to get out of the house and escape into the evening. She took out her bicycle from the front porch, heard her mother say, "Don't be gone too long," and pedaled up the hill and away. On the other side of town, where the houses were less crowded, she'd found a horse that someone kept in a small field. It recognized her now and came up when she whistled, and nuzzled her while she ran her hand down the streak of white on its nose. Sometimes she took a carrot for it.

Or else she went downtown to the confectionery and looked at magazines and sometimes ordered a soda, so that she could sit for a while and watch who came and went, getting popcorn and Cokes to take into the theater. The question that teased her thought was whether Mr. Falconer, who seemed to have as little to do on certain evenings as she, would wander downtown. Once, twice she had passed him on the street and said, "Hello, Mr. Falconer," and he had smiled and said, "Hello, Rachel." He said her name as though only her presence at that moment could have satisfied him. And something caught between them, a little flare. Now she looked for him every time she went downtown, hoping against all logic he might come, knowing she would be there.

He was a painter, and he sent his work up to the galleries in Taos and Santa Fe. Meanwhile he earned a living teaching art in the local high school and junior high. She was in his class, though it was only for juniors and seniors, because she had gotten an excuse from a sympathetic doctor to let her out of P.E. Sinus trouble.

At the beginning of the class Mr. Falconer had shown slides of Indian artifacts and designs on pottery that the Mimbres Indians had made, taking the animals and birds they saw every day for their inspiration. Then he had shown slides of his paintings— sweeps of southwestern landscape in brilliant splotches of color—and spoken about forms and the operation of light. The paintings had taken her breath away—that anyone could produce such marvels!—and she had gone up afterward and told him she wanted to paint just like that.

Now something happened when she saw him. She couldn't take her eyes away from his face. She wanted to stare at him, to seize hold of the smallest expression or gesture, to capture the slight rise at the corner of his mouth when he smiled, the sharp gleam of his eye when it was turned critically on a canvas, the line of his jaw, the geography of his hair. She wanted to devour him in detail, as though she wanted to paint his portrait. But even more, to know everything about him. She found out where he lived and sometimes rode her bicycle down his street, past his house. Her curiosity rose as a tingle in the blood and was unbearable. She had to spy on him.

That one day in the classroom had done it. Mr. Falconer had come up behind her to see what she was doing, put a casual hand on her shoulder as she was painting a picture of the house Henny had taken her by long ago, the old house she had sometimes come back to look at on her own. He had taken the brush from her hand and said, "Let me show you something. You don't have to paint every brick. You can just suggest." And he'd laid two splashes of color on the facade of her house, not haphazardly but with design, and said, "See, that does the trick. Try a few of those." And then he'd said, "Suppose the porch is broken. Those columns don't have to be just on the porch. Suppose you have one over here." And he'd painted a column there at the side in the yard, a broken-off column. Rachel had been enthralled, even though it wasn't her idea. You could do that. You could just make it up.

She walked around with that discovery as though she'd sprouted feathers. She'd thought you were required to make everything look just like it was, but somehow the house with its broken column was real to her. Mr. Falconer had put something into her hands, but she didn't know what to make of it, and she held it ticking like a bomb. What he'd given her was what he was, no separating them, and that drew her like a charm. When she went out into the evenings, she had to find out where he was and where he went, as though he might lead her past the boundaries of what she knew to another realm.

When the light deepened and the surrounding mountains turned indigo, the hard edges of things began to blur, the ugly stuccoed adobe houses and the dilapidated stores on the main street, the dusty, unpaved alleys with thistle and desert poppy growing alongside. It was like a signal: you could walk around unconnected to that, but rather yield to the scent of yellow climbing roses along someone's fence and whatever else hung in the cooling air. Then the walls might separate and dissolve and reveal a stairway you could descend to another realm, if only you knew how.

Disappointment usually greeted her. Sometimes he went into the package store and came out with a bottle he carried up the street and off in the direction of his house. Or he walked into the Buffalo Bar, a rough place frequented by miners and cowboys itching for a fight. When anyone pushed open the swinging doors, the smell assailed those passing in the street, an exhalation of stale beer. She wondered what took him in there. He was always alone. There was a lot of talk about him among the students. Conflicting rumors. One of the seniors in her class said he was living with a Mexican woman because his wife had kicked him out. Said he was always on the bottle.

One Friday when she was coming out of the confectionery with an ice cream cone—she was sometimes allowed to go to the movies on Friday nights if there was something special on—she almost ran into him on the corner. He was looking disheveled and a bit unsteady and he gave her a startled look. "Oh, you've been to the show," he said. "Betty Grable," he said, looking down at her, "And did she get to pick up some broken entertainer from the pavement?" He gave a little chuckle. "And kick up her legs?"

Without acknowledging it, they started up the street together. "Well," he muttered, "we need all the help we can get." He gave a little irreverent laugh.

As they walked he twiddled his fingers at his side. "It's dark," he said. "You know a man was stabbed in the alley down here the other night."

She didn't say anything. He was warning her she shouldn't be walking alone at night. But neither could she stay indoors. She knew where the man had been stabbed. She liked to walk down that alley sometimes, though she didn't after dark. Most of the time, though not always, she kept to lighted streets. She liked to take different ways home.

For a half a block they walked in silence while she licked her cone, butter pecan on top, chocolate below—her favorites. Perhaps he'd taken it upon himself to see that she got home safely. "This town," he said. "It's the bottom, isn't it? Mountains sitting there for time everlasting and in between, the scraps from the pot."

Mountains. She looked at them every morning as she walked up the hill and along the street, up the final hill to where the high school sat on top. Mountains that surrounded you, hedged you in. And if you were up on top looking down, you'd see a collection of dollhouses and creatures running along like ants.

"You've got to get out of it," he said, as if he were giving himself a directive. "Cut your losses, throw your stuff in the rag bag, and move along," he said. "Merrily we roll along."

She gave him a sidelong glance. He wasn't talking to her, she could tell. She worked at the second dip of her ice cream cone. Ahead, the darkened street could have led anywhere, not just out to the highway and to the place beyond, called Chloride Flats, where the high school students parked and made out, but west to the edge of the continent. They could have started walking and just kept going toward whatever territory his imagination was roaming in.

"Where are you going?" she asked him. She didn't want him to leave.

"To hell in a handbasket, young lady." He gave a melancholy laugh. "Just talking to hear myself talk. That's all I do these days."

She waited for him to go on.

Suddenly his mood shifted. "You ever think what it was like out here when it was just the West?"

She'd never thought about it. All she could see now was Indians.

"Rough all right, but you had the place to yourself. You and the Indians and the grizzlies. It must have been something." He thought it over. "People willing to gamble anything. Gamble their money and gamble their lives. For land, for gold. Gambled their lives just like nothing." He snapped his fingers. "And got killed for it." He glanced at her. "Didn't matter."

They were walking past the Catholic church, beyond the parochial school, the playground in between. It was all elevated above the street by a high wall, and steps led up.

"Only now if you live that way. . . . Just try it. Drinking every drop you can hold, throwing caution to the winds. . . ." Under his breath he sang tunelessly, "Moving along, moving along. Only a rolling stone, oh."

None of it was directed to her, she was just an occasion for him to talk to himself. He may as well have stood behind glass. "What are we gambling these days?" he said. "The whole future— We've just got done with Hitler and Hirohito and now we're going to take on Uncle Joe. That'll give us something to do. Hunting Communists."

He went muttering on till they came to her street. No, they weren't going to walk on past, down the highway to wherever the road was leading. Now she wanted only to get away from him.

"I have to go this way," she said. "That's my house up there."

"Home all safe and sound," he said. "Goodnight, little sparrow."

He turned to go up the hill, then turned around precisely as she did and gave her a wave and a laugh. She held up both arms and waved, then bounced down the steps and onto the porch. Her father and mother had gone inside. She opened the door, blinked in the harsh light, and entered.

"How was the movie?" her mother asked.

"Okay."

The room took her into the ordinary in which it sat, day in, day out. Her mother was reading to her father from the *Reader's Digest.* "Do you want a snack? There are some sardines and crackers on the table."

The fourth of Susie's husbands had been a mathematics professor. "Don't know what was in my head when I married him," she said. She was showing Rachel how to put up her hair so that it would make a series of soft curls around her ears and along the curve at the base of her head. They had to be wound in one direction on one side, and the opposite direction on the other. "Maybe I thought if you had brains and a college education, you could live your life without mistakes."

She gave a little savage stroke of the brush that yanked Rachel's hair. "Didn't mean to hurt you, hon."

"It's okay." It was what Susie said that disturbed her. Rachel dreamed of a college education and for that very reason: to go through life in the right way. Her father'd had only two years of college before he went into the navy, and her mother had never gone beyond the eighth grade. Her father was always quoting a phrase he'd taken from a book he'd read in his youth, "the moral obligation to be intelligent." Whatever it meant, it laid such a heavy burden on the reader's shoulders, only a college education might begin to alleviate it. Above all, Rachel didn't want to make any mistakes.

"All he knew about," Susie continued, "was his own penis and a few mathematical formulas."

Rachel had never heard anyone say *penis* before. Susie had said it the way she might have said *marshmallow* or *bric-a-brac* or *cloverleaf.* When Rachel read it in the book her mother had given her after her periods started and which was supposed to enlighten her about all the questions that had long gone unanswered, Rachel thought it was pronounced *pen-is*, as in *pen*. It was not a word she would have asked her mother to pronounce. But with Susie it came right out. Rachel felt a prickling of the scalp, but nothing had shattered and one moment ticked on comfortably into the next.

Susie gave one of the laughs. "Once I remember he was going off to a mathematical conference. You know, where they all get together and spout formulas at each other. That's their idea of a good time. I'm not knocking it, mind you. Maybe if I had some brains myself, I'd find it a regular shivaree. Turn a little more to the left, hon. I'll do the rest and you watch me." She hummed a little of "Peg o' My Heart" and took a bobby pin from her teeth.

"Your husband," Rachel reminded her.

"Oh, yeah. Anyway, he was going off and I said to him, 'Where's your suitcase?' and he said, 'What suitcase?' and I said, 'You know. Don't you want to take some changes of socks and underwear?' And he said to me, 'What for? I'm only going to be gone five days?'"

She gave snort of laughter, reached over for her cigarette, and took a drag. "Can you beat that?"

"At least he washed," Verna, who lived down the street, said, looking up from her *Good Housekeeping.* "I've known some didn't get that far."

"He had a pipe collection," Susie went on, combing and curling. "He was very proud of his meerschaums, let me tell you. He had them in all shapes—bears and birds and mermaids and naked ladies. He'd puff along in class while he was writing equations on the blackboard, show the students he had a touch of the naughty. Well, you could've fooled me."

In the mirror Rachel watched as pin curls were wound up, the rows of them cleaving to her head like a headdress made of hardware. Like her teeth with their braces. All for the sake of future beauty. And she saw something else: no matter what she did, she was never going to be pretty. She'd never be popular like Carla Rae or Mitzi or Annette or Ernestine, who went to the school dances and had dates to the movies at least two or three times a month. Though the others lived on the other side of town where there were houses with yards, Ernestine lived right at the end of her block. Her mother helped run the Dairy Queen, and Ernestine had a job waiting on tables even though she was only fifteen. Rachel had been there once when Ernestine came round to take her order. A couple of high school seniors, basketball players, sat at the counter. They kept ordering things and teasing her, asking for ketchup and mustard and soft drinks and onion rings so they could keep her running back and forth bringing things and talking to them. She moved around in her uniform all quick and cute, with her hair bouncing in a ponytail, carrying herself like she owned something valuable. Rachel knew she'd never look like that.

"Well, that husband nearly got himself in jail," Susie said.

"I thought he was a perfessor," Verna said.

"You think that'll keep you out of trouble?" Susie said. "Only he had it all justified in his head. I'd been in the hospital and we were so poor we didn't have a cent to buy the kids anything for Christmas. That little Bible college he was teaching at didn't pay beans—they expected you to live on piety, they were so full of it. And he went muttering around saying it wasn't right for our kids to go a-begging—he was an educated man after all, valuable to society. And you know what, he went into a store downtown and picked out some toys and marched right out without paying. They didn't charge him with shoplifting, but that Bible school fired him on the spot. And we hardly had anything to eat. Good thing I could set hair."

The next husband Susie had was a tool and dye maker. "I had two intellecshals," Susie said. "I figured I'd go and find me something a little less high-minded." She looked down at Rachel. "I hope your mama has been telling you something about birth control," she said.

"No," Rachel said, "But I don't think I'll have to worry."

Susie gave her a little poke, "Course you will."

"I'm not going to get married," Rachel assured her.

"Don't mean a thing, honey. Don't matter if you stand outside a wedding band or in it. The bedroom or the back seat of the buggy, you'll be doing it one way or another."

It was news Rachel found quite shocking. She couldn't believe it. It had said nothing about that in her book.

She knew Henny was getting worse. Every time Josephine and Fred came into the store, they had something new to dissect, clucking their tongues, shaking their heads over it. The slow course of Henny's forgetfulness had accelerated. Now she'd entirely forgotten how to cook. When Max came home at night, there was no meal on the table. And when he scolded her, she didn't know what was wrong. She didn't know what was supposed to be done with the meat and vegetables; she looked at the pots and pans as though they were strange objects. She couldn't boil an egg.

"I told him, Max, why don't you cook something with her?" Josephine said. "And he gets all red in the face, angry. 'What d'you mean, I'm supposed to cook? She's my wife, that's what a wife is for.'"

He wouldn't eat with her. He would give her something to eat and then go out alone to get a hamburger at the Dairy Queen or out to the Dix Club if he felt like spending the evening drinking. Henny was in the store one afternoon when Rachel came for a moment to see if her father would buy a magazine subscription from the list she was selling for her class. Max wanted to buy one also, it would give Henny something to read. He was doing something for her under the eyes of everyone, including Josephine and Fred. Josephine didn't want to buy a subscription because she knew somewhere she could get it cheaper. Rachel started to hand Max the blank to sign, but he jerked his thumb toward Henny.

Rachel felt uncomfortable. Henny held the pen like some queer instrument whose use she couldn't guess.

"Just sign your name," Max said with a gentleness Rachel was unused to in a voice she'd always found harsh and grating, especially when he was trying to be funny. "Take your time."

The silence gathered around them into a single held breath, tense with their urgency: let her do it, let her not fail. Henny's agitation rose like a beam of radio static. The pitch of the waiting was drawn toward the unendurable, when in a sudden jerky spasm she wrote out her name. The moment subsided. When Rachel looked at Henny's signature, it was an illegible scrawl such as a child would make pretending to write. She should never have come in, Rachel chided herself. And so that no one would ask to look, she dashed out of the store and down the street.

So the news shouldn't have been a surprise to her. She hadn't heard anything about Henny for the past two weeks. She hadn't gone to see her, they'd been so taken up with her father's eye operation. He had gone down to the hospital in El Paso; then, because of the delicacy of the surgery, he'd been in her aunt and uncle's house for over a week. He was taken back for the surgeon to examine his eye, and when he was strong enough, they drove him up to Silver. There he lay in bed most of the day, a patch over his eye. He had to lie down because of the throbbing in his head when he stood up. He sat up for the meals Reba served him on a tray. When the eye was healed and he had recovered, he would go down for the second operation. He'd been fully conscious during the whole procedure, the doctor telling him to look up or look down or to the side. He'd lain there gripping the sides of the operating table. Rachel and her mother moved around on tiptoes.

Rachel had gone by to see Henny on the way home from school one afternoon, but no one answered when she rang the bell. She hadn't thought anything about it. Saturday she told her mother she was going over to see Henny.

"You can't," Reba said with a sigh.

"Why not?"

There was a long pause in which Rachel grew impatient. She hated it when people wouldn't tell her things. "Why can't I go?"

"They've taken her away," Reba said.

"Where? Where have they taken her?"

"To the mental institution."

"She's not crazy."

"Her brain deteriorated," her mother said. "She forgot every-thing. It was dangerous. She'd turn on the stove and not remember. They had to put her away."

Rachel turned and headed out the door.

"Where are you going? I have something to tell you."

But she didn't pause. She ran up the steps and down the street, out of hearing. She couldn't believe it, Henrietta gone. Couldn't believe. Like a light blown out. And the noise she was making, she caught herself at it, like some little kid going down the street all on its own with its own noisy grief. She was never going back home. She'd just keep on going and never look back.

She went up the hill behind the courthouse to the cut-out place in the side of the mountain. She climbed up the pile of shale and sat there for a time. Before she could collect herself, she saw three Mexican boys coming up the hill in her direction. She had no idea what they were doing up there—usually, she had the place to her-self. They had seen her, and she didn't want to be up there with them. She got up, took herself down the slope of shale, and veered away from them. But they were moving in her direction, ready to block her path. They were all bigger than she, though one of them was slender and not much taller. She was suddenly afraid.

"Hey, what's the matter?" one of them said. He was big, already with the build of a man and a heavy face.

She didn't answer.

"You wanna come with us, have some fun?" The slender one reached out to put his arm around her, and suddenly it seemed they were all reaching out for her, toward those vulnerable places where secrets were locked even from herself. She clawed at them viciously, tore herself away, and ran as fast as she could down the hill.

Only when she reached the street, chest heaving, did she stop and turn around. They hadn't followed her. She walked along the street without knowing where she would go. She didn't want to go downtown, there were too many people. Instead she drifted toward the vacant lot on the corner past her house. Sometimes she went down there after it rained, when the water that streamed under the culvert below the street continued on over the rocks and stones beyond, revealing their colors. She went along, picking up the various stones, saving the ones that she liked, taking them home and putting them on her bookcase and bureau on the back porch. Though the colors faded, she kept them until her mother threw them out.

In the vacant lot was a tree she liked to climb. When she was little, she used to climb trees with the boys all the time. And she still hadn't given up doing it, though it wasn't ladylike.

Swinging up easily from the ground, she could see into the Meltons' yard. At the back side of the lot was the shed that both apartments shared, though her mother never put anything in it. The side toward her was charred along the bottom where Gary had tried to set fire to it. It was a wonder, her mother said, he hadn't burned down the whole neighborhood. Now the dog was tied up next to it. He'd had to be tied up because he'd taken to ripping clothes off the neighbors' clotheslines, and one of Rachel's slips had been found ripped to shreds. Reba had made her go over and say that the slip had cost three dollars, and she'd had to stand there while Shirley got a hard look around her mouth. Rachel hadn't wanted to go. Finally Shirley had given her the three dollars.

Now Trigger barked all day long and stood pulling at his chain. "I could kill that mutt," her mother kept saying. "I wish somebody would poison it." Rachel wished Shirley would come out and feed him so that he'd be quiet and she wouldn't have to listen. From the fork she climbed up the next big limb, where she could sit with her legs stretched out and lean against the trunk. It was bigger than most of the trees around town—an old tree. From there she could see the back of Ernestine Dowland's house just around the corner. If Ernestine came along, she'd say, "What'cha you doing up there, guy?" a giggle already on the way up her smooth little throat. And then she'd go past before Rachel could think of something smart to say. But chances were, Ernestine was out at the drive-in with the high school kids she hung around with. About the only time Rachel saw her was at school, or sometimes at the show with her date or at the skating rink, where Rachel watched her go whirling past, the boy she was skating with encircling her with his arm, their two pairs of legs moving effortlessly together. Rachel knew she couldn't do that. She didn't even know how to dance.

She wiped her eyes. Though she knew all along something was happening to Henrietta, she still couldn't believe it. All the while other things were slipping away, the little core of stories remained, all those bright splinters that kept alive the inhabitants of Henny's past, all the lost souls. This was what had bound them, in a way Rachel hadn't known with anyone else. That connection, too, became one of her secrets. She could feel Reba's disapproval, as though Henny were a bad influence. Rachel knew from the tone Reba got in her voice when she said, "What were you doing over there?"

Something was wrong about it, though Rachel couldn't tell what it was. Or if she was a moment late to set the table, Reba launched into a torrent of protest about how she never helped around the house, how she was growing up to be lazy. It was as though her mother was jealous of the time she spent there, jealous of something that didn't belong to her.

And what had she taken away? Stories. Rachel knew these were what Henny had handed to her, stories that were now part of her own memory. But they were Henny's stories, and what was she supposed to do with them?

A door slammed and Gary Melton ran down the steps into the backyard. Rachel saw him bend down, pick up a stone, and throw it at a bird that sat on the clothesline post. Even after the bird flew off, he sent stones in its direction, then turned and threw them over at her yard. He had some kind of speech defect, and it was hard to understand anything he said. He had taken to throwing stones. Shirley was always being called into the principal's office over him, the way he picked on smaller children and tore up things in the classroom. Someone told Rachel his dad was off in the penitentiary for armed robbery.

The afternoon sun was sinking behind the hills, leaving a bright swath on the facades of the stuccoed houses. A truck lumbered down the hill, braked to a stop at the corner, and turned toward the highway. She shifted positions in the tree. She was too old to be climbing trees—that's what her father said.

She'd climbed trees ever since she could remember, swinging on branches, then jumping to the ground. It was no longer easy for her to do it; her body seemed to get in her way. But she did it anyway, skinning up her arms and legs. "Look at what you've done to yourself," Reba would say. "You've got no business up there like a kid. One of these days you're really going to hurt yourself."

She didn't know what to do with herself. She felt guilty somehow, as though the time ought to go differently. There was the time she spent at school and the time she spent doing the dishes and other jobs around the house, the time she spent baby-sitting. Then, with what was left over, she rode her bicycle or went to the show or the skating rink or wandered around town, hoping to run into Mr. Falconer or somebody she liked. Going to Henny's had been different. She wasn't filling up the time with what she had to do or stuffing up the gaps in between.

When she was a little girl, time seemed full of the things she touched or smelled or saw. Almost anything she picked up had filled it. The smell of her dad's witch hazel when she sat in the bathroom watching him shave. The kittens and puppies that tumbled through her hands with their warm animal smells, that she used to dress in doll clothes and push around in her doll carriage. The smell of tar and caramel corn and suntan oil those Sundays they went to the beach and hoisted up the beach umbrella, being very careful, for her mother burned easily. And all the little ceramic cats and dogs she had from the machines that promised you a wallet or a watch, but instead scooped up a handful of candy and one of those little useless made-in-Japans. And playing dress-ups with her mother's cast-off dresses, with Marianne Wheatly and her sister Betsy from across the street, clopping along the street in high heels. And watching her mother clean the oysters her father had brought back from Chincoteague Island, a bushel basket every fall, hoping Reba might open one and find a pearl. All those things had made up the texture of her childhood. Now a line had been drawn down though her life, and all that had broken off into a place only memory could reach.

The dream had caught them up and taken them here. The dream that was supposed to go one way, but that had gone another without their say so, as though there'd been a little hook or quirk that snagged it, a sudden sharp bend in the sunlight that sent things going along an unintended path. This was the way she saw it. Now it looked impossible to go back to the precise spot, take out the twist, and send things on their way again. Henny had told her a story about a young German soldier who'd shot a boy and his mother when they were trying to escape. His orders were to do that, because escapees were enemies of the state. But he told about it with tears running down his face. And Rachel knew those he had killed would always be there to haunt him and he would never be able to make his life what it was before that. The doorway was closed forever. Sometimes half awake she caught the image of a darkened stairway. But she didn't know where it led.

The screen door banged again, and this time Shirley Melton came outside. She clopped down the steps in her high-heeled wedgies, her breasts bobbing like great marshmallows in her white blouse. She had come to feed the dog. She bent over to pour dry pellets from a bag into the dog's dish. "Eat your food, iddy biddy baby. Mama loves you."

Rachel wanted to puke: talking baby talk to that big, ugly mutt. Rachel watched her stand up, put a hand up to her pale hair, and look out to survey what the evening might hold. Apparently nothing of interest, for a moment later she clopped up the steps and inside, the back door slamming behind her. The tag end of the day was left to empty into silence. The air seemed blue, and deepening shadows of trees and houses moved in to occupy the ground.

"Rachel," she heard her mother call.

She felt an impulse to call out, *Here I am. Be there in a minute.* But she kept silent.

She heard the screen door slam and saw her mother come out to the alley behind their yard. "Rachel! Where is that kid?"

Up in the tree, up in the leaves. Rachel looked upward into the leaves glittering in the departing sun. The leaves began to whisper together—they were whispering about her. Then she heard them: *Will the child never grow up? Never grow up? What's she doing up here?* another set of voices asked. *She's too big, too big.* "Rachel," her mother called again. "Rachel." She waited a long moment. "She's never done that before. I could wring her neck."

The other voices just above Rachel's head, took over: *She's too old. Too big for climbing trees.*

Suddenly she was afraid of falling. She had come to the tree for safety and comfort, but the voices in the leaves spoke against her. And from beyond them spoke the other voices: her father's sharp sarcasm and her mother's nagging and complaint; the moaning from Mr. Kober and Mrs. Kober's searing high notes that reached the end of the alley; and Trigger's well-known bark. Voices that made the texture of the day, the warp and woof of one day woven into the next. But Henny had been able to weave all her voices together in a story.

She's forgotten everything. Even how to boil an egg. Just sits all day long looking at those animals or staring at the budgie in its cage.

"Rachel," her mother called again.

"I'm up here," she said, loud enough to be heard.

"I've been looking all over for you. What are you doing?"

"Nothing."

"Didn't you hear me? Your father's all upset. We were just about to call the police. Get yourself over here. He's ready to have your hide. And in his condition."

She didn't want to come down. As in the fairy tales, if she touched the ground, she'd lose the charm, break the fairy spell. She wanted to become part of the tree. But it wouldn't let her, the way it whispered against her. Yet if she set foot on the ground, she'd be an old woman.

Slowly she climbed down and went up the alley.

Her mother stood waiting, quietly now, her anger subsiding into the general low-grade misery she steeped in. "Henny left something for you," she said.

Rachel felt stiff and sore. When she went inside, her shoulders ached. She had gotten chilled.

Waiting for her was the great stuffed clown that had sat in Henny's chair: red and white and orange and blue, a tasseled cap sitting above the wide grin that could have been a grimace. Her gift.

"I guess she wanted you to have it. Though you are a little old for such things."

Her childhood lay somewhere beyond her, outgrown, too small for her. She'd already bumped her head against it. But whatever was growing, unfolding, was as far away as what she'd lost as she stood on this strange and shifting point. Now, thinking back on it, Rachel had a sudden vision: the two of them meeting on a moving stairway, she going up while Henny was coming down. And as they met, paused, Henny had given her a gift, and smiling gently, gentle creature that she was, but in some way powerful too, had handed her this vital and puzzling communication.

III.

They should have fled long ago. It was clear to Reba now that she saw the ad in the *Furniture Retailers Daily*. "Manager required for growing business in Phoenix, Arizona." You could tell nothing from an ad, of course, but suppose they could take over a business with a future. Just run it and see it grow and not have to start out behind the eight ball. Something they could step into. She could learn bookkeeping. Nathan—God grant that he get back his sight—could wait on the customers, so that he could feel he was still in charge. But she knew she would be doing that as well—the lion's share. Such had been her lot in life. But together they could manage, as they'd been managing. Considering all she'd been through, she deserved something better. That was her line of thinking.

She was not certain how to broach the subject to Nathan. Most of the time he wouldn't let her get out the first word, let alone take a suggestion. She always had to placate him, woo him into thinking it was his own idea. But desperation made her bold. She read him the ad during a break when Max was out of the store.

"Write to them," he said. "I'll tell you what to say."

She followed him back to the typewriter. Nathan dictated the letter, and she took it immediately to the post office. It would go out that very day.

Their mood changed. They dared not hope, yet they couldn't keep away from the subject. For the first time in their years there they spoke to one another as though they moved with a common pulse. They saw themselves leaving the town where so long they had eaten the bread of bitterness. Leaving behind the furniture they had carted all the way from Delaware, those worn accessories of their married life. This time they would be making a clean break. They could look for a house. How long they had tripped over one another in that cramped little duplex that wouldn't even hold all their furniture. But to have bought a house meant a capitulation to their fate, announced an intention to stay, to set down roots. As long as they were renting, they could balance against their sense of tentativeness the possibility of leaving: a door always held open.

A house. The house she'd always dreamed of: full of nice things. Silver, linen, crystal. Nice things were enshrined for her in the word *silver.* Silver. The way it slid off the tongue. The way it invited highlights, little fat gleams: the wealth it suggested. It spoke of midnight cruises on glistening dark water, the boat moving through like silk, the sound of light laughter rising beyond. And beyond that a room full of people in formal dress. The strains of a waltz.

New furniture. She could entertain. She wouldn't have to feel ashamed when people come into the house. Even in this nothing-of-a-town were people she'd have been glad to entertain: some of the ranchers and executives at the mines. But how could she? She didn't even have a dining room. No place for the Limoges she had inherited from her mother-in-law, and the things they'd splurged on once when Nathan was flush from his year of selling insurance: her sterling silver and crystal stemware and linen tablecloths. It broke her heart to keep these things in boxes where they were never used. But what else could she do? There was no way to do things right.

And it would be a great satisfaction to her to tell the Goldmans to go to hell. They were the real cause of the trouble—how clear it was to her now: holding on to Max that way. It showed a kind of contempt for Nathan. A callous indifference. They should only have the heartache and worry.

So she entertained herself with prospects for the future, trying to visualize what Phoenix was like, a real city for a change, and Sam Goldman's face when he got the news. She hoped Nathan would give him a piece of his mind, at least have that satisfaction. As for Max, she hoped he would get what was coming to him. He should drop dead. No, let him live, let him clean out the whole store after they were gone. Then let the Goldmans take notice. It would serve them right.

Susie had a visitor. At first Rachel noticed his pickup truck parked sometimes in front of their house, sometimes across the street. From its interior, a tall, rangy man unfolded himself and sauntered across the street and onto Susie's porch; whereupon the door was opened and he was lost to view. Sometimes he reappeared a few hours later and drove off. Sometimes the truck was parked overnight, or at least until the early hours of the morning, for by the time Rachel was ready for school the truck was gone. "You can't even park in front of your own house," her mother would complain,

A tall, lean man with a mustache that Rachel knew only from Westerns, a long, thin, droopy one. He wore a brown Western hat tilted over his forehead, with a design at the front and around the band created by brown and white feathers. He wore no fancy Western shirt, however, but a checkered work shirt and Levis, worn almost white in the seat. His ears Rachel would have described also as tall, and his sideburns were consequently long. Usually he looked to have several days' growth of beard. Sometimes she caught him crossing the street in a booted stride, sometimes pulling up in front. Once she caught him blowing Susie a kiss, a flourish she wouldn't have expected. Then she began to see Susie in the cab of the truck riding with him, very likely out of town.

Then one day Susie came sailing into the store, as Reba put it. Even the delivery boys planted on the stairs felt the force of her entrance. "J.T. and I have come to look around a little," she said nonchalantly.

J.T. stood directly behind her, thumbs looped in his belt, and surveyed the rows of appliances over his mustache. He looked like a man who could take his time but who, having once made up his mind, nothing further would distract by way of opinion. "For starters," he said, "that refrigerator out at the place has about done its day."

Reba wondered what sort of dump he was referring to. Nathan got up to show them the refrigerators. With his impaired vision, he could still get around, though sometimes he misjudged his location and banged himself against doors and furniture. He didn't dare go upstairs. They looked at refrigerators, the biggest model, considered the freezer compartment.

"But we've got to leave the dining room alone," Susie said. "That mahogany table of your mama's is the prettiest I've ever seen."

J.T. looked gratified. "Grandma's actually," he said. "She set great store by it. I can remember when twenty people gathered there for Sunday dinner. And she did most of the cooking."

They settled on the refrigerator, then trooped upstairs in the direction of the bedroom suites. Though most of the furnishings in the store occupied the price range from medium to low—the Las Cruces store offering the prime stuff—they always kept one or two of the more expensive line for the occasional rare customer. Reba followed as Susie and J.T. paused in front of their most expensive bedroom suite.

Susie ran her hand along the bed frame, pulled out one of the drawers of the bureau. "Well, that drawer slides along like silk. I hate drawers that stick." She stood, arms akimbo, considering the layout. "Look at it, J.T. Think that'll go in the guest wing?"

"Honey, anything in this blessed store is yours if you want it. You just do the picking and I'll write out the check."

Reba couldn't believe it. Susie had found herself a Sugar Daddy, and leave it to her to make the most of it. As he stood there, Reba could hardly take her eyes off him. Not exactly her picture of Mr. Handsome. More like something the cat dragged in. Yet there he was, Old Moneybags himself.

"Oh, J.T," Susie said. "I know you'd give me anything." She turned to Reba. "J.T. is the sweetest kisser."

J.T. didn't move. He looked on her and on the surroundings with the same benign if somewhat distant air, while a little twitch happened at the corner of his mouth like a stick moving. Just at the edge of the mustache.

Then Reba looked at Susie, who was reaching back to give a little tug at his hand. She had got her mitts on her meal ticket and wasn't about to let go.

Afterward Reba said again that she couldn't believe it. Yet there it was, after they were all through with the big stuff and some odds and ends: a sales ticket drawn up for fifteen hundred dollars.

They'd had such a terrible month in the store, hardly any business now that the mines were closed down. No one knew when the miners would go back to work. Various customers had skipped payments or come in with sad stories: they would pay when they could. They'd had to repossess some of the furniture, only to throw it into the ditch, after finding it infested with vermin. Meanwhile no one was buying anything new. But this fellow has a balance in his checkbook that could buy out half the store. Reba wondered how some people could have it so lucky.

Thus it was that Susie announced she was getting married— to husband number six. A church wedding at that. Her married daughter was to be the matron of honor, and some of the girls from the frozen food locker and from the drugstore downtown were to be fitted out as bridesmaids. All Susie's family was coming in for the wedding, a daughter from Santa Rosa and two sons from Alta Vista and Las Vegas. A couple of grandchildren as well. Susie's Beauty Parlor was a thing of the past, even before the wedding. Already she was spending her time out at J.T.'s ranch. Before that event took place, she moved out for good, and a family moved in: the Monroes with their two daughters, Xyla and Nelita. In Reba's view the neighborhood was sinking to a new low.

Susie was getting married all in white. "Why not," she said. "Whatever came before, that's all gone. And all that's coming is new. I'm putting everything aside to make room for that."

Rachel had been hatching the question about whether or not Susie loved J.T. the way she did husband number three, or whether she was just marrying him for his money.

"I've never seen anything like it," Reba kept saying. "He's such a sweet kisser," she quoted.

"You should've asked her for a demonstration," Nathan said. "You'd probably have got one."

Somehow when Rachel thought about what Susie said, she was watching her go through a doorway into a place from where she heard fiddle music. There she saw Susie in a group of square dancers. The question she'd struggled with no longer seemed to fit. She let it go and it faded from her mind.

Something was in the air, sending a crackle through it like a charge of electricity. Rachel sensed it, though for a time she had no idea what was going on. But even her mother couldn't quite keep the secret of the letter; Rachel, too, hoped for something from it.

But now something else. Two weeks before, an accountant had appeared at the store after a telephone call from Sam to say that he wanted someone to look over the books.

"It's the figures," Nathan said. "It's hitting close to the bone. Now it's beginning to hurt."

During the time that Nathan had been in and out of the hospital, recovering slowly, sales had hit rock bottom. What had begun as a strike, with the ups and downs of negotiations and the prospects of the men going back to work, had ended in an impasse. The company had actually closed down its operations, delaying any kind of settlement indefinitely. The merchandise sat on the floor.

"It's that bad?" Sam had said, the last time he came up to look at the figures. "It's never been that bad."

Nathan had merely shrugged. You couldn't argue with the facts. All you could do was sit back and wait. Wait for someone like Susie or the occasional newcomer to town to come in for an appliance. But for the rest—what good did it do to dun them and repossess their furniture? Who wanted it back? Sam wasn't pleased, let him do something about it.

"There's money out there," Sam kept saying. And he'd alluded to the ranchers in the area, to the clerks and secretaries, salesman, people in business. Nathan reminded him there were two furniture stores in the town competing with one another, and not enough to go around. Another fact he hadn't fully appreciated when he came.

"You have to be more aggressive," Sam said. "Go after these people—socialize more."

"Like Max?" Nathan said. "So I can give away the store."

Sam hadn't said anything further. Nathan hoped he noticed the miners crowding the half dozen bars along the main street. Sam would have done better with a liquor business up there, if it came right down to it. Now the bars were making more money than the grocery stores.

The day Sam came up from Las Cruces also brought the reply to the letter they had sent to Phoenix. It had come to the house addressed to Nathan. Reba didn't dare open it. But she was so keyed up, she got one of her spells of shortness of breath and had to lie down. Her nerves had been especially bad lately, what with trying to be with Nathan in the hospital, driving back up to take care of things at home. That's what his eye troubles had done for her, forced her to learn how to drive. If she hadn't gotten one of the delivery boys to give her lessons, they would have been stranded. Nathan let her drive only because he couldn't help himself.

Sam was coming home with Nathan for dinner after the store closed. She had to bestir herself and put something on the table. The old skinflint wouldn't think of taking her and Nathan out. She had to walk past the letter, which she'd put under a circular for door chimes, and feel it lying there as she inserted garlic cloves into the cut of roast beef she'd bought and started it in the oven. She tried not to think about it, but the letter kept reaching toward her. She dried her hands, picked it up, fingered the stamp, read the return address, as if all this might reveal the contents. Yes? No? Then she had to take care of the potatoes. She got Rachel to set the table, her slowness driving her almost to distraction, and help her straighten up the living room. Then she was to take a sandwich and disappear the back way to the movies. It was all Reba could do to meet Sam at the door and pretend to be glad to see him.

Max was out—that was the big news he had to tell. The horse stolen, the gate newly locked. That was what he had to tell while he sat at the table in her crummy kitchen shoveling in the food: face made heavy by the gravity of a man's theft from him, but forehead glistening with the moistness of his efforts over the rapid use of his fork. When did a Goldman forget how to eat?

Across from her, Nathan, peering through the thick lenses he had to wear, was eating slowly, saying little. His face was in shadow.

"I did him a favor when he and his family were practically destitute," Sam said. "And he does this to me."

Reba could have laughed in his face. Instead she said, "Would you take another helping of roast beef, Sam. There's plenty. How about some more potatoes?"

Yes, he would take another helping. Delicious, the whole meal. He had a third helping as well before he called it quits, patting his paunch, sighing over the goodness of the food, not forgetting the chunks lost to the keen tooth of ingratitude. Reba's contempt was honed to a fine point.

Finally he was gone. "The letter came," she said.

"The letter?"

She couldn't believe Nathan had forgotten about it. "From the ad. About the store."

"What did they say?"

"I waited for you. I haven't even read it yet."

In a tremor of expectation, she tore open the envelope and read the letter aloud, hardly able to take in the details of what she was reading. It was a larger store than she had imagined: four salesmen on the floor all the time, plus office help. She was given pause when she read the amount of capital they would need. But the amount of profit took her breath away. They would have an income.

"It sounds good," she said, wondering how they could raise such a sum. Nathan's older brother had all kinds of money, sat on the board of several big insurance companies. But they hadn't seen him in years. If he could only be talked into putting something their way . . .

"Yes," he agreed.

She waited.

"They think Max took around fifteen thousand," he said. "But there's no way to pin it on him without a big stink—it wouldn't help the store—and no way of getting it back. So Sam gave him a thousand dollars and told him he was out."

"A thousand dollars!" She couldn't believe it. "He robs you blind and they give him a thousand dollars. They should treat us that well."

"Anyway, he's gone."

"A thousand dollars."

"And not a penny in the business. Serves Sam right. Trying to be the nice guy."

"So what do you think?" she said.

He shrugged. "All water under the bridge."

"I mean the letter," she persisted.

"It's too much," he said. "Too big—even if I could get around. Once, maybe."

"If I helped?"

"How much could you do?" He shook his head. "We don't know the situation. And the investment—my God!"

A little series of explosions went off before her eyes.

"Anyway, Max is gone," he said. "It's something."

She didn't argue with him. It was all over. He had no energy to make a new start. Suddenly there were no dreams left: they'd put in their hand for the last time and found the bottom of the sack.

Mr. Falconer was leaving. There had been rumors he wasn't coming back in the fall, that the principal had asked him to resign. No doubt there were good reasons for that. He was too often seen in the local bars for the parents to overlook the situation. And on certain days in class, it was clear he'd been drinking and was the worse for it. Toward the end he told one of the girls in Rachel's class she was there for something besides wiggling her butt at the boys. Afterward in the hall she stood with a little group of girls gathered around her, spitting out her indignation. She didn't return to the class but got her grade anyway: her mother came to see the principal.

The rest of the students had a party for him the last day of class. The girls brought Cokes and potato chips; one of them had baked a cake. The students went together and bought him a cap on which Julia, admirable at figure drawing, had embroidered, "Sir Value." For he was always talking about the importance of value in their work. He looked at her tenderly when she presented it.

"We're sorry you're going," Julia said.

He hoped they would all continue with their painting, he said, thanking them, but he encouraged them to find some other way to earn a living: that way they'd at least get to eat while they wielded a brush.

They acknowledged the wisdom of this with a little collective laughter.

"Where are you going, Mr. Falconer?" someone asked.

"I haven't made up my mind," he said. "I've been thinking of going to Mexico for a while."

"Cheap rum," one of the mouthier boys suggested.

"Yeah," Mr. Falconer agreed, "and the women are pretty too. How about that, Eric?"

"You got room for me, maybe I'll come with you."

Mr. Falconer clapped him on the shoulder. "I wouldn't be able to keep up." Everyone laughed.

Rachel, still drawn toward him, could not get enough of his expressions and gestures. Yet when she looked in his direction, his face always held a certain shadowiness, somehow impenetrable, that gave her pause. She wanted to envy him, to feel the excitement of going to a foreign place, leaving home. She did envy him, she couldn't get around it. She felt the lure, the thing that pulled at her and wouldn't leave her alone. She had a fantasy of going with him.

Saturday afternoon, the day after school was out, when she was at loose ends anyway, she had to ride by his house one more time, as though to satisfy herself on some score. She'd finished her painting of the house with its broken column off to the side, standing there enigmatically. Did it belong to the house or not? You created something to make an impression and maybe added something else you had never seen. Then when you looked at it, you weren't sure what it suggested. The house sat there with its secrets, its door and windows closed upon them. Things that had happened before you ever got there. But if you walked in the empty rooms what would you know? She made and painted a frame for the picture and took it home and set it on top of her bookcase on the back porch. In front of it and on the sides, she laid out a few of the rocks she had collected. Her mother came and stood in front of it. "Very artistic," she pronounced it.

She'd gone on to do a chalk drawing of a begonia, but Mr. Falconer had told her she could invent her own plant if she wanted to and fill up the page. She ended up with a creation that had huge leaves and unabashed scarlet blossoms with pink centers, like throats, and white stamens. Rather more dramatic than the pink begonia she'd started with.

Now what was she supposed to do? Mr. Falconer wouldn't be around to tell her. She couldn't go back to making bricks like a bricklayer, and suddenly she'd been turned loose to invent whatever fell to her imagination, whole gardens of fantastic flora. A certain thrill came with the prospect, and yet it was scary. Maybe people wouldn't like it. Then what?

He was in the midst of packing when she rode up and had already begun loading some boxes into the trunk of his car. A cow's skull and various bones, some pieces of driftwood, and a couple of good-sized boulders lay in loose chaos around the concrete slab in front that served as a porch. He was going back for another load as she approached.

"Well, Rachel," he said. "You've come to lay your eyes on me one more time before I take off?" He waited as she got down from her bicycle. He acted glad to see her.

She hadn't really expected to see him or intended to stop. As she stood in front of him, unable to think of an excuse for her being there, she felt she'd been caught in some guilty act. "I learned a lot in your class," she said stupidly. "I like drawing."

He gave a slight smile. "You'll never look at the world again with the same eyes."

She looked at him to try to see what he meant. She couldn't remember that things looked different, maybe it was too soon to tell. She didn't know if it happened all at once or gradually. She should go, she thought, but she didn't know how to leave.

"Come in and have something cold," he said. "This packing business is hot work, and I need something to moisten the gums."

She didn't know what she expected to be there inside his place. She found herself in a large room brilliant with sunlight on a disorder of objects. A stove and refrigerator at one end announced the kitchen area, but its clutter of cabinets was more in keeping with the chemistry lab, and between it and the rest was a big sink such as the janitor would have, with no space near it for dishes. The rest was a jumble of easels and tables, chairs with books piled on them, and large ceramic pots here and there with desiccated soil and the remains of plants. Jars with brushes and glass palettes with smears of paint on them, bottles of turpentine and linseed oil still littered the surfaces: canvases, framed and unframed, stood and leaned or curled wherever they'd been set down. Drawings and sketches hung from the walls. From the looks of things it was hard to know what could have been removed. He went to the small yellowed refrigerator and took out a beer for himself, a Coke for her. He appeared more sober and brighter in expression than she'd seen him for a while. "I'm starting a beard," he said. "That would go over big with the folks around here. But I don't think they'll care where I'm going."

A beard. It seemed funny that anyone would mind. "When are you leaving?" she asked.

"Tomorrow. My sister's coming to take the rest of the stuff and put it in storage. I don't have to bother with it." He moved a lamp from where it rested on the one upholstered chair Rachel could distinguish, its rose covering faded and stained. But she didn't want to sit down. Instead she roamed the room, looking at paintings and drawings.

"It's all shit," he said suddenly, coming up behind her where she'd paused before an easel. "No, I mean it," he insisted, reading her expression. "Awful stuff."

She didn't know what to say.

"All for the tourist trade," he said. "Rich Texans with money to burn, thinking they're going to hang a little art on the wall. 'Oh Verne,' he mimicked, 'that'll go so well near the gun rack on the other side of the deer head.'" A little explosion of laughter.

She ran her eye over a series of landscapes—adobe houses and mountains with sunset-tinged clouds.

"The gallery commissioned me to do them," he said. "Even sold some of them. I thought I could do it," he said, "and still keep my virtue—whatever that is. . . ." He gave a laugh. "You don't even know what I'm talking about. Only they told me how it had to be done—so many with mountains, so many with adobes. So many small canvases, so many big ones. So much cactus, so many cattle."

She could hear the grinding edges of his self-condemnation. He was sick with it. He couldn't get over it.

"I've discovered what I am," he said, again with a laugh. "The worst thing of all. I wanted the money, and I gave them the goods. And I had a hot time with it. I still want it. And you know what?—I'll probably go on doing it.

"You think I'm like that?" He looked at her as though he expected her to tell him.

"No," she said, "I don't think you're like that."

"Well," he said. "I'm going to try for it. Make a clean break and go to Mexico and breathe that air. . . ." He had turned away from her. "I'm going to, I really am."

When she went outside again and started off on her bicycle, the sunlight hit her right in the eyes as she rode forward. But something blurred and winked at the middle of her dazzled vision. She could see him every night in the same chair in the cantina, leaving a half-finished painting behind to come and drink with the men. Laughing, gesticulating. Then a dark-haired woman pulling him onto the dance floor. A ring of admiring spectators as they danced and flirted. And his room beginning to fill with the half-finished paintings he came back to. But she had the feeling he wasn't going to be leaving the next day, and maybe not even the day after that. It didn't matter: wherever he went, it would be the same.

The second eye operation Nathan looked toward to salvage what was left of his future, allow him at least to continue in the store. Now that Max was gone. That made all the difference. The tension leading up to his first operation had been unbearable. Nathan couldn't stop thinking about him, his being there in the store while he was gone. On the opaque lenses, clouded by the cataracts, he could see him as if on a screen—at the cash register slipping the bills into his wallet, destroying receipts, distorting figures in the account book. It made him see red.

But then, the antagonism he had felt from the very first kept his nerves like hot wires. Just seeing him standing there in the show window, showing himself off. His pose, the diamond on his hand—like a woman. To impress the Mexicans, who thought he was rich. When they came into the store, they asked for him by name. Just seeing him there like that was enough.

All his posturing and name-dropping. "I was with Fred Foster last night," he said once, with his phony modesty. "President of the Cattlemen's Association. He's building a new place—really lavish. I told him we'd give him a deal."

Big shot: a piece of cardboard. As if Nathan couldn't see through his glad-handing. Naturally Foster would go down to buy his furniture in El Paso. What did Max think he had to offer him? While he sneaked around stealing another man's substance. And trampled on his wife, who was like a child, humiliating her when she couldn't protect herself.

The last time he saw her, in the store one afternoon, Max started yelling at her for mislaying her purse. It was sitting behind one of the chairs. She had searched for it frantically. Finally, it was one of the boys, who had seen her put it down, who came over and gave it to her. "Now hold on to it," Max said. For once, she had spoken up, "Max, you don't have to shout. It's a terrible thing you've done." She was trembling all over. Nathan had been surprised at the fire in her eyes. She looked as though she could have picked up a lamp and swung it at him. She stared at him for a moment, turned away, and sat down. She didn't look at him again.

Now he had that to add to his store of images. Nathan had felt a sudden sympathy for her. He hadn't remembered how deep her voice could be; he'd never seen the fire in her eyes. His image of the Max that trampled her underfoot was laid upon the picture of the hypocrite. On top of that, the thief. Now Henny was gone, and Max was gone, too, for whatever good might come of it.

But curiously, when he went down to El Paso to the hospital, he couldn't relax, couldn't leave the store behind, even though Sam had sent up one of the men he kept on the floor—to help Reba until Nathan had recovered.

"You must try to relax, Mr. Lerner," the surgeon told him. "The eye is very delicate. You're not going help yourself this way."

But the dull repetitiveness kept churning in his mind: fifteen thousand dollars. Fifteen. Enough to buy a house and fill it with furniture. And who knew how much merchandise. Stolen his livelihood. Sucked his blood. Preyed on him.

He could have been rich now himself if he'd wanted to pull a few shady deals. His older brother had made himself a millionaire because he'd had the inside scoop on certain stock deals. Knew just the moment to unload for huge profits. Nathan wanted none of it. And his younger brother had cheated him when he convinced him to sell out of the shirt factory they ran together, Nathan at the plant, his brother doing the sales in New York. Sitting on his *tokhis,* as far as Nathan was concerned. They had made it through the first part of the war on their surplus of materials and backlog of orders. But they were running out, and they couldn't buy fabric except on the black market. His brother Irving bought him out, but had kept all the patterns without giving him any money for them. Nathan guessed something was afoot.

The war had permitted all kinds of profiteering. He could have done some of it with the stocks he had bought and that had gone up, some of them more than double. He himself couldn't stoop to that kind of immorality. But the world was full of people who would pimp for their mothers if they could make an extra dime at it.

In his youth he had been hungry for all the world could offer, as he, along with others of his generation, tried to climb up out of the Lower East Side. Everything beckoned: money—fill your purse. Sell your mind, your talents, your body. The girls had to marry well—that was their avenue out. The men had to hustle in trade. So his older brother had manipulated the stock market and the younger had cheated him. And Max had scraped the pot.

Even though he finally dropped off with the sedative they gave him, when they came to get him in the morning he felt groggy, as if he hadn't slept at all. After the operation, they tried again to calm him with sedatives, and though he felt the tension leave his body, his mind raced on even into his sleep. He dreamed that Max stood before him, and as he watched, Max's body and features began to dissolve, his legs joining together until they turned into a tail and the creature itself went falling to the ground as a snake. Swiftly it moved toward him, and though Nathan resisted with all his strength, wrestling with it until he was exhausted, it bit him on the thigh. And still he could not disengage himself from it. When he looked down, the snake was disappearing into the wound.

He woke filled with horror.

But when he went back to sleep in the late-night quiet of the hospital, Max again awaited him, this time dressed up in his black-and-white-checked suit, flashing his diamond and gesturing coquettishly. More and more enticing and seductive he became, so that Nathan was aroused and began to enter him. He felt a commingling of their natures as they came to union.

He yelled and woke himself up. Toward morning the eye hemorrhaged.

The summer evenings seemed emptier than ever. As usual Rachel fled from the apartment the moment she finished the supper dishes, fled into the twilight and early evening. What drove her out now was even more insistent than the hammering voice of H. V. Kaltenborn or the walls whispering that Max was stealing or the groaning of Mr. Kober on the back porch. It was the pull of something heavier than gravity that made it almost impossible to move. Lead. Everything gave off its dull, poisonous heaviness. When she woke in the morning to what the day had to offer, she lay under a leaden weight. Before her father was well enough to go to the store, she did not get up until breakfast was over—that time of reminders and enjoinders and various complaints—and she heard her mother leave the house. When she got up, her father would be sitting in his chair listening to the radio. He had very little to say. When his condition improved, he went down to the store and told Reba what to do.

In the evenings her parents occupied the two metal chairs on the front porch, her father sitting in the dark glasses she couldn't see behind, her mother reading to him one of the stories in the *Ellery Queen Mystery Magazine* or an article from the *Reader's Digest*. The same heaviness hung over the porch. Her mother's desires no longer ran in front of her, scattering like a flock of chickens. Only now the leaden ache of disappointment, sometimes accompanied by the wheezing organ next door, where old Mrs. Pennington played her hymns.

Rachel had temporarily abandoned her bicycle; she now preferred to walk. She still received the same admonition, "Don't be gone too long. Be home before dark." She set off with a prickling of resentment and pushed that time as far as she could.

When she slipped through the gate, Xyla and Nelita were playing hide-and-seek across the street with some of the kids from up the block. She paid no attention to them. Their house had ceased to exist since Susie had gotten married and moved out. Once Rachel had seen them together downtown, the tall figure of J.T. striding along with Susie on his arm. He was guiding them in stately fashion down the street, as though observing the many and possibly unnoteworthy activities of men from above his mustache, while she looked up into his face and chattered away, seemingly oblivious to everything around her. Rachel had crossed the street to avoid them. They seemed enclosed, special, complete; she had no desire to break into the circle of their engaged affections.

Though she sometimes had a soda at the confectionery, there was no expectancy in it. Mr. Falconer would no longer walk in the door or appear suddenly on the street. He had lingered around the town a week or two after their parting at his house, and just as unpredictably disappeared, whether for Mexico or somewhere else no one knew. A Mexican family had moved into his house. And Henny was long since gone. They had all been there, a set of distinctive, continuing presences that helped make up the fabric of her life. Then they had disappeared as though the waters had closed over them. It was strange to her how places forgot you as though you'd never been. Not long after school was out, Shirley Melton and her parents had moved as well, for her mother a long-awaited event. And though Rachel was glad to be rid of Trigger's barking and Mr. Kober's groaning at night and Mrs. Kober's ice pick of a voice, she sensed once again the breaking off of the familiar. It was a smaller version of what happened when she left Delaware, when all she had known broke off and became the past. She didn't know what to pull out of that emptiness, if there was anything in it for her to hold on to. It was like trying to remember a dream when you were waking up and watching it dissolve even as you reached out to capture it. What was there to wake up to now—to come along and take the place of disappearing things?

She hadn't been able to walk past Henny's house, not while Max was still living in it alone and not now that he had left. If she walked in that direction, she detoured around it.

This evening she had no idea where to go. Sometimes she walked up to the top of the hill and sat on the steps of the dormitory of the little teachers' college located there with its cluster of unremarkable brick buildings and watched the sunset from the steps. But she didn't feel like doing that tonight. She thought of going to see the horse, but didn't feel like doing that either.

She could only set herself in motion, turn down one street and then another as though wandering were a fate imposed upon her and she was doomed to find as many ways through the town as possible. A maze of interconnected excursions that led nowhere, only back upon themselves with no way out. Perhaps as in the fairy tales, Henny and Mrs. Lee had set an enchantment upon her when she'd taken and eaten the pear that had been offered her. And nothing existed to break the spell.

Something hung in the air like longing, pressing the street under its shadow when the dust had settled and the houses leaned back from their time in the ordinary into a twilight repose, and the street itself became the haunt of dogs led by their noses, and night-stalking cats and winos. Smells rose from the dark, the smell of piss from the lampposts, from the alleys; the residue of water in the ditch. The smell of trees with dust-coated leaves settled over by coolness. And above, the stars scattered like handfuls of brilliant dust. What was she supposed to do in this world? Walk down by the Catholic church, but not enter. Past the newspaper office, the bowling alley. Places other people went; things other people did. But for her only to pass by.

Down to the center, to the ditch, where the water gathered and swept all away.

Something hung in the air like warning, something the darkness held like a finger pointing at her back. She didn't know how its shadow was linked to her, but she herself could arouse it just by walking down the street. Something could happen to her, as it could have the day she met the Mexican boys or the night when Mr. Falconer told her about the man being stabbed in the alley. Rough hands reaching out in the violence of longing.

She didn't understand the things that happened at night. She'd heard that the priest ran naked through the streets then. Everybody said so. The parishioners objected, and a delegation from the church had gone to the bishop. She didn't know why a priest would want to do such a thing. Running, running in the dark, making a crazy zigzag through alleys and streets. What was he running from or toward? Ordinarily, she'd have thought it nasty for anyone to run around without a stitch on, but for a priest to do it made it somehow awesome, a strange and bewildering rite. She wondered if it was quite safe for him to be on the streets like that.

She was passing alongside houses whose windows opened onto the street. She could see right into someone's kitchen. A young woman was feeding a baby in a high chair, food all around its mouth and dribbling down its chin. The baby opened its mouth like a bird and banged a spoon against the top of the high chair. Mother and baby. Yellow kitchen walls, a bright flowered tablecloth on the table. The mother murmuring and holding out the spoon. The baby teasing her, resisting, making a mess. The stove with pots and pans hanging on the wall above, the flowered tablecloth: all belonged together in a picture. And the mother didn't appear to mind that the baby was making a mess. She kept up a little crooning of encouragement and aimed the spoon into its mouth.

She couldn't see herself doing that, Rachel decided. Never being in a kitchen with a baby. *What are you saying?* she could hear at her back: *A big girl like you. Almost old enough for marriage and divorce and children flying into the future.*

She couldn't stand the thought. There were the two sides, the side that obeyed the ordinary, that did not rise up very high or sink very low, and over that her mother presided. And there was the other, which could rise up very high like those airy plants that had no roots but just a brief term of growing in the air. Those that sprang up out of the water, self-created, moving on the impulse of their own dreams, unaware of the shadow, that insubstantial trailing thing that rose and grew powerful. She could see it, see the one Henny had pointed toward, propelled by the power of an idea, a single race of blue-eyed, blond-haired giants. The dark man himself, whose shadow fell over all of Europe, catching up all the small shadows. And around her here, little lives all trailing their shadows. What was she supposed to do there in the street as it grew dark?

No one seemed to know where Max had gone or what he had been doing the several months since, as Reba put, he left with his tail between his legs. But now he was back. Reba caught sight of him at noon one day when she was driving Nathan home from the store. She couldn't believe her eyes, couldn't believe Max would be brazen enough to show his face, considering the damage he had done. But there he was on the sidewalk in front of the bakery. In a moment he would be walking past the store. But to her surprise, he veered off suddenly, stepped from the curb, and walked right in front of the car. She stopped short as a matter of reflex, almost lost control.

"Can you believe that?" she said, "I almost ran into the bastard. He wasn't even looking where he was going."

"Too bad you didn't kill him," Nathan said. He wondered if Max had seen them.

"He looks like a ghost," she said. "He didn't even have a jacket on." Indeed it was a shock to see how much his appearance had altered. He looked as though he'd been on a bender and slept in the streets or hadn't fully recovered from an illness. His face was pale and drawn, and his white hair blew in the wind like chaff.

"He didn't look to the right or the left, just came right on coming." She couldn't get over it.

Nathan called to mind the time Max had walked into the door. It was peculiar. He'd been walking out of the store and just kept on going, right into the thick plate glass of the front door. And he must have hit it hard because the glass broke down the middle and he was so thoroughly dazed he couldn't go out for coffee for at least half an hour. He suffered a bad cut on the forehead. The same thing. Would never look where he was going.

A strange mood came over Nathan, as though he were being visited by a miasma, something inescapable that had come into his life and would never depart. Knowing Max was back, even if he couldn't see him, vexed his thought. What did he want now? For Sam to buy him off again?

Indeed, Max had been to Sam Goldman: he'd been sick, he told Sam, and needed money for treatment. He had no insurance. He was down on his luck. Sam gave him a hundred dollars and told him not to come back.

"It's what he deserves," Reba said, when she discovered this a few days later. "When I think of all the grief. . . ."

"I knew right from the start," Nathan said. "I could see right through him. Like looking through a dirty window into a dirty room." It was the one satisfaction left to him, that he'd been the impeccable judge of Max's character. *See,* he wanted to say to Sam Goldman: *you he cheated for years. I knew immediately.*

Josephine made certain they knew the smallest details of Max's whereabouts. He had been to see them too, sitting in their living room, haggard and dissipated looking, to ask for money, but they hadn't given him a dime, Josephine said. She had no idea what he was living on. He'd gone round to see his cronies at the Elks Club and the Chamber of Commerce. Mechlin, who ran the drugstore, had seen him at one of the booths drinking coffee.

On the front porch in the evening Nathan and Reba chewed over these scraps, morsel by morsel. Max had tried to get a job selling insurance, wasn't that a laugh. Fortunately, everybody knew his number by this time, Reba said. There was some discussion of this. Nathan wasn't sure. But Josephine would have blabbed, Reba insisted. Nathan wasn't sure Sam had told her. It would reveal him for the sucker he was. He could have said the business was down, Max wasn't pulling his weight. Reba was certain Josephine would have sniffed it out anyway, with that nose of hers. Nathan acknowledged the possibility: you sneezed on one side of town and Josephine was saying Gesundheit on the other. Anyway, Reba said, it was all those fair-weather friends, all those people Max had given discounts to, given the stuff away to for years for a song—his notion of goodwill. Generous with what other people paid for. Let him see how far it got him.

Rachel caught whiffs of these conversations as she crossed the porch and fled into the evening. Then she saw him.

She had bought a copy of *Seventeen* and was glancing down at the cover as she turned the corner. A shadow fell on the page like a stain, and when she looked up he moved past her. His eyes looked straight in front of him and held an expression of blank unseeing, as though he were looking beyond the street, beyond her, to something that transfixed his vision. Whatever it was, it did not appear reassuring. It was as though he'd looked upon something that had trapped his gaze forever, allowing him no alternative. He could have walked into a brick wall, but only because, like a steamroller, he had to continue; it was the only possibility for him to make whatever stood in his path get out of the way. Rachel found herself moving off to one side to allow him room. And when he passed, a mere shadow of himself, for she saw a piece of wreckage, she found her heart beating in her chest, a tingling in her fingers.

Then suddenly, perhaps two weeks later, Max was dead.

They embrace. The camera zooms in for a closeup and catches the flower in her hair and her smile as she looks up into the face of the man who, having struggled with storm and shipwreck, has now won her love. Their arms clutch, their bodies cling, their lips merge into a kiss, the sideways tilt of the head that avoids the clash of noses. And there is the long breathless breath, the climactic moment that has decided their fates. Now they emerge and walk off together hand in hand. The music comes up in a great wave, the screen goes blank—and it was all over.

The lights came on, turning the viewers out of the darkness they'd subsided into and forcing them back to themselves. The theater was full of kids who'd sunk down into their seats and put their feet on the seat in front, and eaten their fill of popcorn, dropping their cartons to the floor, along with the cups and straws from their Cokes, squirming and wiggling, talking, booing and cheering, necking in the back rows. Now they rose and moved noisily toward the exit. Rachel stood up and joined the throng. They'd paid her way to the movie—she didn't have to use her allowance—while they went to the funeral. Such largesse did not fall her way very often. Whether it would take anything less than somebody's death to evoke it was a question she left aside for the time being.

She came outside blinking and yawning, trying to see in the hot light of the afternoon on the street. It was always like that when you came out of a show; you yawned and blinked, even though it was the middle of the day. The light hit you square in the eyes, dazzled away what was on the screen: you woke from a dream.

She'd have liked to keep hold of it: the tropical island studded with palm trees, the waves lapping up to the white sand beaches, the plumage of parrots and cockatoos and birds in brilliant flashes of red and yellow and orange. The color made her heart ache, the sheer vibrancy of it. Then the night sky swarming with stars. And as you watched the girl, shy and beautiful with her long dark hair, and saw the man who had come to fill her longing, with smiling eyes and a sweet soft mouth and good muscles in his arms, it seemed that somewhere it existed, the love so great, that growing from that final kiss it could endure forever. And happiness like the brilliance of birds, like the ocean wavering between blue and green and the sky exploding with stars—the landscape to enfold you and take you in and make your dreams come true.

The street was full of people. A short, fat Mexican woman passed her with her kids chattering around her, a little old woman in black, her head covered with a shawl, moving slowly behind her. High school boys with nowhere to go in particular jostled one another on the pavement; one got shoved off the curb into the street. The old men in front of City Hall, with a couple of policemen who came out of their station, stood passing the time of day. Cowboys and miners in worn jeans and boots. The miners, no longer out of work but getting their first paychecks in months, were headed toward one of the bars by way of celebration. Perhaps there would be a fight; there usually was on Saturday nights.

She had nothing to do the rest of the afternoon. Her mother had left supper for her, something for her to heat up. Her parents were going to eat out after the funeral, something they rarely did. There was really nothing for her to do.

They'd given her money for ice cream as well. She went into the confectionery to kill a little time reading magazines. A sign at the front said, "Don't read the magazines," but she pretended to be looking for one to buy. Nobody said anything. Sometimes she got to finish whole articles and stories. She no longer bought comic books, since her father had shamed her out of them, though she sometimes borrowed them and read them on the sly.

Summer issues on the shelves. Girls in bathing suits lolling in the sun, with their bright smooth faces awaiting a tan. Being smiled at by boys in swimming trunks, their tanned arms holding beach balls—both poised for pleasure. Pages of cosmetics and hairstyles and clothes; articles on the figure, the complexion, the etiquette of dating: all the accoutrements, directions, warnings, and encouragements needed to become one of those enviable creatures basking in the sun. All safely enclosed between the covers of a magazine. She closed the magazine and put it back. She bought a double-dip cone, chocolate and butter pecan, and left.

She wished she had a way out to St. Mary's to the swimming pool, the only one in town. By the time she walked there it would be closed. She didn't want to go home; there was nothing to do there either except read or play monopoly with herself. She felt restless, at loose ends. The movie had left her feeling strangely hollow.

Even then she could make a certain distinction: her father had wanted something to take him beyond this place of mud and dust. He'd always wanted it, some kind of life that they'd never really had but it seemed they might attain. And he'd struggled and struggled, against everything that prevented him. And thought he knew the way. Now he'd failed: the sun had turned black and fallen from the sky. Her mother had had to look on and watch the promised riches slip away before she could get her hands on them. And she was bitter and full of blame for those who'd prevented her. Her father had found the world full of fools and knaves, while her mother saw a world full of the lucky ones, who could look at things through rose-colored glasses and never know what she'd been through.

She walked toward the intersection with the flagpole in the middle, the signal point toward which the high school kids steered their cars, "dragging Main," as they called it. Then abruptly she stopped and turned around. She knew where she had to go. She had to pay a visit to Henny's house, only she had to get there the way they'd gone the first time.

She walked by Mrs. Lee's grocery and glanced in the window. A younger woman, perhaps Mrs. Lee's grown daughter, was behind the counter. Then she turned past the store to go by the old house, the boardinghouse that she had made into her painting.

Solidly it stood with its pillared porch and brick that had been painted over: Slater's Boarding House, a weathered sign announced. She'd never seen anyone leave or go inside. She wondered who would live there. If anyone saw her picture, they probably wouldn't know this was the house she'd had in mind. It was mostly her imagination. But Mr. Falconer had pushed her in that direction. She wondered where he was.

She had turned up the street to go past the opposite side of the parochial school, by the playground, when she heard someone calling her. At first she couldn't make out the figure in the doorway of the little house across the street. Then she saw that it was Shirley Melton. She hadn't known exactly where she'd moved. Shirley was calling for her to come over. Though she didn't want to particularly, she crossed the street and found her in the doorway, clutching her bathrobe around her. She was alone. "Come inside," Shirley said. Rachel thought it peculiar for her to ask, but she saw that she was frightened.

"Do you believe in ghosts?" Shirley asked her, when Rachel had sat down in a living room even smaller than the one in the duplex.

"I don't know," she said. "I've never seen one."

"I've seen a ghost," Shirley said. She looked dazed and pop-eyed. Clearly she did not know what to do about it. "I really have."

Rachel didn't doubt her. She was certainly scared enough to have seen a ghost.

"What did it do?"

"It was my sister's husband," she said. "It came and told me to turn off the burner on my gas stove. Isn't that strange?" she announced.

"Was it on?"

Shirley looked at her. "No," she said. "It wasn't even on."

Rachel agreed that it was strange. When she was out on the street again, she wondered why the ghost hadn't had something more interesting to say—if he was going to come like that and scare poor Shirley nearly out of her wits. She hadn't seen an adult really scared before, and it struck her as odd to have Shirley looking to her for comfort or help or some proof of her sanity.

But a ghost, she thought, would scare you.

She kept on walking—

The one thing Reba knew as they stood waiting for the service to begin was that she made a good appearance. She was wearing a hat made of Persian lamb, her own creation from what she'd managed to salvage from the full-length coat her mother-in-law had left her. The two daughters had been not just green but purple with envy that their own mother should make special mention in her will that her elegant coat should go to Reba, the daughter-in-law. Such a signal mark of her favor. Thinking about it was enough to bring tears to her eyes. Reba had worn the coat until the fur was smooth, then cut it down to a jacket, and finally pieced together enough for this hat. Let Josephine, standing on the other side, dressed in the *schmattas* she dredged up from some basement sale, get an eyeful. The trouble was that no one in this one-horse town could appreciate the finer touches. They were worse than the Mexicans with their outlandish colors and vulgar tastes. It didn't matter how much money they had, they only knew how to spend it on liquor and a good time. These were people you couldn't educate to anything better. And you had to knock yourself out trying for just a little touch of sophistication. The men were coarse and the women were frumps. Trying to impress them was a pure waste of time.

Unless you were Max. Who had he been trying to kid? His lodge brothers?—who didn't give a damn about him. They were giving him a Masonic funeral—figure that one out. The Masons in their white gloves and white aprons formed two lines leading to the open grave. The pallbearers stood near the hearse ready to remove the coffin. They were waiting, she wasn't certain quite why. She looked around to see who hadn't come. Sam Goldman hadn't bothered to put in an appearance. She didn't see MacGregor, the president of the Chamber of Commerce. Indeed she hardly recognized anyone she knew.

"It isn't much of a crowd," she whispered to Nathan with some satisfaction. "What happened to all his pals he was so chummy with?"

"Be quiet," Nathan said.

A surge of resentment rose up. He depended on her for everything now, yet he still treated her like a child. She hoped the service wouldn't drag on too long. It was Sunday, the one day she could relax. Always things waited for her, demanding to be done now that she had taken on the whole burden of the store as well as the house. Nathan was still talking about when he'd be back on his feet, telling Sam that with the new medication it would be soon now. His sight would return and Reba wouldn't have to help out. But it was no use talking. Now with the glaucoma his days in the store were over. Sam was wise to his condition. It didn't take any genius to figure things out. And she could see it coming: it was only a matter of time before Sam would let her go, tell them he'd found a new manager. She'd gotten wind of it from Josephine that he was looking for someone, even though she suspected Josephine wasn't supposed to let the cat out of the bag. That was what you could expect from people: they'd kick you aside like a dog without thinking twice. As if she weren't perfectly capable of handling the store. . . . And after all that Nathan had been through. And Sam not willing to listen. A thousand dollars they'd paid that bastard!

She looked out toward the hills. A beautiful spot to be buried in, out there with the highway trash. First a bunch of unstuccoed adobes where the poorest Mexicans lived, where there weren't even sidewalks and the thistle and weeds took over. Then a graveyard for old cars and, past that, the city dump. One discard after another. On the other side of the highway was the Mexican cemetery with its wreaths of garish artificial flowers and weathered wooden crosses canted at various angles where the wind had left them. The sight of it had filled Reba with distaste. But for the Anglos it wasn't so wonderful either, even with the granite headstones. You couldn't get a blade of glass to grow in this godforsaken spot. Even so, it was more than Max deserved: they should have thrown his carcass to the vultures, let it serve some purpose.

But if they were going to do it, she wished they'd get it over with. What were they waiting for? The resurrection? Letting them stand there all day.

It seemed to her she'd been waiting all her life for something good to happen. When she married Nathan, he was going to be a rich man—that's what he told her. His mother had given the boys ten thousand dollars to start the business. It was to be only a few years. There would be a big house, maybe even a yacht. Then she wanted her money back, and they'd practically gone under. For the daughters. For their dowries. So they'd struggled along. Even the war didn't help them, when so many had made a killing. And then this great opportunity that was supposed to put them on Easy Street, give her the things she'd always wanted. The Goldmans had them, and Rose Goldman as uncouth as they come. Josephine had her share, with her rentals and her bargains. Only Reba still waited.

For nothing.

There was a sound of a car door slamming, a scrape of footsteps on the gravel, and Reba was aware of what they had been waiting for. When she looked around, she saw one of the Masons guiding a woman toward the group of mourners. They moved around the edge of the small group to the side opposite Reba, and people opened a space for her by the side of the grave.

"My God," Reba whispered to Nathan, "they've brought her here."

"Who?"

"Henny," she said. "Can you imagine that?" She couldn't help staring. It wasn't clear whether Henny knew where she was or why she was there. She looked at the man who had escorted her to that spot as though for reassurance. Then she stood motionless, composed. She hadn't aged, Reba noticed. If anything her face seemed smooth as a girl's, as though she were beyond trouble, without a care in the world. Somebody was there to look after her, see to her meals. She was beyond it. Reba shifted uneasily. The way Nathan was standing was a weight on her. And right now she couldn't see any way around it.

It was difficult for Nathan to stand there unable to see. He felt a certain weightlessness. The ground was no longer solid under his feet but threatened to move and shift beneath him. Only Reba's arm gave him something concrete to hold on to; even so, there were moments he was afraid of losing his balance and pitching forward. Once he was there he wondered why he had come. What was the purpose of his standing there over Max's useless clay?

"Is Sam here?" he said to Reba.

"No," she said. "Probably couldn't be bothered."

It had struck him during the past months that Sam did not act particularly grateful to him for having uncovered Max's embezzling. He wanted just to push the whole thing under the rug and forget it as though it had never happened. Under the rug that had been pulled out from under them. After all his struggle and heartache.

"We are again called upon to consider the uncertainty of human life, the immutable certainty of death, and the vanity. . . ."

So it was beginning. Nathan shifted to find an easier position to stand. He found it hard to listen to the service for the other voices pressing upon him.

You're a fool. It could have been Sam's voice in his ear.

He had to protest. But a man's principles.

Principles. So go and play the high and mighty. There's a strain of larceny in everybody.

But was that a reason to ignore it? And the evil he did.

So go fight with your shadow. Have fun and good luck—down in the muck.

Look what Max did to you. And you wouldn't fight.

So why would I have to? So, a bastard. So why cry over it? Peanuts. A wave of the hand. Nathan could almost see the off-hand gesture. *When you've been in politics like me, you get a tough hide. Under the surface it goes on all the time. Grease to make the wheels go round.*

So now Max was dead, and where was the triumph?

He was there, Henny was there. He was there for as much reason as Henny was. And what had brought him?

"Brethren, we come here on this occasion with saddened, subdued heart and softened affection. . . ."

He caught the scent of flowers and his thoughts fell away, swooned from the moment as though down a passageway. Once in his youth he'd found strawberries growing in the cemetery he passed through on the way to school. The sweetness of their taste. The years had not blotted out the trace of the sensation. And all that flooded back—the crowded streets of the Lower East Side, with the peddlers hawking their wares, the press of garment workers and young men trying to hustle their way along. His family struggling; his father, a seller of lace. Active in the synagogue. Once as a boy playing football in a vacant lot, Nathan had been kicked in the nose, his nose broken. Again he smelled and tasted. The taste and smell of his blood as he lay on the ground. His father coming, picking him up, carrying him home. Being ruined even before the First World War, when he could no longer import goods. Dying of diabetes when Nathan was sixteen. His mother grieving and grieving until she died herself. . . .

Trying, trying to get out. Hanging on the intellectual fringe down in the Village. Scribbling verse. Looking for a hot tip for the Stock Exchange. Money, the money that hadn't been there for him to become doctor, lawyer, engineer. Till his mother came into some inheritance from a brother. Business then. In your own business. He'd known those who'd struck it rich.

So it had been offered, his opportunity: to come West and make good. Be his own boss. Not knocking on other people's doors, as he'd done selling insurance. His investment would make him an equal. For money meant something in the world. The difference between living the life you wanted and not living it. And he had been struck down when he'd only asked for . . . Oh, the losses.

Suddenly a great wrenching wail rose up, coming as from a great depth, breaking to the surface and rising beyond them. An animal cry of pure grief.

"It's Henny," Reba whispered at his side. "She must know what's going on."

The sound shattered him like a blow. Henny: who existed for him now only in that one sound. He tried to see her, to get an image of her face. Broad and square, he remembered.

Wholesome, no harm in her. Like a loaf of bread. He could call to mind little more than the pose of her patience, as she sat like a fixture in the store. Those long afternoons of waiting, broken only by Max's belittling and bullying, or his testy humor. He could make fun of her, he knew how to do that.

Nathan had never given her more than a hello, how are you, some small talk about the weather or the miners about to strike. Then he'd had other things to do. Left her to sit there with her broad peasant face and her dark hair. Old country. Large frame and strong hands. Like she'd be more at home in the fields than anywhere else. Always in dark clothes, sometimes with lace around the collar or at the front. Formal somehow. Belonging to another place, another time. And then only a woman losing her hold on the world.

Weeping now over Max, who could only victimize her. The wail continued, followed by a long sobbing refrain, as though drawing together the echoes of griefs without number in the long history of grief. It contained all that one might imagine of grief, including his own—rising from a great whelming source to mirror it, send it forth.

She was only this rising sound. Nothing else remained of her, except now that terrible power of sound. Terrible, yet powerful. It made her something more, something beyond anything he'd known, but containing all that he now knew.

Reba, who had only his helplessness, his bad nerves and depression, and Rachel, who would grow up beyond him, fight her way out of the house as soon as she could—he had abandoned them long ago. Now he was afraid of the future, of what they would have to remember. And what he was going toward. He had grown so heavy with this life, taken in so much foulness, he could not give anything back. No, he would have to sink himself into the earth, suffer the mortification of worms and dust, let the molecules that held all together fall apart. Then he might be free once again to move blindly toward some distant light.

And Henny was all that he could see, looking into the mirror of all his griefs, all he had lost. Robbed, yes, and all the time assisting the thief.

"Who shall separate us from the love of God? Shall tribulation or anguish . . ."

Separated, oh, entirely. The blackened stone crumbling beneath his feet.

". . . or persecution, or famine, or nakedness, or peril, or the sword?"

Henny's sobbing was beginning to subside like the aftermath of a great wave calming. He could still hear an occasional sob, rather like that of a child who, after the paroxysm, is still overtaken by a spasm. The spell had passed, perhaps those around her offering her a murmur of comfort, a hand on her shoulder.

Soon they would be laying the white lambskin apron on top of the coffin and, upon that, the sprig of acacia in the hope of a glorious destiny beyond the world of shadows. He knew the ritual from his time as a Mason himself.

Yes, all calm now. But his face was wet with tears, and he could not stop weeping.

In front of Henny's house she felt the pull toward the hollow of its emptiness. The windows were blank, the door shut fast upon absence and departure. Rachel could smell its closed-in dust, as in the old attic of the house of her childhood. Around the porch the weeds had sprung up, and a bolt had fallen out of the gate, so that it sank on one hinge into the yard. This was what happened when the life went out of things. The weeds took over, visited by grasshoppers. Henny was gone and Max was dead, and Rachel was there to know it.

Out of the center of the strangeness she felt, she was suddenly caught up in what still offered itself, as though she was left holding whatever they had dropped. Something that wouldn't remain still in the dust-closed silence. She was remembering how she'd come to this house the first time, walking into the living room, seeing the animals on the wall in their poses of cleverness and patience and knowledge. And then into the kitchen, still warm with baking and filled with the odor of spices. The tinkling of the music box. The clown, with its melancholy mirth. And the dark form of Henny turning toward her, offering her cookies, showing her the coins her son had sent back from the war, taking out her hair and letting it fall in a loose cascade to her waist. Telling her stories. They were all there together, these images, like a crowd of ghosts, summoned from forgetfulness. They stood as though waiting for someone to offer them blood and allow them to speak: Henny and her son, Henny's father, and the boy who had tried to seize the heart of the Evil One.

Objects and gestures and tones and voices, all the bits and pieces. Once she had picked up a glass ball on the mahogany table with the woven runner from Belgium and found that it contained a snowfall. A tiny world with snow falling over little streets and houses, and when she held it up it filled with light like the gel of the eyeball. Only taking light and motion from an outside hand. Then the snow fell soundlessly, without coldness, perpetually white in that enclosed eye. Otherwise it sat quietly. But with a little shake all the snowflakes were in the air again. She wondered if they always fell the same way.

This was a place where she had come and could come no longer, but when she took them with her, the things that had fallen kept falling, continually stirred up to fall again. And with that, the intimation of what would keep on happening. The things she lived here, now melting like snow, never disappeared for good and all. She could see the snowflakes, each unique crystal, falling, all the things that ever existed falling to the earth again, leaving behind a little spark.

She couldn't stand there all day, couldn't look at the house any longer. She let go of it and turned away, as though she'd been given what she came for.

Where to now? She didn't know when the funeral would be over, whether her mother and father would stop back at the house before they went on to dinner. Perhaps she should go back. She was at loose ends. She could have gone to the funeral if she'd wanted, but she'd had no desire to go. She'd never been to a funeral; she'd never liked Max. She was glad she'd come to Henny's house instead.

Wait, a voice prodded her, *you haven't answered the questions.* He was running after her, skipping really, for he seemed to have a limp. And his voice was high and shrill, though with a certain sweetness. The clown's. She hadn't heard him speak before. Questions? *Of course, questions.* He tilted his head. *Question: Why did the Evil One Laugh? . . .* Because it tricked the young man into feeling pity? He waited. Or because it tricked the young man into thinking he was any match for him at all? She was stumped. *Question: And why did the human lose?* He wasn't finished. Because he grew puny with the weakness of pity? Or because he felt such sympathy for what he hated most? The clown put a finger alongside his nose. *Think about it,* he said. And she knew she was stuck with him forever.

She paused at the corner. If she got home just before her folks arrived, it wouldn't matter how long she was gone. She had come this far. She might as well go the rest of the way, in yellow light accompanied by blue shadows. The sun gathering up its gold, from where it lingered in sharp rectangles on the sides of houses. Down the hill past Henrietta's, you turned left and then you had to continue on dirt streets where thistle and desert poppy grew undisturbed along the side and horned toads and lizards scurried through the grass. Then suddenly you looked upon a great open space between the houses, as though the town had given out and didn't intend to go on further. In front of you was the field.

There the sky opened out and the mountains stood before you, solid as walls, reaching upward beyond the town, those mountains that had once been below the sea. She looked at the mountains every day now, every day as she walked to high school. They were always there, blue-purple in the morning sunlight, deepening to indigo at the end of the day, sometimes with clouds over them casting irregular shadows. Encircling her and her mother and father. Ever since they had come to this place, the mountains had bound them, shut them in with their pulsing, oppressed desires. How was she to escape?

Her mother had wanted money, so that she could tell everybody to go to hell. If you had money, people looked up to you and you could do what you pleased—that's what she kept saying. And her father . . . Rachel knew what he wanted, could see the shape of it as it slipped away, eluding him even as he grasped and struggled. He'd wanted a place where he could be free. That was his dream: to be his own boss, not to have to knock on anybody's door. And even more, to stand head and shoulders above the common herd. Beyond their petty lives.

These were the dreams that melted in the fluid and opaque regions between sleep and waking and haunted the daylight. Haunted that savage and dusty town, where the ditch roared with water and the streets overflowed and turned to mud. Or where the drought ruled the countryside and everything shriveled down to the cactuses and tumbleweeds in vacant lots thirsting in the dust. Everything, a struggle. The miners on strike, the company closed down. The Mexicans who lived in the poorest houses and got drunk in the bars. And Max stealing and her father defeated, her mother wailing in the shadows.

When she reached the field, she didn't see the horse. She whistled and waited, but still he didn't come. The afternoon was deepening toward twilight, and the sun was a bright blaze on the horizon. She saw that the moon was in the sky, above the mountains rising away from the foothills. The moon greeting the sun, the light handing the world from gold to silver and back again, while the land glimmered underneath. For a moment she was held breathless.

Rachel, you are in the world. You knocked at the door and entered it, through the iron gates. That is real, if nothing else is. But the rest, what of that? And maybe you'll wait all your life, waiting to know. Picking up bits and pieces, weaving and unweaving, trying to create a pattern from all the bright and dark threads, so many, so tangled. How difficult to pick it out of the common life.

She didn't hear it, but it had come up, perhaps from a small cluster of trees on the far side of the field. Now standing beside her was the horse, putting its head over the fence. It nuzzled her hand, and she stroked its nose. "Hello, boy," she said, patting its neck. "I don't have anything for you today. Next time I'll bring you an apple." She bent down and pulled some of the longer shoots of grass on her side of the fence to give to him. "I wish you were mine. I'd ride you."

She wondered if anything good could ever happen in her life. So many terrible things had happened, and she herself had done no one any good by being there. She wanted to be grown up—that's what she'd been waiting for. She imagined herself climbing on the horse's back, galloping off into the distance, leaving everything behind, her father and mother and all that had happened, just riding onward and never looking back. But the trouble was, it would be herself that was doing it: she couldn't get rid of that.

Nor the shadows. The shadows that were always there, in the daylight, not just the dark, though that's when you saw them more distinctly. Whatever made her mother say, "Be home before dark," even though she liked the dark, liked the way the evening blunted the edges of the houses and toned down the ugliness of the streets. The threat of the dark always hung in the air and made Mr. Falconer tell her about the man who was found dead in the alley. She thought of the priest who ran naked through the streets, perhaps wanting to be a shadow himself, to bring what the daylight hid but could not be kept secret. She, too, knew secrets—about her uncle. He had his secrets. And so did Mr. Kober, whose moans she had heard from the back porch. And secrets about Max's stealing had whispered in the walls, and all that had happened to her father. Now Max was going into his grave, and who knew what he had done? The shadows that followed her toward twilight followed everybody. While the sun moved across the sky, they came and lengthened and trailed in the darkness, meeting and crossing and growing.

The horse stood in front of her expectantly. "Good horse," she said. She wished she could be a cowgirl and do something splendid the way they did in the movies. Like capture the outlaw who had terrorized the town, robbing and shooting. Then folks could settle down again, and everybody would be so happy they'd all go on a picnic and set off fireworks. Then she could wander off alone. The horse would be there waiting for her; she would put on his saddle and bridle and leap lightly onto his back. "Come on, boy," she'd say, and he'd gallop off, strong and beautiful and swift and full of power. And he'd take wing and leap over the mountains.

But that was the movies. She could almost see herself as she stood now, as though the years had fled by and left her far from where she was: solitary, standing there in the outlines of youth, not yet filled in by flesh or experience. And maybe you will wait all your life, wait to know, weaving and unweaving, trying to make the garment that is not just a shroud for the past. She hardly knew what to want, what to try for.

The light, moving past gold, past silver, for some moments holding the luminescence of alabaster, was fading. She was getting hungry and it was time to go home. It would already be dark when she arrived.

"Good-bye," she said, and turned toward the street.

Midway up the hill, she paused and looked back. The horse was still there, watching her go.

About the Author

Gladys Swan is the author of six books of fiction, including *A Visit to Strangers* and *Do You Believe in Cabeza de Vaca?*—both available from the University of Missouri Press.